NORTH PARK COLLEGE
An Annie Mercer O'Dell Story

By
Kenneth Lee McGee

To My Wife and Kids

I want to thank all those people who helped make this story come to life.

Chapter One

Detective Keith O'Dell carried a large suitcase in each hand as he struggled up the stairs to the third floor.

"Annie, would you have chosen the top floor if there had been an elevator?"

"No, of course not. What fun would that have been? This is the last trip, Daddy."

"Thank God for that. I won't be able to sleep tonight, I'll be so sore."

"I could have carried one of the suitcases."

"Now you tell me."

He dropped the suitcases with a thud outside of her room. He dabbed the sweat off his forehead with his handkerchief before it ran into his eyes. He smiled with pride as he looked at his seventeen-year-old daughter, Annie Mercer O'Dell. She wore blue shorts and an old, white t-shirt with a Fridays At Five logo on the front and a list of concert dates on the back. Her short, curly brunette hair, though covered at the moment by a blue baseball cap with the initials SHPD on the front in capital letters, accented her doe-like brown eyes. She stood five feet, two and a half inches tall in her bare feet, and not much taller in her dirty white sneakers with blue shoelaces.

The narrow hallways of Howe Hall, the dorm for freshman girls on the campus of North Park College in South Hampshire, overflowed with swarms of excited young girls looking for their rooms and moms and dads carrying suitcases, boxes of books, pillows, blankets and other prized possessions. Many of the girls were going to be living away from home for the first time.

"Maybe my roommate will be here by now. I can't wait to meet her. Oh look! There's Lainey."

Annie spotted one of her best friends, Elaine "Lainey" Novicki, in the hall.

"Annie! Did you just get here?"

"No, this was our last trip. Daddy carried everything for me. Are you all moved in?"

"Finished an hour ago. Adrien helped Father and Cindy

should be back any second."

Cindy Mackens was Elaine's roommate and best friend. They met at age four and lived across the street from each other the entire time. Adrien Coyle, a senior at North Park, happened to be Elaine's boyfriend.

"Can I see your room?" Annie asked.

"Sure, I'm just down the hall. Hello, Mr. O'Dell."

"I'll talk to you in a second, Lainey. Just need to catch my breath. Did your father manage to get all your stuff up here without having a heart attack?" Detective O'Dell asked.

"Sure, he used the service elevator down at the other end of the hall at the back of the building," Elaine answered as she pointed.

Detective O'Dell looked up at Annie as he bent over with his hands on his knees.

"Daddy, I swear I didn't know about the service elevator." She held her hands up to proclaim her innocence.

"And you claim to be a detective." Dad sighed.

"Do you still love me?"

"Of course I do, but you will pay for this."

"Have you met your roommate yet, Annie?" Elaine asked while leading Annie down the hall to her room.

"Not yet, but I know her name. It's Erin Bezick and she went to high school in Nebraska."

"How do you know that, Annie?" Dad asked slowly as though he already knew the answer.

"I looked it up on her school record."

Annie looked at her father, who shrugged.

"Just remember, Annie. Grandpa isn't here to bail you out if you get in trouble."

Grandpa Liam O'Dell was the principal of Roosevelt High where Annie and her friends attended.

Annie leaned back against Elaine's desk. "Do you know which room Trish Eiffert or Rachel Lowery are in? Or what floor?"

"Trish is on two and so is Rachel, I think. I saw them both earlier." Elaine opened the suitcase on her bed.

2

"Can you believe Diana Ahronson chose North Park College over Princeton. Did she and Damon break up or something?" Annie asked.

"I haven't heard anything about it if she did. She will join a sorority for sure."

Annie moved toward the door. "Let's see if we can hook up with Trish and Rachel and grab something to eat later."

"Sounds good. Isn't it great we all have cell phones now."

Annie looked at her father.

"All right! I'll get you a cell phone, Annie."

"Thanks, Daddy."

"I'm going to head home, sweetie."

"I'll walk you to the car." Annie paused in the doorway, "I'll see you in a bit, Lainey."

Annie walked beside her father to his car. This would be the first time they ever lived apart. Annie's mother, Amy Catherine Mercer O'Dell, passed away when Annie was five and Dad raised her by himself. They got to the car and paused. Dad looked at Annie and started to get misty-eyed.

"Daddy, I'm only twenty minutes away the way you drive."

"I know, sweetie, but the house will seem so empty without you. Except for the boarder who rented your room."

"You better not rent out my room. I plan on coming home to do laundry."

"Good. That means I'll see you twice this year."

Annie hugged her father and he held her tightly. She caught some other students staring at her, but she didn't care. She loved her father and he was just about her best friend in the world.

He kissed her forehead, then got in the car. He rolled down the window and pointed a finger at her. "Make sure you study hard and go to classes. No partying all hours of the night and no beer!"

"Daddy, I'm underage. Where would I get any beer?" Annie asked with a grin.

"Give me a kiss and I'll go home."

Annie leaned in the car and kissed Dad once more. "I'll call you sometime if I can borrow a phone from someone."

The scene was similar at Humphrey Hall, the freshman boys dorm—except it was mostly the mother's who were getting emotional about leaving sons behind. Elisabeth Franklin, a light-skinned African American woman in her early forties, accompanied her son, Mace, to his room. Mace's thirteen-year-old brother, Keyshon, who had been born with Down Syndrome, carried a large suitcase with pride.

"Thanks, little buddy. Was it heavy?"

"No, not a bit. It was as light as a suitcase full of bricks. But I'm getting strong."

Mace walked outside with his mother, who raised both sons without any help from their father, and asked, "Do you want me to come home on the weekends to help with Keyshon?"

She looked at her son and for an instant thought of their father. She remembered how her family advised her against a relationship with Bill Franklin. They warned her about the prejudices some people still held about racially-mixed marriages. In the end they were proved right because he abandoned his family after the birth of Keyshon. She had not seen, or heard from him in over ten years.

"Keyshon and I will be all right. I want you to enjoy yourself at school. You are welcome to come home to visit, but I don't expect you to come home simply because you feel I need help."

After embracing, Mace watched his mother and brother get in the car and head home. He ran back upstairs to his room. He claimed his side of the room he would be sharing with Solomon Berkshire.

"I'm Mace Franklin."

"Solomon Berkshire. Nice to meet you, Mace. Are you the basketball player from Roosevelt?"

"The very same. How did you know I play ball?"

"I went to Mannheim Catholic and was at the game when we played against you guys."

"You went to Mannheim? I thought maybe you were Jewish."

"Yeah, I get that a lot, but I'm not. Not even Catholic, for that matter, but that's where I went. Is Mace your real name or just a nickname?"

"It's the only name I got. Mom saw it somewhere and liked it."

"Are you here to play ball?"

"Only way I could be here. Got a full ride."

Mace sat on his desk and watched as Solomon unpacked.

"What is that thing?" Mace jumped down to take a closer look.

"This is my laptop computer." Solomon proceeded to share the technical details about his new computer. Mace was totally confused but realized one thing.

"You're a computer geek. Sweet! Maybe you can help me out with your computer, and I can help you meet girls."

"I could use some help in that department."

Randy Braun, another recent Roosevelt High grad, also had a room in Humphrey Hall, one floor below Mace.

Meanwhile over at Asner Hall the scene was less chaotic. Asner was a coed dorm for upper-class students. The parents were used to having their child in college now, so it was less emotional.

Later that evening the group of Roosevelt grads met in the center of campus.

"I'm hungry," Mace said.

"What else is new?" Annie replied.

Adrien pointed. "If we want pizza, Beggar's is the closest. It's decent and cheap enough for college kids."

"Sounds good to me," Mace said while rubbing his belly.

Mace and Trish dated in high school but she dumped him over the summer for another guy. Mace felt a little uncomfortable seeing her, but Trish was friends with all the girls and didn't have any problem talking to Mace.

"How have you been, Mace? How are your Mom and Keyshon doing?" Trish asked.

"They're okay. Keyshon doesn't understand I won't be home every night yet." Mace thought about the adjustments his younger brother would have to make. "Are you still together with... what was his name?"

"Tyree Boyce. He's a senior here."

"Did he go to Roosevelt?"

"No, he's from Detroit."

Annie listened as Mace and Trish talked. After Trish and Mace broke up, the long friendship between Annie and Mace changed. They discovered a physical attraction that surprised both of them. That attraction was complicated by the fact Annie's father and Mace's mother were in a relationship, also.

"Rachel, who is your roommate? Have you met her yet?" Elaine asked.

"Her name is Ashley Zeigler, and I just met her briefly. She is going out with her parents tonight. She's from some little town downstate. She has a laptop computer, and I think she's some kind of computer whiz."

Mace looked at Solomon and nodded his head. "Solomon has a laptop, too. Maybe you could introduce him to Ashley. They might have a lot in common."

"Why, just because they both have computers?" Rachel asked.

"You can never tell."

They commandeered two tables in a corner of the restaurant and ordered pizza and pop. Mace and Annie sat across from each other but did not speak or make eye contact. Neither one knew what the reaction of their lifelong friends would be if they discovered Mace and Annie had possibly become more than just good friends. Annie and Mace weren't exactly sure about the status of their relationship now.

After a couple of hours, the group called it a night and everyone headed back to their rooms, or apartment in the case of Adrien.

Annie watched Mace and Trish walk back together. *Don't even think of trying to get her back, Mace. Just because she was your first lover doesn't mean she feels the same as you do.*

Annie got back to her room and saw her roommate.

"Hi, I'm Annie O'Dell. You must be Erin."

6

"Hi, Annie. I'm Erin Bezick."

"Do you need any help unpacking or anything?"

"I just unpacked some clothes. The other stuff can wait." Erin adjusted the headband keeping her shoulder-length brown hair out of her greenish-gray eyes.

"How long did it take for you to get here? How did you get here anyway?" Annie asked.

"It took forever! My parents brought me this time. They're staying in a hotel tonight."

Annie and Erin shared background information.

"I grew up in Kearney, Nebraska. How about you?"

"Born and raised in SoHam." Annie sat on her bed. "That's what we call this place. Have you got any brothers or sisters? I'm an only child."

"I'm the oldest. I've got a younger brother and sister."

"What do your parents do?"

"They're both high school teachers in Kearney. Yours?"

"Daddy is a detective in the robbery division here in SoHam. Mom passed away when I was five."

"Oh, I'm so sorry."

"Thanks. Daddy raised me by himself. I'll have to introduce you to my friends tomorrow. If you ever want to learn more about the city, just let me know. I can give you a guided tour." Annie laughed and said, "I know all the neighborhoods and can tell you which ones to avoid."

"I don't plan on leaving the campus very often, but I would like to know where the nearest mall is located," Erin said.

Chapter Two

"According to this, the local, and extremely wealthy, Barclay and Peterson families established North Park College in 1865 as an independent comprehensive college which offered degrees in liberal arts and sciences." Annie read from a pamphlet later that night as she lay on her bed.

"How long has the city been here?" Erin asked, as she set some family photos on top of her dresser.

"Since the 1850s. I learned that in history class at Roosevelt High."

"That's where you and your friends attended, right?"

"Yeah. I'll take you there someday. It's this huge three-story building that takes up a whole city block."

Erin sat on the edge of her bed as Annie read more.

"The campus of North Park occupies seventy-three acres atop a bluff on the north side of the Kinmundy River. The Riverwalk extends from downtown SoHam all the way through the campus and is a favorite attraction to locals and tourists alike." Annie sat up. "Is this as boring to you as it is to me?"

Erin laughed. "Probably not. You've lived here all your life, and I've only been here for a few hours. I want to learn more about SoHam." Erin grinned and said, "See, I'm already referring to it by its nickname."

"Okay, just let me know if you get bored." Annie lay back down on her back. "The campus was once the western edge of South Hampshire, but the city of over 150,000 has now expanded beyond the college. Duh! All we have to do is look out the windows and we can tell." Annie rolled her eyes, then continued, "With over 3500 undergraduates and nearly 500 hundred graduate students, North Park is large enough to attract the best students from nearly all fifty states and even some foreign countries." She paused, then laughed.

"Why is that funny?"

"If you knew some of my friends, you would understand. Some of them are not the sharpest knife in the drawer."

"Is there more?" Erin plugged in her alarm clock.

8

"The admission standards are high, but every year some places are filled by local students with potential. Eighty-nine percent of the full-time teaching faculty of over 150 have doctorates or terminal degrees in their fields." Annie flung the pamphlet toward her open closet. "So much for the propaganda."

"Do you like sports, Annie?"

"Yeah. I like basketball the best. Probably because of my friend Mace. He was the best player on the team last year and they won the state tournament. He's here on a full-ride scholarship."

"I like football better because I dated one of the guys."

"The football team plays in SoHam Memorial Stadium. They have to share it with the local high schools, but Daddy told me the college is going to build its own stadium on the edge of campus. They, I mean, we've got a fairly new gym. They hold concerts there and I've been to a few with my friends."

While not on the same level as Notre Dame, the athletic department had grown tremendously in the last twenty years. The teams competed in the prestigious Prairie States Conference.

"I didn't have much of a chance to check out the campus today, but I did when I visited last year. One of the things that really impressed me were the buildings," Erin said.

"Aren't they neat? I really like the red brick and all the ivy covering them."

"I walked around campus on my visit last year. All the buildings are pretty close together. It should be easy to get to classes."

"Did you see the student union building?" Annie asked.

"Is that the new one?"

"Yeah. It's across from Old Main and I think it's the only one on campus that looks modern."

The campus buildings were a mixture of the old and the new. Old Main, built of locally quarried white limestone, was the oldest building on campus and housed the administrative offices. The actual name of the building was The Barclay-Peterson Administration Center but everyone referred to it as 'Old Main.'

"I really like all the mature trees. It makes the campus feel like a park."

"And the river is close. I read that the Quadrangle is the sight of the original brick building which housed the entire college. That building was razed in 1905 and the area has been the quad ever since."

"I remember it's got a lot of benches and brick sidewalks. I saw a lot of students hanging out there."

"I'm going to get ready for bed." Annie grabbed her nightclothes—a t-shirt and old gym shorts. "Do you have a car, Erin?"

"No. My parents told me I could have one next year as long as I keep up my grades."

"I've got one. It's a Honda Prelude that used to belong to Grandpa. The SoHam Transit Authority runs buses from most parts of the city to the college, so it's pretty easy to get around even without a car."

"That's good. I think I'll take you up on your offer to see the city as long as you keep us out of the worst areas."

"Cool! There are a lot of neat neighborhoods. Oh, if you need to do laundry, just let me know. I'm going to take mine home and you might as well do yours there, too. It's a lot cheaper than using the laundromat."

"Thanks, Annie. I'll see you in the morning. I hope they have good food at the dining hall."

"It's edible," Annie joked. "Actually, it's pretty good, but it's customary for the students to complain about it. Good night, Erin. I think we're going to have fun this year."

Chapter Three

Classes started September eighth. Annie's first class started at nine every morning but she finished by two o'clock every day. Her roommate Erin had an eight o'clock class on Monday, Wednesday and Friday but didn't have any class until ten on Tuesday and Thursday. The staggered class schedule made getting ready in the mornings much easier. Each room in Howe Hall was equipped with a private bathroom. One of the advantages of a smaller, but extremely well endowed college. The freshmen boys dorm, Humphrey, was not as modern. The boys shared a communal facility—one on each of the five floors. Mace and Solomon didn't seem to mind.

Solomon walked into his dorm room one evening, set his backpack on his desk and turned to look at Mace.

"Why do you look so cheerful?" Mace asked.

"I met someone," Solomon replied.

Mace closed his textbook and spun around in his chair. "Spill it."

Solomon sat on his bed. "So, I was minding my own business when Rachel Lowery walked up."

"Whoa! How do you know Rachel?" Mace asked.

"We're in the same English class and we set next to each other. I don't really know her."

"Yeah, I get it. Go on."

"Okay, I was heading to Jordan for lunch and Rachel and this other girl approached me. I was shocked she even said hello because she's like a prom queen if you know what I mean."

"She is hot," Mace said while blowing on a finger.

"But she did and then she introduced me to her roommate." Solomon paused to boot up his laptop.

"So, what's her name, dude?" Mace asked after a moment.

"Oh, It's Ashley Zeigler and she's into computers."

"Sounds like a match made in geek heaven. Is she hot?"

Solomon tilted his head back and forth. "She's maybe not as smart as me, but she knows her way around a computer."

"Yeah, whatever."

"We ate lunch. Ashley and myself. We were talking about computers and I don't think the other people could follow."

"Were you using that computer lingo you use on me? If so, I totally get why no one can understand you. It's like speaking Russian or Chinese."

"I can speak some Mandarin," Solomon said.

Mace rolled his eyes and reopened his book. "I know you ain't talkin' about oranges."

"Apparently, Rachel and Ashley are getting along swell."

"That's just peachy," Mace replied without looking at Solomon.

Trish Eiffert and her roommate, Hanita Ladinae, were not as lucky. Their personalities clashed. Trish came from a home where both parents were professionals. Her father was a judge and her mother was a doctor. Hanita came from a less than idyllic broken home in Chicago's inner city. Her older brother had been shot and killed by a rival gang in a drive-by. She came to North Park on a basketball scholarship. This personality conflict convinced Trish to try to join a sorority.

"Cindy, since we're sharing a room and our class schedules are the same, I feel in addition to being best friends, we're sisters," Elaine gushed as they returned to their room after dinner.

"Do you think we have a chance to land positions on *The Chronicle*?" Cindy asked. "We know we're going to major in journalism and it would be perfect if we could work on the college paper just like we did at Roosevelt."

"My goal is to be the editor by next year," Elaine said.

"I'll be satisfied just to be a part of the team," Cindy said while brushing her blonde hair.

Elaine and Cindy shared matching views when it came to boyfriends. They were waiting before becoming sexually active.

The Jordan Dining Hall, named in honor of Miles T. Jordan the first mayor of South Hampshire, was the main dining area on campus. Other options included a cafe in the student lounge and a coffeehouse, but most students ate at Jordan. The Roosevelt High gang was no exception. They tried to meet everyday for lunch, if classes allowed, and met for dinner almost every night. They settled upon a regular spot where they met and it soon became known as 'Rough Rider Central.' This was where they shared the latest news about fellow Roosevelt grads.

Rachel, Elaine and Cindy were having dinner one evening when Trish joined them.

"Hey, guys, did I tell you Diana Ahronson is in my ten o'clock English Composition class?"

"No, you didn't say anything, Trish. How is she? Have you talked to her?"

"She's fine and she and Damon did not break up, so everyone can ignore that rumor. We talked about joining a sorority together."

"Rachel, do you think you'll join a sorority?"

"I haven't really thought about it. There really aren't many fraternities and sororities left. It's becoming a thing of the past."

"All the more reason for me to join one. They are becoming more elitist about who they select," Trish said and sounded rather uppity.

Mace, Solomon and Ashley joined the group and Annie and Erin arrived a couple of minutes later. Solomon and Ashley were constantly together now. Randy Braun arrived and stood behind the empty chair next to Annie. He was breathing hard and his face was red from exertion.

Annie looked over her shoulder and asked, "Are you okay, Randy? Did you run all the way here?"

"Just part of the way. Guess who I saw coming out of the Student Union just now?"

"Wait! Don't tell me, I know. Was it Halle Berry?" Mace asked.

"Real funny, Mace. I saw Matthew Sullivan."

At the mention of his name Annie looked first at Randy, then across the table at Mace. She hadn't seen Matt since early June when he took her to Derrick Keasling's graduation party.

"So he's back in town after all. Do you think he's living on campus?" Mace asked with a mouth full of fries.

13

Randy sat down next to Annie. "He would be in our dorm if he was and I haven't seen him around."

Mace looked at Annie, but she was not looking back. She developed a sudden interest in her green beans. Matt Sullivan was the only son of Cormac Sullivan, who was thought to be a local crime figure in the city.

"I heard Matt was sent to New York City over the summer to avoid some minor local trouble," Randy whispered. "You know anything about that, Annie?"

"How would I know anything about Matthew Sullivan," Annie said and then looked at Mace.

Annie had dated Matthew and he was one of the first boys to ever kiss her.

"No reason," Randy said. "Could you pass the salt please."

Cindy held a fork in her hand as she glanced around the table and whispered, "Matt cultivated a reputation as a 'bad boy' in high school and rumor has it he's one of the likely candidates to be the father of Victoria Madison's child. I don't like to spread gossip, but that's what I heard.

Annie picked at her green beans again and wondered if Matt would try to call or see her.

"How can you even be sure he's going to school here, Randy?" Elaine asked while handing him the salt. "Maybe he was just visiting the campus."

Randy covered his mashed potatoes and gravy with salt and said, "He was carrying books. I doubt he would be carrying books if he was just visiting. Oh, he was with a girl and she seemed to be very interested in him."

"Did you recognize the girl?" Elaine asked.

"No, she wasn't from Roosevelt. She looked older, too."

After dinner Mace joined Annie as they got ready to leave.

"Can I talk to you, Annie?"

"Sure, what's up, Mace?"

Mace held the door open for her as they walked outside.

"Are you okay with Matthew being back in town?"

"Why not? He lives in SoHam. The city's big enough for both of us," Annie answered sarcastically.

"That's not what I mean and you know it. Don't cop an attitude with me, girl."

"It doesn't matter, Mace. I'm over him. We only went out a couple times."

"You let him kiss you and what about the night in Peoria?"

Annie stopped walking and grabbed Mace's arm. "How do you know about that?"

"I have ways of discovering things just like you, Nancy Drew. I know you were in the pool alone with him in that little bikini of yours."

"Nothing happened, Mace! The only thing he did was kiss me."

"I know." They resumed walking. "Keyshon was asking about you today."

"How is he doing?"

"He misses me, but he's doing okay. Wanna go with me Saturday morning to see him?"

"Sure. I want to stop and see Daddy, too. Do I have to drive?"

"We can take the bus if you'd rather."

"No, I'll drive."

Mace bounced his basketball against the wall while waiting outside of Howe Hall for Annie early Saturday morning.

"About time you got down here," Mace said.

"Have you been waiting long? You could have come upstairs, you know."

"I wasn't sure if men were allowed on your floor."

"Men aren't, but you could..."

"You're real funny, Annie," Mace said.

Fifteen minutes later they turned into the Mayfield neighborhood. After a right turn onto Oakland Lane, Annie pulled into the driveway at the Franklin home.

"Anyone home?" Mace shouted as he and Annie walked in the front door. "Mom! Keyshon! Where are you guys?"

There was still no answer. Mace walked through the house.

"I don't think there's anyone here, Mace. Did they know

you were coming home this morning?" Annie asked as she sat down on the living room couch.

"No, I was going to surprise them."

"Well, I guess they surprised you instead. Can we run over to my house so I can start on my laundry?"

"Do you need any help? I could sort it out for you."

"It's already sorted, Mace. Why on earth do you want to see my dirty laundry?"

Annie smacked his arm as Mace grinned and she realized why.

"Will you grow up?"

On the way to her house, Annie's thoughts kept returning to the news of Matthew Sullivan's appearance at North Park. She questioned if her interest in him over the summer was solely based on his reputation. She accepted that as part of the reason, but she knew there was more to it. She looked at Mace and asked about Trish.

"Do you know how Trish met Tyree? Do you know him?"

"I only know him by sight. I've never talked to him."

"Do you think they're..."

"Don't go there," Mace interrupted. "I don't want to even think about that. It doesn't matter anyway and how about Matthew Sullivan. What will you do if you run into him?"

"I'll be polite and say hi. I doubt I'll see him though."

They pulled up in the driveway.

"Hey! That's Mom's car," Mace said.

They parked and ran into the house. Dad was having breakfast with Mrs. Franklin and Keyshon. Keyshon was the first to see them.

"Annie!" Keyshon yelled at the top of his voice startling his mother and Detective O'Dell. Keyshon ran over to Annie and hugged her.

"How are you, Keyshon? What have you been doing this week?"

"I went to school all week. Mace! You're home, too. Did you and Annie get married yet?"

"Not yet, little brother. Do you think we should?"

16

"Maybe not. I think I will marry Annie instead."

"Hi, Daddy. Hi, Mrs. Franklin. We stopped by your house but no one was home."

"We came over here early this morning, Annie. Your father is taking us grocery shopping."

"I came home to do laundry. Do you mind if Keyshon stays with us while you and Daddy do the shopping?"

"Are you sure you don't mind, Annie?"

"He misses Mace. Look at them."

Mace was dribbling his basketball and Keyshon was guarding him.

Keith and Elisabeth ran out to do the shopping while Mace and Keyshon stayed at the O'Dell house with Annie. Annie started on her laundry.

Keyshon followed her into the laundry room. "Annie, do you live with Mace at the college?"

"We don't live in the same building, Keyshon."

Keyshon waited while Annie loaded the washer. He followed her back out to the living room.

"What's on your mind, little man?" Mace asked.

Keyshon looked at his brother. "Can I come to a basketball game sometime. I want to see you play and sit with Annie."

"You can come to all my games if you want, Keyshon."

"And you can sit right next to me, too," Annie replied.

"Great! People will think I'm cool if I sit with you, Annie."

Annie shook her head. "You've got it wrong, Keyshon. People will think I'm cool if I get to sit next to you."

Keyshon grinned.

The next Thursday Trish Eiffert shared some good news with Elaine and Annie.

"Diana and I are part of the Alpha Phi sorority now. They accepted both of us."

"That's great, Trish," Elaine said. "I guess this means you will both be living at their house, right?"

"Yes, Diana and I have already moved out of the dorm. We are sharing a room. Now I don't have to put up with that hoodlum

17

from Chicago. She scared me at times."

"Come on, Trish. Cut her some slack," Elaine said. "We don't know how difficult it must be to live in that world. It has to be so different than SoHam."

Annie wondered if she should investigate further into Hanita Ladinae.

"You can still call us and we can do things together," Elaine said.

"I will, Lainey. Tell Cindy and Rachel the news for me okay. I gotta run. Diana and I are going out to dinner with her parents."

Annie watched Trish hurry away, glanced up at Elaine and asked, "How long do you think it will take for her to forget about the rest of us?"

"Trish isn't like that," Elaine said. "She'll still hang out with us. We've been friends for a long time."

Within a week, Trish made new friends at the sorority and soon was too busy for her old friends. Trish didn't realize, and it could never be spoken of in official terms, but she was accepted to fill a quota. She was one of three 'minority girls' in the sorority.

Chapter Four

"Hey! Are you picking me up, or do I have to walk over to your dorm?" Mace asked Annie over the phone.

"For crap's sake! Your dorm is a block away and the parking lot is even closer. Get your butt over here. I'm not picking you up. Just meet me at the car in ten minutes." Annie hung up and shook her head.

"Who were you talking to?" Erin asked as she sat at her desk twirling her elastic headband around a finger.

"Just Mace. He was trying to convince me to pick him up at Humphrey Hall. We're picking up Keyshon and bringing him to the game. He thinks I'm his personal taxi. Are you coming to the game?"

"I don't have a ride unless I take the bus."

"Just ask Lainey or Rachel for a lift. I'm sure they won't mind."

"Okay, but I have to finish reading three chapters."

"I'll save you a seat. Just look for us."

The first home football game was at noon against Augustana State College of Cedar Rapids, Iowa. Mace and Annie picked up Keyshon and took him to the game. They met their friends and sat together in the half-full SoHam stadium. Keyshon was happy just to be with Mace and Annie. North Park won the close game on a touchdown late in the fourth quarter. As they were leaving the stadium, Annie ran into Matt Sullivan. Literally! She was walking around a corner of the building after making a pit stop and she and Matt bumped into each other.

"I'm sorry, Annie. I didn't see you. How are you?"

"I'm all right, Matt. How have you been? Are you taking classes here?"

"I am. I decided to come back home for college. New York was a little too crazy for me."

Mace and Keyshon saw Annie talking to Matt and walked toward them.

"Are you living in a dorm?" Annie asked

"No, I'm commuting from home this semester. Are you

living in a dorm?"

"Yeah, I wanted to experience the whole college thing and staying at home with Daddy wouldn't quite cut it."

Mace and Keyshon stood behind Annie without saying a word.

Matt nodded his head. "How about you, Mace? I heard you got a basketball scholarship."

"Yep! Full ride. I'm living in Humphrey Hall."

They were all quiet for a moment until Matt asked, "Would you mind if I call you sometime, Annie. We could talk about old times or something. Maybe even grab something to eat."

"Maybe. I'll let you know, Matty. See you around."

Mace grabbed Keyshon's hand and they moved a few feet away to let Annie talk to Matt in private.

"Come on, Annie. Give me a break. We used to be friends. We had some fun together. Remember the time we spent in Peoria."

"I remember it, Matty."

"Didn't you like kissing me? You seemed to like it at the time."

"I should go, Matt." But before she did, she dug into her purse and scribbled on a piece of scrap paper and handed it to Matt. "This is my cell number. You can call me sometime."

"See you around, Annie O'Dell."

Matt watched as Annie walked toward Mace and Keyshon.

"You are looking better than ever, Annie," Matt whispered under his breath.

Annie turned to look at Matt as she reached Mace. He smiled at her, but she just turned away.

"You all right, Annie?"

"I'm fine, Mace. I just didn't expect to run into him today."

Keyshon grabbed her hand. "I don't like that guy, Annie. I think he wants to marry you so he can kiss you. Please don't marry him, Annie."

"I won't, Keyshon. I promise. Come on, let's go get milkshakes at Burger Bob's. Everyone is going to be there."

When Annie, Mace and Keyshon finally got to Burger

20

Bob's, Elaine, Cindy, Adrien and Bryce were already waiting. Solomon and Ashley walked in talking about computers. Randy Braun and Erin Bezick showed up a few minutes later. They grabbed some tables in the corner and the conversation turned to college life.

"Do you guys like the food at Jordan?" Elaine asked. "The *Chronicle* is going to run a story about the company with the contract. I hear kids complaining about the food all the time. Personally, I don't think it's that bad. What do you think, Erin?"

"Some days it's better than others, Elaine."

"Please call me Lainey," Elaine said and then turned to Randy Braun. "What do you think, Randy?"

"I think it depends on what kids are used to eating at home. I think they do a pretty good job. I mean they can't make tacos or pizza every day."

"Why not?" Mace asked.

"Because there are some kids who don't like to eat pizza every day, Mace. I know you find that difficult to believe, but it's true."

"Annie, you are being rather quiet. Are you all right?" Cindy asked.

Mace nudged Annie's shoulder. "She ran into Matt Sullivan after the game. She's probably thinking about him and ignoring us."

Annie smacked Mace's arm. "I am not thinking about Matty. I just don't have anything to say."

Mace looked at Annie and could tell she was thinking about Matthew.

"I like milkshakes! When I go to college I'm going to have chocolate milkshakes everyday," Keyshon announced.

Mace laughed as he patted Keyshon on the back. "When you get to college you can have all the milkshakes you want, little buddy."

Keyshon listened to the conversations, but he stayed close to Annie, since he didn't know the other kids as well as he knew her.

Cindy and Bryce sat close together and held hands. She

whispered to Elaine, "I'm gonna head back to the room. I need to work on a paper. Bryce will give me a ride. I'll see you later, okay."

"Sure, Cin. I was going to go over to Adrien's for awhile, anyway. I'll be home around nine."

Annie listened and wondered if Elaine and Cindy had worked out an arrangement so they could have time alone with their boyfriends. Bryce and Cindy left, still holding hands.

Elaine continued her interview. "Now what about the dining hall. Any suggestions."

Solomon and Ashley both answered at the same time.

"More computer hookups!"

"Do you guys ever think of anything other than computers?"

"Sure, we think about software, operating systems, hard drives and processors, too," Ashley answered.

Eventually, everyone was ready to leave. Annie and Mace dropped Keyshon off at home. Keyshon hugged Annie for a long time before he would allow her to leave.

"I miss you. Will you come and see me again?"

"Of course I will. You make sure you do a good job at school."

"I will. I'm the smartest guy in my class."

Annie broke off the hug and waved as she got in her car.

Mace looked at Annie and asked very seriously, "Are you still thinking about Matt?"

"You know me too well, Mace. Okay, I was thinking about him. Do you think he really is the father?"

"I try not to think about that. If Victoria doesn't know, then why should we care?"

"I heard she's going to give the baby up for adoption, then come to North Park next semester."

"Who told you that?"

"Laura Russell told Rachel and Rachel told it to Lainey and Cin and they told me."

"Remind me to never tell you guys anything."

"I can keep a secret if I need to, Mace."

Twenty minutes later Annie parked the car and she and Mace headed to her dorm. They looked at each other wondering what the other was thinking. They hadn't kissed since moving onto campus.

"It's still nice out, Annie, wanna go for a walk? The Riverwalk is close by."

"As long as we don't stay out too late. I need to finish some reading tonight."

"I promise I'll have you back by midnight."

"What are we going to do until midnight?"

Mace grinned at Annie.

"You are terrible, Mace Franklin. Are you trying to take advantage of my inexperience with boys?"

"Yes, do you think I stand a chance?"

"Not tonight you don't."

"I bet if I was Matthew Sullivan you wouldn't say that."

"Screw you, Mace Franklin!"

Annie stopped walking, turned around and started to walk away.

Mace grabbed her arm before she could get away. "I'm sorry, Annie. I shouldn't have said that. Come on, let's go for a walk, please."

"As long as you don't mention his name, okay?"

"I won't mention what's his name again."

"I never let him do as much with me as you have, Mace."

"I'm sorry if I seem a little jealous. It's just that he doesn't care about you the way I do. He will just use you if you let him."

"And you won't?"

"That was a low blow."

"I'm sorry. I know you love me as a friend, but that doesn't make it okay for us to... you know."

"And just because Matt is 'not' a friend doesn't mean it's okay to 'you know' with him." Mace suddenly felt uncomfortable talking to her about sex. Something that hadn't happened before.

Annie faced Mace. "But Matty is a friend. I know he wants to be more than a friend at times, but he's still a friend."

They kept walking and Mace tried to hold Annie's hand but

23

she wouldn't let him.

"Stop it! I'm not going to hold hands, or anything else with you."

"Sorry, you don't have to bite my head off."

They kept some space between them as they walked along in silence for a time.

"Did you hear how Lainey and Cindy were talking? It was like they were arranging who was going to be alone in the dorm room and tonight was Cindy's turn."

"What are you talking about?" Mace asked.

"Didn't you hear what Cindy told Lainey?" Annie asked.

"I guess I didn't pay any attention. Besides it's none of our business. If Cindy wants to spent some time alone with Bryce, that's her decision. It's not like she is totally ignorant of what guys want."

"I suppose I should get used to the fact college kids sleep together. I can't imagine Lainey and Adrien doing that though," Annie said.

"Even if they don't sleep together they probably make out. They are humans, you know."

She poked Mace in the side. "You can be a real creep at times, but you're still my friend. Do you think Solomon and Ashley make out?"

"I refuse to answer that question."

"They probably kiss like two computers connecting." Annie laughed, then turned serious. "I walked in on Erin and Randy a couple days ago."

"Erin and Randy Braun? No way! I would have thought she had better taste and higher standards."

"Do you think Erin is pretty?"

"Not as pretty as you, sweetie pie," Mace teased.

"Good answer, but not the correct one. Do you?"

"Yeah, she's pretty and has a nice build. Were she and Randy... you know?"

"No! You creep! They were just sitting on her bed. They were both fully dressed."

"What did you do?"

24

"I went downstairs to the lounge and read a book until Randy left."

"So you cannot swear the defendants did not engage in sexual activity while you were out of the room. Please answer the question." Mace grabbed her shoulders and grinned at her.

"That is correct. I cannot swear to it, but I did ask Erin later and she divulged all the juicy details."

"And you are going to share them with the court now."

"Not in a million years, your honor! You can torture me and I will not reveal anything." She moved the back of her hand to her forehead.

"How about part of the juicy details?" Mace asked.

"How about we go back to my room and maybe create some details of our own."

"Really?" Mace was surprised.

"No! But I need to get back anyway."

"Fine. I need to find a new girlfriend."

"Does that mean I'm not your girlfriend, Mace?"

"Do you want to be?"

"I'm not sure anymore, Mace. Maybe what happened was just wrong. We never should have kissed like that."

"I was thinking the same thing, Annie. I don't want to lose your friendship, but I want to have a girlfriend."

"Maybe you should talk to Erin or maybe Rachel."

"I thought Rachel was seeing Ben Barnes?"

"Oh yeah, I forgot about that. They make a nice couple. You should talk to Erin though. I don't think she's real serious about Randy and they didn't do anything when I was out of the room."

When Mace and Annie entered her room, Erin was at her desk studying.

Annie closed the door with a bang, but Erin didn't react, so Annie hollered, "Erin, I'm back and Mace is with me."

Erin turned around. She was wearing earbuds and didn't hear them come in. She removed the earbuds and smiled.

"Hi, Annie. Hey, Mace. What were you guys doing?"

"Just taking a stroll along the Riverwalk."

"Did you have a good time?"

"We were just walking and talking, Erin. Nothing else."

"Hey, Erin, are you going to be studying much longer?" Mace asked.

"I'm finished. Why?"

"I was just thinking maybe you and I could go for a stroll along the Riverwalk. The night is young and it's a beautiful night."

Erin looked at Annie. "Would you mind?"

"No, why would I mind? Mace and I are just friends."

"Give me a minute and I'll go with you."

Erin used the bathroom and Mace gave Annie a high-five.

"You better behave, Mace," Annie warned.

"I won't do anything I haven't done before," he replied.

"Mace!"

"I meant with you, Annie. Not Trish."

"Keep your hands to yourself if you wanna live," Annie said.

Erin was ready to go and she and Mace went for a walk. Annie got ready for bed. She put on an actual pair of lightweight pajamas and sat at her desk to study. Erin and Mace walked for a few minutes along the asphalt path.

"Is there anything between you and Randy?" Mace asked.

Erin stopped walking and looked up at Mace. "Annie told you, huh?"

Mace nodded. "Is there?"

"Not really. He's okay, but there's no chemistry between us."

"No heat, huh?" Mace asked as they continued walking.

An occasional cyclist and two guys on roller blades passed them. They came to a bench and sat and talked as they listened to the sound of the Kinmundy River as it flowed lazily along.

"Do you like living here?" Mace asked. "What's it like in Nebraska?"

"It's not like a foreign country," Erin said, then she described her hometown of Kearney.

They stopped talking after a time and looked into each other's eyes. Mace kissed Erin and she kissed him back. After a

26

few minutes of kissing they returned to Howe Hall.

"Would you like to come in?" Erin invited Mace in without realizing Annie was in her pajamas. "You can stay for awhile, but then I have to get to bed."

"I won't stay too late, Erin. I need to do some studying myself."

Erin unlocked the door, pulled Mace inside, then quickly closed and re-locked the door.

"Annie, we're back."

Annie, sitting at her desk, turned around to face them. Mace noticed she was in her pajamas and not her usual nighttime wear. She pulled her knees up to her chest. "Did you guys have a nice stroll? You weren't gone all that long."

"We had a good time. We walked along, then found a bench and got to know each other a little better."

Annie looked at Mace, narrowed her eyes and frowned.

Erin sat on the edge of her bed and patted the spot next to her. Mace sat down and Annie turned back to her studying. She tried to ignore the sound of Mace and Erin kissing. She finally turned around and cleared her throat.

Mace got the hint and stood up. "I should get going, Erin. I really need to study for a couple hours."

"If you really need to go, it's okay. Will you call me tomorrow? Maybe we can study together."

Erin stood up and walked over to the door with him.

"Sure, I'll call."

Mace and Erin embraced and kissed as Annie watched.

"Night, Mace, go home. See you later." Annie waved.

"Good night, Annie."

Chapter Five

Six weeks had passed since the beginning of the semester at North Park College. The Roosevelt High gang settled into routines. The daily gatherings for lunch and dinner became less frequent. Elaine and Cindy become very involved with the school newspaper and their boyfriends. Solomon Berkshire and Ashley Zeigler were joined at the hip and never far from their computers. Mace anxiously awaited the start of basketball season. He kept in shape by running five miles every day. He and Erin Bezick still dated. Randy Braun acted like a typical freshman living away from home for the first time. He partied all weekend. He made new friends who shared his desire to get wasted and stopped hanging out with the kids he knew from high school. Trish and Tyree never socialized with her old friends. Diana Ahronson hadn't changed. She was genuinely liked by everyone she met. Damon Barclay flew home from Princeton University every other week to see her. They started dating during their junior year at Roosevelt High. Sightings of Matt Sullivan happened on occasion, but he spent most of his time working at The Hungry Lion, or studying at home.

Everyone found a partner except for Annie O'Dell. Not that opportunities didn't present themselves. Several of the older guys on campus asked Annie for a date, but she refused them all. At just seventeen, she wasn't ready to start dating every guy who asked. A wise choice since most of the guys were only interested in sex. There were two guys she would go out with. One was Mace Franklin, but he and Erin seemed to be getting along just fine and Annie didn't want to interfere. Mace even took Erin home one weekend. Annie stayed on campus because her father and Elisabeth Franklin had taken Keyshon to visit his maternal grandmother in Wisconsin. Mace and Erin had the house to themselves all weekend. When they got back to campus on Sunday, Annie assumed they slept together but didn't say anything to either of them.

The other guy Annie thought about was Matt Sullivan. She was still drawn to him and, though she didn't like to admit it, part of the attraction was his 'bad boy' reputation. Although she had given Matt her cell phone number, he hadn't called. She was not about to call him. She kept busy with her classes and concentrated on her studies. There were times when that was not easy because Erin brought Mace up to the room to study together. They studied, but Annie knew sooner or later they would finish and start kissing. Erin would kick Mace out before they went too far. One night after such a study session Annie and Erin talked.

"Annie, are you sure it doesn't bother you when Mace comes up to see me? I know you guys are just friends but..."

"I don't mind Mace being here," Annie said as she got ready for bed. "I get to see him at least. I don't even see Lainey or Cindy much anymore."

"I know Mace likes to tease you."

"And I tease him back even more."

They both giggled. Erin took her pajamas into the bathroom to change but left the door open.

"Mace is always telling me about his little brother and how much Keyshon loves you. Keyshon misses you, Annie. Whenever Mace calls him, he always asks about you."

"I miss Keyshon, too. Have you met Keyshon yet?"

"I saw him at the game against Augustana, but I didn't get much of a chance to talk to him."

"Keyshon is the sweetest kid."

"I've never really known anyone with Down Syndrome before. I've seen kids with that, but I've never really known them."

"Can I ask you something, Erin? You can tell me it's none of my business if you don't want to answer."

Erin walked out of the bathroom and sat on the edge of her bed. "You want to know about the weekend I was with Mace. It's okay, Annie. I don't mind you asking. I'm sure Mace might have told you a few details."

"He just told me you guys went to Sandusky's and Darby's on Saturday. I know Mace and Trish... Oh, maybe I shouldn't say anything about Trish."

"I know all about Trish, Annie. Mace really liked her, but I think he's totally over her now."

"Yeah, it hurt him when she dumped him, but he has a

thick skin. He hides his feelings from friends really well."

"He can't hide his feelings from you though. You know each other so well."

"I guess so. Sometimes he lets his guard down with me. Has he ever told you anything about his father?" Annie asked.

"No, not a single word and I didn't want to pry."

"He left after Keyshon was born and Mace hasn't seen him since."

"No wonder he doesn't talk about his dad."

Annie looked at Erin but remained quiet for a moment. Erin could tell Annie wanted to ask more about the weekend.

"Annie, I can tell you are dying to ask, but are reluctant to pry, so I'll just tell you. Yeah, we slept together and it was my first time. I know it wasn't Mace's first time."

"Was it everything you hoped it would be," Annie asked.

Erin lay on her side facing Annie. "It was pretty good. I used to think my first time would be on my wedding night, but I didn't want to wait any longer."

"Speaking of longer," Annie said and then glanced at the clock.

Erin laughed and moved onto her back. "I didn't time it, but Mace didn't exactly rush things along if you get my meaning."

"Sorry, but I wanted a general idea of how long it takes," Annie said and then flopped onto her back. "I'm not totally naive, but I've heard all sorts of stories. This one girl at Roosevelt said she and her boyfriend stayed in bed for three hours and others have said it only takes a minute."

"I imagine ours was five minutes at least," Erin admitted.

Annie stared at the ceiling for a time, then turned on her side and asked, "Did you take precautions?"

"Mace did. I wouldn't let him otherwise. He told me about some cheerleader from high school who got pregnant and isn't even sure who the father is."

"Victoria Madison. She knows who the father is, but she likes to pretend she doesn't for some reason. She should be about ready to have the baby, I think."

"No way would I let that happen to me. I would get an

abortion before having a baby. What about you, Annie? If you were pregnant would you have the baby?"

"I guess I haven't even thought about it, Erin. I'm still a virgin."

"It only takes one time, Annie. If you ever go ahead and do it, make sure the guy uses protection. You should even use protection yourself."

"Daddy would freak out if I was on the pill."

"He wouldn't need to know and there are other methods besides the pill. You don't tell your father about everything you do, do you?"

Annie twisted her hair. "There's not much Daddy doesn't know about me."

"Would you tell him if you had sex?"

"He would probably know because I would look different. I would have a guilty look on my face. You know he's a detective, right?"

"Mace told me. Well, at least now you are in the dorm so he won't know if you have a boy sleep over with you."

"Daddy would still know somehow and I wouldn't lie to him if he asked."

Chapter Six

Mace knocked on Erin and Annie's door the night before the official opening of basketball season.

"Oh, gross! You can come in, but don't you dare touch us," Erin said as she put her hand against his chest. "It's November and cold. Why are you so sweaty?"

"I just ran five miles as hard as I could," he answered.

Annie went into the bathroom and came out with a washcloth and towel. She threw them at him and said, "You can use these since they were already in the dirty clothes pile."

That bit of information didn't phase Mace. He wiped off his face, arms and dried his hair.

"Finally, we can practice basketball. I can't wait until tomorrow. This is why I've worked so hard to get in the best shape of my life." He handed the washcloth and towel back to Annie.

Annie used her fingertips to hold the sweaty material as far away from her as she could before throwing them into the bathroom. "Are you going to be able to keep up with your studies?"

"As long as I don't sleep more than an hour a day. Maybe two hours if I'm lucky."

"Are you going to have time for me, Mace?" Erin asked as she smiled.

"I will fit you into my busy schedule somehow, Erin."

"What about me, Mace? Are you just going to forget about me?" Annie plopped down on the edge of her bed.

"What was your name again?" Mace teased.

Annie threw her pillow at Mace, then stuck out her tongue and made faces at him. Mace moved closer and started to sit on Erin's bed.

Erin pushed him away. "Don't even think about sitting on my bed, you smelly man."

Mace turned around and approached Annie with his hands out. "I'm going to make you pay for that. I could have been injured by that pillow and not been able to play ball."

"You better leave me alone, Mace Franklin!" She scooted

back against the wall. "Are you supposed to be Frankenstein?"

Mace lowered his arms. "There's no one here to protect you now, Annie O'Dell. You are all mine."

"That was the worst imitation of a monster I've ever seen," Erin said.

Mace turned around and began marching toward Erin as the monster.

Annie jumped off of her bed and leaped onto Mace's back. "You better leave Erin alone, you bad monster."

Erin put a hand to her mouth. "I wish I had a camera handy. You should see how silly you guys look."

Annie slid to the floor and pinched her nose. "You need a shower and don't even think of smelling up ours."

Mace took two steps toward the bathroom before Annie grabbed him.

"No way, Jose," Annie yelled.

"Can I at least sit down? I'm exhausted from my run."

"Not a chance," Annie said.

He looked at Erin hoping for some sympathy.

She shook her head. "You have to stand by the door."

"Can I sit on the floor?"

"Yeah, sure," Annie said. "The have to replace the carpeting anyway."

Erin laughed and soon Annie and Mace were laughing also.

"Are you going to come to the games, Annie?"

"No! Why would I want to see you play ball? You'll be sitting on the bench the whole game if you even make the team."

"You should go home so you can rest. You have a long day ahead of you tomorrow," Erin said as she pointed to the door.

He stood up and held out his arms. "Do I get a kiss before I go?"

"I don't know?" Erin scooted against her desk. "Annie, do you want to give this sweaty guy a kiss?"

"Yuck! No way! He's all gross and sweaty. I think I need a shower just from touching him."

Mace grinned. "How about we all take a shower together? That will save water."

"Why would we want to shower with you, Mace Franklin?" Erin asked.

"Yeah! Why would we want to see your skinny body in the shower with us beautiful women?" Annie asked.

"Because you know how sexy I look."

"Gag me with a spoon!" Annie stuck a finger in her mouth. "Did going for a run scramble the few brains left in your head?"

Erin and Annie teased Mace about his body. They knew he didn't have an ounce of fat on him and most girls would have considered him very sexy indeed.

"Should we flip a coin and the loser has to shower with Mace?" Erin asked.

"Do you have a coin with two heads?" Annie asked Erin. "We could both call tails and neither one of us would lose."

"You mean you would both lose. Actually, you would both win since you would have the honor of showering with me." Mace was teasing them and they knew it. He looked back and forth between them. "What no takers? I guess I'll have to shower alone."

He pulled his sleeveless sweatshirt over his head and both girls looked at his muscular chest. When he untied his sweatpants and started to drop his them, Annie yelled, "Stop it! Don't you dare. There's no way I'm letting you take a shower in my bathroom."

"Why not?" he asked.

Annie looked at Mace, then at Erin. "Oh, God! Erin, please tell me you didn't let him use our shower."

"You weren't here."

"I'm gonna throw up." Annie furiously waved her hands. "Don't tell me if you guys had sex in there."

Mace grinned. Erin smiled. Annie swore.

Mace put his shirt on. "I need to go. Who is going to give me a good night kiss?"

Annie and Erin looked at each other as they shook their heads.

"Rock, paper, scissors?" Erin asked.

"Sure, count of three."

Erin lost.

"Best out of three!"

"Okay." Annie reluctantly agreed.

Mace shook his head.

Erin won the nest two rounds.

Annie kicked her desk. "Crap! I should have quit when I was ahead. Now I've got to kiss him."

"Come to daddy and give me a kiss, sweet pea!" Mace grinned stupidly as he held out his arms.

"Call me that again and I've give you a reason to redshirt this year."

Mace walked over to Annie. She looked at Erin.

"I won fair and square."

"But he's *your* boyfriend!" Annie exclaimed.

"My point exactly. Why should I have to kiss him when he's all sweaty and smelly?"

Annie groaned and said, "One kiss and make it quick."

Mace leaned over and kissed Annie's cheek without touching her anywhere else.

"There, I didn't get my sweat all over you, Annie."

"Thank you, Mace." She smacked his butt. "Good night, sexy!"

"Good night, Annie. Love you!"

Mace kissed Erin good night on the lips and she walked him to the door.

"Good night, sexy girl. See you tomorrow."

Mace smiled as he made his way to his dorm.

Erin leaned against the door. "He is very sexy."

"He is a good kisser and he does have a cute butt." Annie giggled, then turned red. "Not that I've ever seen it. I have kissed him, but I've never seen his butt."

"It doesn't matter." Erin sat on the edge of her bed. "Are you really upset that we showered together?"

"What? No, I was only kidding. How was it?" Annie joined Erin on her bed. "I'd be afraid of slipping and breaking my neck. How would I ever explain that to Daddy?"

They both giggled.

November fourth was the first actual day of basketball practice. Coach Robert Bazetich blew his whistle and gathered the players on the bleachers in front of him. Mace Franklin looked around at the other players. He recognized most of them. Mace sat next to Javarius Mays, who played for Chicago Simmons.

"I'm glad we're on the same team now," Javarius fist-bumped Mace. I didn't like losing to you last year."

Mace grinned and asked, "Why did you choose North Park? You could have gone anywhere."

"I wanted to stay close to my mother and grandmother," he answered.

Despite standing six-eight, Javarius could handle the ball as well as Mace. He combined the ability to shoot from the three point line with the moves and strength to take the ball inside.

Also returning to the team were six players who saw a lot of action last year. Kevin Murphy, a senior and the team captain, was a tough-as-nails point guard who grew up in the Irish section of South Boston. His leadership both on and off the court was the glue to this team. Damian Gibson, a six-nine front court player, led the team in both scoring and rebounding last season and returned for his final year. The rest of the players who saw action last year were either juniors or sophomores. The third freshman recruit was small forward Arnett Robinson from Detroit's Finley High School where he led his team to the state championship game before losing. He was in street clothes because of an injury which would keep him on the sidelines for another month. His grandmother raised him after he lost both parents in a gang shootout.

After a fifteen minute talk, Coach started the drills. For thirty-two years he had stressed conditioning to his team and Mace now appreciated his extra running. The players sprinted from one end of the court to the other and Mace won every sprint. Coach took notice. He knew Mace was athletic, but did not expect him to be this quick.

Chapter Seven

The North Park Redbirds opened the season two weeks later against Rockford College. Mace's friends from Roosevelt sat in the section behind the bench. Erin and Annie stood and hollered at Mace before the game. He spotted them and waved.

"Oh, Mace, you're our hero," Annie teased.

Erin blew him a kiss.

"Hey, Franklin, is that your fan club?" Javarius Mays asked. "You haven't played yet."

"They're just friends," Mace explained.

The starting lineup was Murphy, Gibson, Cunningham, Odom and Young. Mace Franklin was the first man off the bench. He played both the point and shooting guard. The Redbirds blew Rockford out of the gym and ended up winning by thirty-five points. Mace played twenty minutes and scored ten points. He added three assists, two rebounds and no turnovers to his record.

After the game Mace met Erin and Annie in Jordan Dining Hall to grab some food.

Annie and Mace followed with their trays as Erin led the way to a table.

"Not a bad start, Mace," Annie said. "I thought you played better than Alex Young. Coach Bazetich should start you instead."

"I think he started Alex because he has more experience," Mace said over his shoulder.

"Why didn't Javarius start? He's the best player on the team."

Erin found an unoccupied table and they sat down.

"He was five minutes late for practice Wednesday and Coach really let him have it. He told Javarius if he's late again he will sit for an entire half."

"What if he has a valid reason?"

"Coach is fair. If someone has a valid reason, he doesn't punish them too much."

"What would he consider a valid reason?" Annie asked because she knew Mace would have a smartaleck answer.

"Oh, you know. The usual stuff. Parents killed in a plane

37

crash. Heart surgery might excuse you. Basically, if you are breathing you are expected to be on time."

"He sounds mean," Erin said while pouring French dressing on her salad.

"He's tough, no doubt about that, but he really cares about his players. A lot of his former players come back to see him. I think that says a lot about him."

Annie noticed some people walking in. "Isn't that Kevin Murphy?"

Mace turned to look. "Yeah, it is and the other guy is Scott Cavanaugh. He's on the team, too. He's a walk-on."

"What's a walk-on?" Erin asked.

"It means he doesn't have a scholarship to play ball. He's on the team because he just loves to play. He's from the same neighborhood in Boston as Kevin."

"Who are the two girls with them?"

"Not sure, but it looks like we are going to find out."

Kevin waved at Mace and walked over with his friends.

"Nice job today, Mace. I know Rockford isn't much competition, but you played a good game."

"Thanks, Kevin. This is Erin Bezick and she's Annie O'Dell."

"Hello, ladies. These are my friends Scott and Holly Cavanaugh and Lisa Kamen."

"Do you want to join us, Kevin?" Mace asked.

"Sure, if you don't mind."

"Not at all. Grab a chair."

"Would you happen to have a wee bit of Irish in you, Annie O'Dell?" Kevin asked as they ate.

Annie smiled at Kevin's accent. He sounded as if he had just arrived from Dublin.

"My family came from County Kerry originally, but my father was born here and so was I."

They kept talking and Annie deduced Scott and Holly were twins.

"Are you a couple?" Annie asked after finishing her burger.

"Holly and I have been going out since high school," Kevin

said as he put an arm around her waist. "And Lisa and Scott have been together for three years."

Mace introduced Erin as his girlfriend and claimed Annie was an old friend.

"I like to tease Annie, but she's a good sport about it."

Annie kicked him in the shin.

"Ow! Did you do that on purpose?"

"Oh, sorry. It was just a reflex on my part." Annie frowned.

"Erin is a good Irish name. Are you part Irish?" Kevin asked.

"My mother's maiden name was Collins and her grandparents were both from Ireland."

"Mace, do you have any Irish blood in you?"

"Me da had a bit of Irish blood in him."

Mace tried to sound Irish but only succeeded in making everyone laugh.

"Well, then I christen this table 'The Dublin Pub' since everyone is at least part Irish."

The girls started talking together as the guys talked about basketball.

"So, Mace, I hear you are a local SoHam kid. That true?" Kevin asked

Mace nodded. "Lived here all my life. Went to Roosevelt High with Annie and played ball for four years."

"Scott, Holly and I grew up in South Boston. Our fathers are both cops. Lisa is from St. Louis and has roomed with Holly all four years."

"Annie's father is a SoHam detective in the robbery division. Annie's mother died when she was five and her father has raised her by himself."

"You don't have to tell him everything," Annie said as she poked Mace in the arm.

Kevin could tell Mace was very fond of Annie even though Erin was his girlfriend.

"That's cool. My father is in homicide and Scott's dad works in administration," Kevin mentioned, as he glanced at Annie. "There are still a lot of Irish cops in Boston."

"How did you guys end up in SoHam?" Mace asked. "It's a long way from home."

"North Park was the only decent school that offered me a scholarship. Scott and I knew we were going to go to the same college. He tried out as a freshman and stuck as a walk-on. Holly has an academic scholarship and Lisa's grandparents live in Newcastle."

They finished eating and Kevin stood up. Everyone else followed suite.

"We gotta run. It was nice to meet you ladies." He high-fived Mace. "I'll see you at practice."

Mace smiled. "Later guys... and ladies."

Annie waited until Kevin and his friends were gone, then she smacked Mace's shoulder.

"What was that for? I didn't do anything."

"You told him everything about us except our parents are dating."

"I didn't tell him anything to embarrass you," Mace said.

"You came close," Annie insisted.

As they walked out Erin whispered, "Are you pleased the captain of the team wants to be your friend?"

"Yes, but I think he realizes I'm the most talented player and will be getting all the attention from the media soon."

Annie kneed him in the back of his hamstring. "Big talk from someone who hasn't started a game in his career."

As Mace, Erin and Annie headed to Howe Hall, Annie commented, "Kevin and Scott are really handsome and that accent is so darling. I could listen and stare at them all day."

"I'll remember to tell him at practice."

"Don't you dare, Mace Franklin! I'll never be able to face him if you do."

"Holly and Lisa seem really nice," Erin said.

"Can you imagine growing up in South Boston. I hear it's a pretty rough neighborhood."

Annie reminded them, "Can't be any worse than parts of SoHam."

Chapter Eight

"Are you still planning to meet Mace's mom and brother today?" Annie asked Erin on the way to the dining hall Sunday.

"Yes, and I'm little nervous. Can you come with us?"

Annie shook her head. "No can do. I need to study this afternoon. There's Mace." Annie pointed and waved. "You'll do fine. His mother is really nice."

"Good morning, ladies," Mace said. "You are both looking fine today."

"Stuff it, Mace," Annie said as he opened the door.

When Mace got home, he saw Detective O'Dell's car in the driveway.

"Hey, Keyshon! I'm home."

Keyshon ran to the living room to see Mace.

"Hi, Mace! I miss you. Where is Annie O'Dell? I miss her more than you."

"Are you making a joke, little brother?" Mace said as he hugged Keyshon.

"Yes, I miss you more, but I love Annie more."

"This is Erin Bezick."

"Is she your girlfriend now, Mace?"

"She is so don't you be putting your moves on her. She's my girlfriend."

"Hi, Erin, I'm Keyshon."

"It's nice to see you again, Keyshon. I saw you at a football game earlier this year," Erin said.

"I went to a couple games and I'm going to see Mace play basketball."

"Where's Mom?"

"In the kitchen, Mace. I'm making some potato salad."

"Come on, Erin. I'll introduce you."

Mace and Erin walked into the kitchen followed by Keyshon.

"Hi, Mom."

"Hello, son." She turned around and wiped her hands on a towel. "It's good to see you and who is this pretty young lady?"

"This is Erin Bezick. She's Annie's roommate..."

"And she's Mace's new girlfriend, too!" Keyshon informed his mother.

Elisabeth smiled. "This is Keith O'Dell. Annie's father."

"Hello, Erin, it's nice to meet you." He shook hands with Erin. "Annie has told me how much she enjoys having you as a roomie."

"Thanks, Detective O'Dell. It's nice to meet you. Annie is such a sweet friend."

"Annie? My Annie? Sweet? Are you sure you're not talking about someone else?" Detective O'Dell asked as he rubbed his jaw.

Erin laughed.

"Are you kids hungry?" Elisabeth asked. "I could make some soup and sandwiches."

"Not really. We ate lunch at Jordan."

"That works out perfectly then. Keith is going to grill some burgers later."

"We need to study a couple of hours, Mom."

"That's all right. Keith and I are going to take Keyshon out to see Liam for awhile."

Mace looked at Erin and explained, "Liam is Annie's grandfather—her dad's father."

"He's a high school principal, right?" Erin asked as she looked around the spotless kitchen.

"Yes, indeed."

Keith, Elisabeth and Keyshon drove out to the farm to see Liam while Mace and Erin studied. They actually studied. Mace tried to make a move on Erin, but she reminded him why they were there.

"We have to finish studying. Maybe if we get done early, we can kiss, but no sex. Understand?"

"I get it. Your message is coming across loud and clear."

"Good."

Annie planned to study in her room, but discovered she needed a book from the library. She threw on her coat, grabbed her backpack and headed to the library. After finding the book she needed, she sat at a table in the corner. She was concentrating on

42

the book and didn't notice as someone came up behind her. She felt hands on her shoulders and jumped.

"I'm sorry. I didn't mean to startle you."

She looked over her shoulder and smiled. "Hi, Matty. I didn't even hear you."

"Hi, Annie. I saw you sitting here so serious and all. I thought I would come over and say hi. If you're busy, I can leave."

"No, don't go, Matty. I'm just about finished."

"Are you hungry or thirsty? Maybe we could go somewhere and talk."

Annie tapped a finger against her mouth. "We could go over to the Union and grab something."

"That work's for me," Matt said.

Annie put her notes in her backpack and returned the book to the stack where she found it as Matt followed. She placed the book on the shelf and turned to face Matt. He looked at her and placed his hands on her shoulders.

Annie felt her heart racing as she looked up at Matt. *Should I let you kiss me or not?*

He moved a hand, lifted her chin and kissed her confidently. She wasn't sure whether to break away or enjoy the kiss. She decided to kiss him back.

"We should go, Matt," she said a bit flustered.

"Right! I don't know what came over me. You just look so pretty, Annie. Is that a new dress?"

"No, but I don't wear it very often."

Matt looked at the dress again as they stood facing each other. He moved a hand to the front of her dress and touched a button.

"I like dresses with buttons. You look so good in this dress, Annie."

"You kinda mentioned that, Matty. We should go. I'm getting really thirsty."

"Okay. I'm buying, all right."

"In that case maybe we should go somewhere more expensive," Annie said with a grin.

They left the library before Matt kissed her again and

walked to the Student Union. Matt bought sandwiches and bottled water. They sat at a table by the large windows that made up the front wall of the modern building. They talked about classes and Annie kept looking into his eyes and smiling. They ran out of things to talk about and were quiet for a moment.

"Have you talked to Victoria lately?" Annie asked.

"Not for a while. She's due any time now."

"I heard she was going to give the baby up for adoption."

"I heard that, too."

"How do you feel about that?" Annie asked after she took a long drink of water.

"Annie, the baby's not mine," Matt said slowly with emphasis.

"How can you be sure? You admitted you were with her."

"I was with her, but I used protection every time that whole weekend."

Annie looked surprised. "Maybe it didn't work."

He clenched his hands into fists. "Trust me, Annie. The baby is not mine."

"Even so, you were with her and people have seen you around campus with other girls. Have you been with them?"

"I haven't slept with every girl I take out. I've never slept with you." He relaxed his hands and grinned.

"I'm not going to ask how many you have slept with. Have you ever been checked by a doctor?"

"I always use protection, Annie, but yeah, I've gotten tested and I'm clean."

"Good."

"How's your father? Is he still seeing Mrs. Franklin?"

"He's fine, and, yes, they are still dating."

"You seem to be all right with that now."

"I'm perfectly okay with it."

Matt stared at Annie for a moment.

"Did you ever tell your father about the night in Peoria?"

"What about that night? Daddy knows I was in Peoria."

"So you never told him where you slept that night."

Annie stared out the window and felt her face get warm.

44

"No, I never told him and I'm not going to tell him or anyone else. Lainey and Cindy don't know I was with you that night. Derrick Keasling and Kristen know, but they won't ever tell anyone."

"Don't forget Tony Bertucci knows, too. He was the one who picked you up, placed you on the bed and covered you."

"He is such a teddy bear. Whatever girl falls in love with him will be so lucky."

"Do you remember anything more about that night?"

"Not until Kristen woke me up in the morning. I remember reaching for the phone and realizing I was in bed with you."

"I woke up a couple times during the night. You kicked off the covers and were next to me."

"You didn't do anything, did you, Matty?"

"You had your back to me and I put an arm around you but I didn't take advantage of you, Annie. I swear!"

"Are you ready to leave, Matt?"

"I'm ready to leave here, but not ready to say goodbye. I want to spent more time with you."

"It's too cold to go for a walk."

"Know anywhere else we could go?"

Annie looked at Matthew and made up her mind.

"My roommate Erin is gone for the day. Would you like to come up and see my room?"

"Just to see your room, right?"

"Yes, Matty. I'm not one of your other girls."

They walked over to Howe Hall and climbed the stairs to the third floor.

"Do you have to announce I'm on the floor or anything like that?" Matt asked.

"No, why on earth would I do that? Do you want the whole dorm to know I'm showing you my room?"

"I just thought since this is a girl's dorm, you might have to...never mind."

"This is my room."

"Is it as messy as your room at home?"

"My half is, but Erin is a neat freak. Don't look for any dirty clothes laying around. I put it all in my laundry basket."

"Wouldn't think of looking."

Annie let Matt in the room and he could tell immediately which side was Annie's.

"Nice room. Let me guess which side is yours," he said as he stepped over a sweatshirt.

"Stop it! I know you can tell. I can't help it if I'm a slob. I'm just too lazy sometimes."

"You are a very pretty slob, Annie O'Dell."

Matt took Annie in his arms and kissed her. She kissed him back and soon they were using tongues.

"Matty, I'm not ready to do anything with you."

"I won't force you to do anything, Annie. I promise. You can trust me even though we're alone."

"Promise you won't? I like it so much when you kiss me."

"Will you let me touch you, Annie? I want to touch you so much."

"Just don't touch me..."

Annie looked at where she didn't want Matt to touch her.

"I won't, Annie."

She kissed him again and Matt moved his hands to her lower back. Annie pressed her body close to Matt as they kissed and touched each other. She let Matt excite her even more. He picked her up in his arms and carried her to the bed. He set her on the bed and moved next to her. They pressed their bodies close to each other. Matt moved a leg on top of her. She kissed him more urgently and Matt put a hand on the front of her dress as he kissed her deeply.

"Matty, you know just how to get me excited."

"Are you ready to do more?"

She ran a hand through his thick hair. "What do you want to do, Matt?"

"Will you let me undo your dress a little, Annie?" he asked as he toyed with a button.

"I've never done that before, Matty."

"I promise I won't hurt you, Annie. You can tell me to stop at any time and I will."

He kissed her lips and then her neck.

46

"I don't have a bra on, Matty. I'm just wearing a camisole under my dress."

"I could kinda tell, Annie. I have some experience," he said while still kissing her neck.

"You've probably seen lots of girls naked before."

He lifted up and looked into her eyes. "I've seen a few. Have you ever let anyone see you?"

She moved her head back and forth on her pillow. "No, not even partly undressed."

"So I would be the first?"

"Yes. You won't try to make love to me will you?"

"Not today, Annie. I'm not prepared."

"You don't have a condom."

"No, and I won't have unprotected sex with you, Annie. I wouldn't let what happened to Victoria happen to you."

"If I let you undo my dress a little, will you not tell anyone? Not ever?"

"I'll never tell anyone, Annie."

Annie nodded. "You can undo my dress if you want. Please go slow, Matty."

"I will, Annie. You will like it."

Matt kissed her and Annie closed her eyes. He undid the buttons holding her dress together very slowly. He kept kissing her and pressing his body against her. He undid all the buttons, which went all the way to her waist, and opened the top of her dress so he could see her camisole. He placed a hand on her camisole and could feel her breasts. The top of the camisole was held together by a string tied in a bow—much like a shoelace. Matt gazed into her eyes as he slowly untied the bow and undid the string. He kept kissing her mouth, then began to kiss her neck. He worked his way down to her chest. Annie kept her eyes closed. He dreamed about being able to make love to her. He kissed her again and slipped his tongue in her mouth at the same time he moved his hand under her camisole. Annie trembled as Matt touched her. She opened her eyes and looked at him.

"You look so beautiful. I've always wondered what you would look like and now I know."

Annie lifted her arms above her head. Matt placed a hand on her breasts.

"Move on top of me, Matty," Annie whispered softly.

"Are you sure, Annie?"

"Yes, I'm sure."

"I will keep my promise, Annie. I just want you to feel what it's like to almost make love."

"What are you going to do?"

"Will you trust me to keep my promise?"

"I trust you, Matty. I don't want to get pregnant though."

"You won't. Believe me I don't want to die and your father would kill me if that happened."

"He might kill me if he ever learns what we were doing even now."

"You are so beautiful, Annie. I could stay here with you all night."

"You can't do that, Matty. Erin will be coming home sometime."

They were sitting on the edge of the bed kissing later when Annie heard a key in the lock and the doorknob turned.

"Should we have called Annie to let her know we were coming back early?" Mace asked while waiting in the hallway.

"Why? Annie doesn't ever have any boys over. She is probably at the library, anyway."

Erin opened the door and she and Mace kissed as they walked into the room.

"Erin! Mace!" Annie screamed. "I didn't expect you guys home so early."

"Hi, guys," Matt said with a smile.

Erin turned and stared at Annie and Matt for several seconds. Mace stood behind Erin.

"Annie, I'm sorry. I should have called first," Erin finally said.

Annie looked at Mace. She felt as though he could see right through her and knew exactly what she and Matt had been doing. Annie forgot her dress and camisole were undone and still opened. Matt looked at Mace and Mace stared back with clenched fists.

Mace was close to losing his cool and Matt sensed it.

"I should be going, Annie. I'll call you tomorrow," Matt said as he stood up.

"Bye, Matty," Annie said softly.

Matt kept an eye on Mace as he edged past. He took one more look at Annie and then left quickly, which just made things worse because now Erin and Mace both assumed the worst. Mace closed the door and Annie flopped back on her bed with her legs over the side.

"Talk about bad timing," Mace said after several seconds of no sound other than the ticking clock.

"Shut up, "Mace!" Erin smacked his arm and then asked, "Are you all right, Annie?"

Annie covered her eyes with her arm. "I'm fine. I'm just so embarrassed." Annie's lips quivered and she began to sob.

Erin came over and sat next to Annie on the bed. She closed Annie's dress as best she could and looked at Mace. "Maybe you should go."

"Yeah, good idea." He turned to leave.

"No, don't go, Mace," Annie said.

Mace walked over and stood beside the bed. He tugged her dress down to cover her legs.

"Did Matt use protection, honey?" Erin asked.

Annie moved her arm and shook her head. "No, he didn't have any."

"I'll kill him!" Mace made a fist and smacked one hand into the other. "Annie, I swear I'll pound him for taking advantage of you."

Annie sat up quickly. "No, Mace! Stop! Let me explain. He didn't have a condom, so he didn't have sex with me. We did other things but didn't have sex. I'm sorry. I just got carried away."

"What are you saying, Annie?" Erin asked.

"Matt and I didn't go all the way," Annie whispered.

"Are you sure?" Mace asked as he looked at her dress.

"I'm sure, Mace! Don't you think I would know?"

"Tell me what happened," Erin said as she put an arm around Annie's shoulders.

"Matty saw me in the library and we ended up here. We were kissing and I let him... do things. I wasn't thinking straight. He undid my dress and he saw my..."

"You don't have to say anymore, Annie. The important thing is that you're okay." Erin gently squeezed Annie's shoulders.

"I'm still going to break his neck when I see him, Annie," Mace said as he paced back and forth.

"No you won't, Mace Franklin! It was just as much my fault as his. I let him do what he did."

Mace sat on the bed next to Annie. She looked up at him and cried again. Mace held her hand as Erin wiped her tears away.

"Do you hate me now, Mace?"

"No, I could never hate you, Annie. I might hate Matthew Sullivan for what he did, but I still love you, Annie. You're my friend."

"Do you need anything, Annie?" Erin asked.

"I just need to get up."

Annie realized her dress wasn't covering her as much as she thought. She held her dress closed as she looked at Mace. "I'll be right back," she said as she ran into the bathroom.

Erin watched Annie dash into the bathroom and then smacked Mace's arm. "Were you looking down her dress, Mace Franklin?"

"I glanced down when she looked down," he admitted.

"So you saw what I saw and what Matt saw, too."

He shrugged. "I couldn't help but see. I just looked for a second or two, then I looked away."

"Don't let Annie know, okay. She feels bad enough that Matt Sullivan saw her. If she knows you saw, too, it would embarrass her even more."

"I won't say anything."

"Have you seen Annie like that before? Tell the truth."

Mace stood up and walked to the middle of the room. "Not since we were kids."

"Was that the only time?"

He turned to face Erin and held up a hand. "Yes, I swear."

Annie walked out of the bathroom. "What are you talking

about? I heard you say something about when we were kids."

"I didn't say anything, Annie."

"Mace Franklin, don't you start lying to me. You've never lied to me before, so don't start now."

"Annie," Erin said slowly.

Annie walked over, stood in front of Erin, put her hands on her hips and said, "I want to know."

"All right, I'll tell you," Erin said as she stood up and faced Annie. "I asked Mace if he was looking down your dress and he did for just a second."

Annie looked at Erin and then turned to face Mace. She looked up at him. "It doesn't matter. I'm not embarrassed you saw me, Mace. I hope it doesn't bother you that Mace saw me, Erin," Annie said without looking back at Erin.

Erin put her hands on Annie's shoulders. "It doesn't matter. I'm just glad you are all right, Annie. He could have taken advantage of you so easily."

"He promised he wouldn't and I trusted him. I just hope I don't see him for awhile. I will be embarrassed when I do."

"Do you want me to leave, Annie?" Mace asked.

"Yes! You should leave so I can talk to Annie," Erin said. "You should have left right away."

"No, please don't go, Mace. Stay with me. I'm dressed now. Will you ever be able to look at me the same way?"

"I still think of you the same way. You don't need to worry, Annie. I'll never stop being your friend."

"Oh, Mace. I'm so ashamed for what I let Matty do. I could have stopped everything before it even started, but I didn't want to. I wanted him to kiss me all over. Matty made me feel special."

"TMI, Annie," Mace said as he made a face and cringed.

"Hush. I've always told you stuff," Annie said.

Mace moved closer and held Annie in his arms as she cried. Annie rested her head on Mace's chest as he kissed the top of her head.

"Everything will be all right, Annie Mercer. You're strong enough to overcome this, girl."

51

Chapter Nine

Monday morning Erin got up early to meet Mace for breakfast. She checked on Annie before she left the room. Mace was waiting outside Howe Hall for Erin.

He kissed Erin and asked, "How is she doing this morning?"

"She is still zonked. It took her a long time to get to sleep last night."

"I hope she will be all right. She's never done anything like that before."

Erin grabbed his arm and gave Mace a dirty look. "And just how do you know that?"

"Don't look at me like that. I just know, okay. We've been friends a long time."

"I know you've kissed her and not like a 'friend' kiss either." Erin squeezed his arm harder.

"We have kissed, but I never did what Matt did to her."

Erin let go of Mace and began walking again. "You can't lay all the blame on Matt Sullivan. Annie is partly responsible, too. She could have said no, or better yet, not let him in the room when I wasn't there."

"Matt just seems to know which buttons to push with Annie, and he uses that to get what he wants from her."

Erin rolled her eyes. "Do we have to spend all morning talking about Annie and Matt. After all she is still a virgin. Now she will hopefully be a little smarter about boys."

"Fine! Excuse me for caring about a friend," Mace said.

"Don't get on my case," Erin said. "I know you care about her."

Annie woke up a few minutes later, stretched her arms over her head, looked across the room and saw an empty bed. She closed her eyes and thought about Matt Sullivan. *Why did I get so carried away? I shouldn't have let him in the room.* She showered and dressed. She put on her coat, grabbed an apple and a bottle of water from the small refrigerator, picked up her backpack and headed out the door. She prayed she would not see Matthew

Sullivan on her way to her nine o'clock class. She hoped not to run into any of her friends, but Elaine and Cindy saw her and came up behind her to talk.

"Good morning, Annie. How are you this beautiful morning?" Cindy asked.

"Hi, guys. I'm all right. How have you been? I haven't seen you for a few days."

"I'm doing great!" Cindy exclaimed.

Annie stuck her hands into her coat pockets. "How can you be so upbeat this early on a Monday morning?"

"She thinks she's in love," Elaine said.

"Well, I am in love," Cindy insisted. "You're not the only girl at North Park who can be in love. Just because I haven't been dating Bryce as long as you and Adrien have does not mean we can't be in love. Isn't that right, Annie?"

"I don't know anything about being in love. I just know I'm never going on a date ever again."

Elaine and Cindy looked at Annie and then each other.

"Are you sure you're all right, Annie. You sound upset about something. Did you go on a date with the wrong guy or something?" Elaine asked.

Annie huffed and then said, "I suppose you could say that."

"Who was it, Annie? Do we know him?" Cindy asked.

"I don't want to talk about it right now, guys, okay?"

"You don't have to now, Annie, but if you want to talk later just call us. Maybe we can have dinner tonight. Do you have any plans?"

"No."

"Okay, let's do dinner at seven so Mace and Erin can make it."

"All right. I'll meet you guys at your room and we can head over to Jordan from there."

"See you later, Annie."

Elaine and Cindy hurried to their class while Annie walked to Lancashire Hall for her Introduction to Education class relieved Elaine and Cindy didn't press her for more details. She was doubly glad Matt didn't know her class schedule. She felt bad enough he knew the location of her room.

Mace arrived early for basketball practice. He got ready in the locker room and stepped onto the gym floor to begin his routine. He stretched to loosen up, ran sprints, shot free throws and worked on his ball handling skills. All of this before practice started. Coach Bazetich took notice of Mace's work habits and the extra time he put in.

At four o'clock sharp Coach blew his whistle and gathered the team on the bleachers. "Rockford College did not provide much competition, but I was pleased with the effort for the most part. Anyone expecting playing time must be excellent on defense. I can't stress that enough."

During the last hour of practice Coach let the team scrimmage. He let Mace play with the starters for part of the scrimmage. He kept a close eye on how Mace fit in with the other guys. Coach Bazetich was pleased with what he saw and decided to make a change.

At 6:45 Annie and Erin knocked on the door to Elaine and Cindy's room. Cindy opened the door.

"We'll be ready in a minute. Lainey just wants to change. How did classes go today?"

Erin answered but Annie was still being very quiet.

"Not too bad for a Monday. Remind me not to sign up for any eight o'clock classes next semester. I need more sleep."

Elaine was ready so they headed to Jordan. Mace was sitting with his friends Kevin Murphy and Scott Cavanaugh and their girlfriends. The girls loaded their trays and joined Mace.

Annie whispered to Erin, "I'm glad Matt doesn't live on campus and I've never seen him in the dining hall."

"Good evening, ladies! Welcome to 'The Dublin Pub' tonight," Mace said as he pulled out a chair for Erin.

"What are you talking about, Mace?" Elaine asked.

"I forgot you haven't met my friends. This is Kevin Murphy, Scott Cavanaugh and his sister Holly. Lisa Kamen over here. May I introduce Elaine Novicki. We call her Lainey and she's definitely not Irish. This is Cindy Mackens. Do you have any Irish blood in you, Cindy?"

54

"No, sorry," Cindy said as she sat down. "Is that a prerequisite to sit at this table?"

Mace shook his head. "Not really, but everyone else is Irish, or at least part Irish."

"Including you, Mace?"

"I have a little bit of Irish in me."

Annie grinned but kept quiet. She sat next to Mace and across the table from Kevin Murphy. Erin and the other girls talked about classes, then about boyfriends. Annie hoped Erin wouldn't say anything about Matthew. Mace noticed Annie was still not her usual self and didn't tease her. She stayed close to Mace and kept her head down so she didn't have to look at the other kids.

Mace whispered softly to her, "You don't have to worry about Matt now, Annie. You're with me and Kevin is one of the toughest guys I have ever met. He's not afraid of anything and has seen it all. South Boston is a really rough place to grow up."

"I'm not worried about Matty right now, Mace. I'm more concerned about you and me. Can we talk later, please?"

"Of course we can, girl."

"Thanks, Mace."

Kevin watched as Mace and Annie talked quietly. He sensed something was different about Annie today but didn't pry. He asked Annie a couple questions she could answer with a yes or no because he realized she was reluctant to talk. Thirty minutes later everyone was finished and ready to leave. Mace said good night to his new friends. Elaine and Cindy headed over to the library to do some research for the school paper.

"Erin, would you mind if I talk to Annie for a bit?"

"Of course not. Are you okay, Annie?"

"I'll be all right, Erin. I just need to talk to Mace. I'll see you back at the room."

Erin hugged Annie and whispered, "Things will get back to normal in a couple of days, Annie, and you won't even think about Matthew Sullivan anymore."

Annie smiled at Erin and hugged her back. "I won't be out too long."

"Take all the time you need, Annie. I'll be in the room

when you get back." Erin headed back to Howe Hall.

"Where should we go, Annie?" Mace asked. "We can't really talk at the library because Lainey and Cindy will be there. It's too cold to walk around outside."

"Anywhere is okay as long as we can talk privately without any other kids around."

Mace thought for a moment.

"I know a perfect spot. Follow me."

Mace took Annie's hand and she followed him to Humphrey Hall. She realized where they were headed.

"I don't want to go up to your room, Mace."

"We aren't, Annie. There is a room next to the lounge on the first floor no one ever uses."

"Are you sure there won't be any kids there?"

"I'm positive. I've never seen any kids there except maybe on Sunday."

Mace took Annie through the lounge and she saw the sign next to the door. It read 'Clarkson Chapel' and she knew they would have privacy here. She followed Mace into the small dark chapel and they sat on a bench in the back row in the corner. No one else was around.

"What do you want to talk about, Annie. Is it Matthew?"

"Not really. Maybe in a way it is. I'll get over what happened between us. I'm just glad it wasn't worse. If you guys had walked in a few minutes earlier... I don't want to think about that."

"Good, because I don't want to have a picture in my mind of Matt Sullivan on top of you with his hands all over you."

Annie giggled a little. "That would not have been a pretty sight."

Mace held Annie's hand as she started to cry. He put an arm around her shoulder and let her cry on his chest as he kissed the top of her head.

"How am I going to face Daddy? He will take one look at me and know I did something."

"I know your father is a very good detective, Annie, but he isn't God. He doesn't know everything."

"He knows everything about me," Annie said as she wiped

her nose with her hand. "He will see a change in my eyes."

"Maybe not. Besides, he loves you. Do you think you're going to lose his love because of what happened one time with Matthew Sullivan?"

"No, I suppose not. I won't be his innocent little girl anymore though."

"You are still pretty innocent, Annie. Can I ask you something?"

"What?"

"Did you have your eyes closed when Matt was in bed with you?"

"Not all the time."

Mace laughed. "Why doesn't that surprise me?"

Annie poked Mace in his side and grinned. "I watched a little when he was undoing my top. I was shaking when he first put his hand on my..."

Mace waved a hand. "I don't need all the details, Annie. I can imagine what he did."

"Does it embarrass you I let him see me partially naked?"

Mace moved his arm from around Annie's shoulders to the top of the bench. "I wouldn't say it embarrasses me. I mean I wish he hadn't seen you. I kinda wish I didn't see you."

"You are so sweet to me, Mace. I don't mind that you saw me. At least my panties were still on when you got there or else you might have passed out."

"Gross!" He moved his arm and quickly scooted away from her. "Too much information, Annie O'Dell."

"I do believe you are blushing, Mace Franklin," she said as she giggled.

"If you didn't have your underwear on, you and Matt would have still been doing it."

"How can you say that, Mace?" she asked as she smacked his arm. "That's gross!"

"Because if he had been having real sex with you, he would have made it last for as long as he could."

"It took him a couple minutes, Mace."

"You really are innocent, Annie. He was in a hurry because

he knew he couldn't really have sex with you. If he was... just take my word for it, Annie."

"When you look at me now are you picturing how I looked yesterday? I don't care if you are. At least now I don't have to worry about being so modest."

"Just because I saw you once doesn't mean you should let me see you again."

"I didn't mean I was going to let you see me on purpose. Are you picturing how I looked now?"

"No way, girl. As far as I'm concerned you are still my sweet little friend and always will be."

"Thanks, Mace. I feel better now, but could you hold me for a little longer?"

"I'll hold you as long as you need me to, Annie."

Mace held Annie close for a few minutes as she rested her head on his chest. She sat up and kissed Mace's cheek.

"Are you ready to go back to your room now?" he asked.

"Will you walk with me? All the way to my door?"

"Of course I will, but it will cost you."

They stood up and Annie looked up at Mace.

"I love you, Mace. I hope we can always be friends."

"I love you, too, Annie O'Dell."

Mace hugged her and she trembled in his arms for a moment. He held her close until she stopped. Mace walked beside her all the way to her room. He kissed her forehead before she went inside.

"Thank you for walking me home. I'm sorry I was being such a big baby about this."

"It's all right, Annie. You're my friend and I'm here for you."

Chapter Ten

Annie picked up *The Chronicle* on her way to Jordan Hall and noticed an article about the basketball team as she ate lunch with Mace and Erin.

"Should I read it out loud?" Annie asked.

"Since you have the only copy, it might work better than me trying to read your mind," Mace teased while adding crackers to his chili.

"Fine! Feed your ugly mug while I read," Annie said. "The North Park Redbirds won their first five games of the season against soft competition. The first real test of the year will be the Monday night road game against the Lewiston University Flyers. One unexpected bright spot has been the play of newcomer Mace Franklin." She stopped and looked at Mace. "Don't get a big head. This is just some college guy's opinion."

"Please continue," Erin said. "His skull is too thick for his head to get any bigger."

Annie snorted, then continued, "After coming off the bench in the first game, Franklin has taken over the starting spot alongside Kevin Murphy. With a strong front line of Damian Gibson, Darrion Cunningham and Javarius Mays, the Redbirds are a strong rebounding team. The offense, under the direction of Murphy, has improved every game. Franklin has averaged 10.8 points a game and less than one turnover a game. His defense is improving every week." Annie paused and Mace looked up from his chili. "The reporter must not have seen that guy slam dunk over your head in the last game."

"Hey, that dude was six inches taller than me and I got caught in the paint on a switch," Mace said.

"Yeah, whatever," Annie said and folded the paper.

With the campus of Lewiston only forty miles away in Lockhold, Indiana, Annie and several of the other students decided to make the trip to see the game.

"Can't you finish that paper later?" Annie asked Erin as she got ready to leave.

"No, I put it off and it's due tomorrow. Who's going?"

"Lainey, Cindy and Bryce." Annie used her fingers to tick off the names. "Adrien can't go so Christopher Braun is going. I'm riding with Holly and Lisa. Since you can't go, I might see if Solomon and Ashley are interested."

"Tell Mace I'm sorry if you see him. I'll know better next time."

They took two cars. Annie squeezed into the back seat with Solomon and Ashley. They arrived in Lockhold, joined the other people entering the gym and found their seats.

"Wow! It's pretty loud." Annie put her hands on her ears for a second.

Holly leaned close to Annie and shouted to be heard, "You've probably never been to a game here before. This place gets really loud and rowdy and this is before the game has even started." Holly pointed to the other side of the gym. "The Lewiston students are in that section behind their bench and all along the lower section over there. They are called Flyer Fanatics and they stand up for the whole game. They don't lose very often at home. I don't know if we've ever beaten them here."

Annie leaned close to Holly and said, "This is a real cozy gym. It seems like all the seats are right on top of the floor."

"I know the players don't like coming here," Holly replied.

Elaine tapped on Annie's shoulder from behind and asked, "Where is Erin?"

"She needed to finish a paper for her English Lit class so she stayed home. Where is Adrien?"

"He is on duty tonight. He works on the campus security staff."

"I didn't know that."

"This is his second year," Elaine explained.

Annie talked to her friends from Roosevelt as they waited for the game to begin. She seemed to be back to normal after her encounter with Matt Sullivan. Annie had told Elaine and Cindy only part of the story. She was afraid they would criticize her for allowing Matt in her room while she was alone.

"Annie, there is this really cute guy in my Elementary Math

class. He sits next to me and we have gotten to know each other a bit. He doesn't have a girlfriend. Maybe I could introduce you to him sometime. What do you think?" Cindy asked.

"Maybe, what's his name?"

"Reid Smagala. He's actually a second year student from Chicago. He seems really nice, Annie. We could meet for dinner at Jordan and you could check him out."

"I'll think about it, Cindy, but I've never thought much of blind dates."

The game got under way and the Redbirds got off to a fast start. The Flyers scored the first basket, but then North Park went on a fifteen point run. The Flyers never got closer than nine points the rest of the game. Mace played his best game of the year and led the team in scoring for the first time. He finished with nineteen points, four steals, three assists and only two turnovers. Javarius Mays played his best game with eighteen points and thirteen rebounds. He was instrumental in shutting down Radzic Cembrzynski the high scoring forward for the Flyers. Kevin Murphy tied a personal high with thirteen assists in the game. It was a very happy team on the bus ride back to SoHam.

The North Park fans left the gym, headed out to the parking lot and talked about the game.

"Didn't Mace have a great game tonight?" Holly said.

Annie nodded. "He seems to be getting better every game. He's a better defensive player than Alex Young. Alex is probably a better shooter though."

"How come you seem to know so much about basketball, Annie?" Solomon asked as he and Ashley walked behind Annie.

Annie walked backward as she answered Solomon. "I've always been a fan and I've gone to so many of Mace's games that I guess I just picked up little bits about the game." She turned around and then told Holly, "I'm glad your brother got to play."

"He even scored four points."

"Annie, do you want to ride back with us?" Cindy asked. "We could talk about a time for you and Reid to meet."

"Let me ask Holly if she minds. I don't get to talk to you guys as much as we used to."

61

"I don't mind, Annie," Holly answered. "You can ride with Lainey and Cindy. The geeks probably won't even notice. Can you understand any of the stuff they talk about?"

"Only some of it. Those two are a perfect match."

"Yeah, if they ever have a baby it will have a harddrive for a brain and a processor for a heart."

On the drive back to campus, Annie sat in the back between Elaine and Cindy. The guys claimed the front seats.

"Do you have any plans for dinner tomorrow, Annie?" Cindy asked.

"Not really. I'll probably meet Erin and Mace."

"Why don't you bring them and we can all get together around seven or is that too late?"

"Seven would work. Mace usually has practice till six or so."

"It might be more comfortable for you and Reid to meet when there are other people around. It won't seem like so much of a blind date that way."

Bryce looked in the rearview mirror and smiled at Annie. "Cindy has been trying to find a guy to set you up with all semester, Annie. No one has been good enough though. She finds something wrong with every guy she meets."

"I have not. Annie is perfectly capable of finding a guy on her own," Cindy answered.

Annie said, "I guess I just haven't been looking very hard."

"Well, there is always Matthew Sullivan if you get desperate," Christopher joked.

"That's not funny, Christopher. Annie and Matt have dated before, but he always seems to have a new girlfriend every week. Annie deserves better than him," Elaine said.

"He's not all bad, you guys. He can be very charming when he tries," Annie said in his defense.

"That's for sure," Bryce said. "He has a reputation for charming girls right out of their clothes and into his bed."

"Bryce!" Cindy poked the back of the driver's seat. "Keep your eyes on the road and stop talking about Matthew Sullivan and his experience with girls."

Christopher ran a hand through his shoulder length blonde hair and turned to look at Annie. "You should be careful around him. I hear he likes girls without a lot of experience. He likes to make sure they are experienced after he has finished with them though."

Annie stared at Christopher. *Like you've got a lot of room to talk. You've been out with lots of girls, too.*

"Will you guys stop talking about Matthew Sullivan already," Elaine said. "I think Annie gets your point."

Annie stared out the window and blushed as she thought about what happened the last time she was with Matthew. *I hate to admit it, but if I'm truly honest with myself, I think I have some real feelings for Matthew Sullivan. Yeah, he's had plenty of other girlfriends, but he said that nothing really happened with most of the girls he dated and I believe him.*

Chapter Eleven

"Hi, guys! Did you choose the mystery meat or the pasta?" Annie asked as she looked around the cafeteria. "Lainey and Cindy are supposed to be holding our table for us."

"I took the pasta," Mace answered. "Coach wants me to put on a few pounds."

"I see them over there," Erin said. "Is the guy with them your blind date?"

"He probably wants the extra weight to be muscle, Mace." Annie spotted their friends. "It's not exactly a blind date. Just an opportunity to meet and talk to him."

They walked over to the table.

Mace pulled out a chair for Erin and said, "Everything I eat turns to muscle. Just look at this fantastic body."

"We'd rather not while we're eating," Elaine answered.

Annie sat next to Mace and across the table from the guy who must be Reid. She stole glances at him as he talked to Cindy and Bryce, but she didn't say anything to him as she ate.

After waiting for about ten minutes, Cindy decided to take action. "Annie, this is Reid Smagala. Reid, Annie O'Dell. I've known Annie forever I think."

"Hi, Annie. It's nice to meet you. Cindy has told me a lot about you," Reid said with a smile.

"It's nice to meet you, too, Reid. Don't believe half of what she tells you."

"It was all complimentary, I assure you."

Reid tried to make small talk with Annie as they ate, but she was rather quiet. After they finished eating, Reid took Annie's tray for her.

Cindy followed him and asked, "What do you think about Annie?"

Reid glanced over his shoulder to make sure Annie was still sitting at the table. "She is kinda cute, but doesn't she ever talk? I tried to engage her in conversation, but she didn't respond much. Does she even have a personality?"

"She's not usually this quiet with us, but she can be a little shy around new people," Cindy answered. "Are you going to ask her out?"

He glanced at Annie again and shrugged. "I'll see how it goes."

"I think you guys would make a good couple," Cindy whispered as she and Reid headed back to the table.

About ten minutes later everyone got up to leave the dining hall.

Cindy gently shoved Reid in Annie's direction. "Ask her to do something."

Reid got Annie's attention. "Would you allow me to walk you back to your dorm, Annie?" he asked as Cindy grinned.

"If you would like to join us, you're welcome. I'm going to walk with Mace and Erin," Annie answered rather noncommittally.

The four of them walked back to Howe Hall together. They could see their breath in the cool, crisp December air. A light flurry of snow fell, but disappeared as soon as it touched the ground.

"Would you like to sit in the lounge for a while, Annie?" Reid asked figuring if she refused he wouldn't bother asking her for a date.

"All right, but I can't stay down here very long. I've got to read three chapters tonight for Psych."

Mace watched as Annie and Reid hung back. "See you later, Annie. I'm going to study with Erin in the room."

"See you, Mace. Should I knock first before I enter?" Annie asked with a grin.

"That would be a good idea unless you want to see the mighty Mace in action."

"I'll knock first."

Erin smacked Mace's arm. "We're just going to study, Annie. You can come up to the room at any time."

Reid steered Annie toward a couple of unoccupied chairs in the corner and they sat down.

He glanced around the lounge while he waited for Annie to say something. When she didn't, he said, "Cindy told me you graduated early from Roosevelt High."

"Yes, I earned enough credits and most of my friends were

a year ahead of me, so here I am. Where did you go to school?"

"Chicago Lakeshore. I graduated four years ago and worked full-time for two years to save enough money for school. I've lived in Chicago my whole life."

"So how old are you?" Annie asked.

"I'm twenty-two. How old are you?"

"Seventeen," she answered softly because she thought this might cause him to lose interest.

"Oh! I didn't realize you were so young."

She grinned. "I didn't realize you were so old!"

They both laughed. Reid looked at Annie. He wondered if she was too young for him to date even casually. He had just about decided she would be too young, but then she put a finger to her lip in a way that looked enchanting. He decided to give it a shot—after all he really liked her eyes.

"Would you like to have dinner tomorrow?" Reid asked. "Just the two of us perhaps."

"Just dinner?" Annie asked hoping he wouldn't try to get her back to his room.

"Maybe we could go over to the union after dinner, or if there's something else you would like better."

"I'll have dinner with you, then we can play the rest of the evening by ear and see what happens."

"What time do you want to meet?" Reid asked.

"How about six?"

"That's okay with me. I'll meet you by the fountain outside the Student Union."

Annie and Reid talked for another half hour before she needed to get back to her room. She didn't offer to let Reid come up though. She wasn't ready to let him know which room she and Erin shared. She hoped Cindy hadn't told him already. Annie climbed the three flights of stairs and knocked on the door to her room to warn Mace and Erin. She entered and Mace and Erin were actually studying. Erin was on her bed and Mace was at her desk. Mace turned around when Annie entered.

"So how did it go with Reid? Did he ask you out?" Mace asked.

"We're meeting for dinner tomorrow night, then we might go somewhere. Did you know he's twenty-two?"

"No, I didn't," Mace answered then turned back to study. "He's pretty old for you, Annie."

She walked up behind him and looked over his shoulder at the textbook. "It's just dinner, Mace, but Daddy would definitely say he's too old for me."

"You're right about that," Mace said. "Do you want me and Erin to go with you?"

Annie thought about it. "No. I'll be all right, but thanks anyway. We're meeting at the Student Union and going to Jordan for dinner. Not sure if he'll want to do anything after that. I'm pretty sure he thinks I'm too immature for him."

"No doubt," Mace teased.

Annie thwacked the back of his head.

"You're not immature for your age," Erin said.

Mace and Annie stared at her.

"Sorry, I guess that didn't sound right, but you get my meaning."

"We'll be in the dining hall somewhere if you need us," Mace said.

"I don't think Reid will try anything in front of the whole dining hall."

"It would be the last thing he ever tried if he did," Mace promised.

"You don't have to be my superhero guardian, you know. I can take care of myself," Annie said but then added. "But I'm grateful you are willing to look out for me."

Chapter Twelve

Annie shivered as she walked back to her dorm after the last class the next afternoon. *I need to run home and get my winter coats this weekend.* She came around the corner of Lancashire Hall and ran right into Matt Sullivan. She was startled because she certainly didn't expect to see him waiting for her.

"Hi, Annie. How have you been?"

"I've been fine, Matthew. What do you want?" Annie asked as she kept walking.

"Hold on, Annie! I just want to talk to you."

Annie stopped and faced Matt. "I'm not sure I want to talk to you."

"Oh, Annie, don't be mad at me. I kept my promise to you that day. If I really wanted to, I could have made love with you." He noticed her shivering. "You're freezing. Do you want my coat?"

She shook her head. "I know that, Matty. Thank you for not taking advantage of me when you so easily could have."

He stared at her. "I get the sarcasm."

"Ya think."

"Are you telling me you didn't like it? Is that what you believe?"

"You know I like kissing you, Matty. That's not the problem and you know it."

"What is it then?" He removed his coat and slipped it over her shoulders.

"Thanks, Matty."

"No problem," he said.

"Why haven't you called me since then? Too many other girls to sleep with?" she asked as they started walking.

"I've never hidden the fact I see other girls, Annie. I've always been honest with you, but I agree, I should have called you. Do you have a new boyfriend yet?"

"I don't have a boyfriend, but I've actually got a date for dinner tonight and he's twenty-two."

Matt grinned. "I'm impressed. You're dating older men."

68

"Well, we're not exactly dating. I just met him yesterday. Cindy set me up with him."

"How are Cindy and Lainey doing? Are they still with... whoever?"

"Adrien and Bryce, and yes they are."

"I'm sorry I haven't called, Annie. I should have, I know. I've been working for my father at the restaurant and between that and school I haven't had much time for a social life. I've only had two dates since I saw you, and I hate to admit this, but I was thinking about you while I was with them. I don't even remember their names."

Annie stopped and looked up at Matt. He smiled at her. She knew she shouldn't but she smiled back at him. "Just two dates, huh? I'm headed to my room. If you want to keep talking to me you can go with me, but it's too cold to stand out here and freeze."

"I'd like that, Annie. You have always treated me better than everyone else."

Annie gave him a dark look.

"I didn't mean it like that. I meant you never treated me like a piece of trash like other kids did."

"I never thought you were as bad as most kids thought. You didn't help matters by acting like the 'bad boy' all the time—trying to be so tough. I know you better than that, Matty. You can be really sweet if you want to be and I don't mean when you put on your charm because you want to get a girl into your bed. Deep down you are better than that. You just don't ever let anyone see that side of you."

Matt changed the subject. "I heard Mace is on the starting team. He must be doing all right."

"Yeah, he is. He is going out with my roommate Erin."

"I've met her before, remember?"

"Oh, right."

Annie and Matt kept walking and were soon at Howe Hall. Annie stopped and Matt faced her.

"I've missed you, Annie O'Dell. I always like talking to you even if that's all we do."

"I've been thinking about you, Matty. For some reason I

still like you. I should hate you for what you did, but I don't."

"That makes me happy, Annie. I wouldn't like to think you hated me."

Annie looked into Matt's eyes and saw a gleam. He smiled and her heart skipped a beat.

"What?" he asked. "Are you looking at my scar?"

"No, you've had that little scar on your forehead ever since we met."

"Yeah, some kid through a jar full of dirt at me."

"Will you carry my backpack upstairs for me?"

"Sure. Why didn't you ask me earlier? I would have carried it for you."

"I wasn't sure I wanted you to until just now."

Matt took her pack and they went upstairs. Annie opened the door expecting Erin to be home. Instead she found a note on her desk. Erin was with Elaine and Cindy and wouldn't be home until after dinner. Annie turned around to face Matt and handed him his coat.

"Was that a note from Erin?"

Annie nodded. "She won't be home until later. I guess we are all alone."

He looked around the room. "I see you cleaned up your side."

Annie looked up at Matt. He dropped her backpack on the floor and took her in his arms. He kissed her and she kissed him back.

"Just kissing today, Matty! I have a date later."

She wrapped her arms around his neck and he put his hands on her bottom and held her close. She pressed her body into his as they began using their tongues to excite one another.

"What time is your date, Annie?" Matt asked when they paused to catch their breath.

"I have to meet him outside the Union at six."

"That gives us plenty of time, Annie."

"Just kissing, Matty. I'm not going to get undressed or make love with you."

"I'll do whatever you want, Annie, and I won't do anything

you aren't ready for. I promise and you know I keep my promises."

He kissed her again and she lifted her legs and wrapped them around his waist. He held her and moved toward the bed. He stopped beside the bed and lowered her onto it.

"Is it okay if I join you?" he asked.

She patted the space next to her.

He slipped in next to her and they began kissing as Matt moved on top of her.

An hour later Annie was giggling as Matt teased her. "I did not undress you! You still have all your clothes on."

"I guess technically you are right but..."

"But what?" he asked with a shrug. "We both have every thing on we started with."

Annie lay on her back with Matt next to her on his side. He smiled at her and kissed her again. He looked down at her body.

"I don't think your argument would stand up in court, Matthew Sullivan. Look at me!"

"I am looking at you and I like what I see. I wish I could see more."

Matt looked at her again. She closed her eyes as Matt touched her stomach with his fingertips. Although Matt did not remove any of her clothes he did 'rearrange' them, as he put it. Her shirt was partially unbuttoned and her jeans were unzipped. Annie turned onto her stomach and lifted her upper body with her elbows. She lifted her feet into the air and moved them back and forth.

"Where are my shoes? You took my shoes off, Matty."

"You're right. I'm sorry I took your shoes off. Do you hate me?"

Annie giggled again. Matt put a hand on her back under her shirt. Annie relaxed as she lay flat on the bed again. He gently rubbed her back for a moment. He could feel the warmth of her body. He put his hand on her lower back and slipped it under her jeans.

"I should get up and take a shower."

"Do you need any help, Annie?" Matt asked with a grin.

"I think I can manage by myself. Daddy hasn't had to give me a bath for a couple years now."

"Too bad."

Annie turned to face Matt. She kissed him, then sat on the edge of the bed.

"Are you going to wait while I change?"

"I'll be here. Go ahead and take your shower... alone."

"Maybe someday, Matty... but not today. I know you have protection with you today. I'm sorry I wasn't ready to let you use it. Do you think you can wait much longer?"

"I can wait as long as it takes, Annie. How much longer do you think you will be able to wait?"

"I don't know, Matty. I really don't know."

Annie grabbed some clean underwear from her dresser and took her shower. She dried off, put on her underwear, wrapped her towel around her and walked out of the bathroom. Matt was still on the bed as he watched.

"Don't stare at me, Matty."

"What are you going to wear on your date?" Matt asked.

"Jeans and a shirt. Why?"

"I think you should wear a dress. Show this guy how good you look. You should wear the dress you wore the last time I saw you."

"You only like that dress because of the buttons."

"That is part of the attraction," he said.

"Stop grinning at me. I don't know if I should wear a dress. It's cold outside," she said while holding up the towel with one hand.

"You won't be outside for long and it's not that bad out. You do have a coat, right?"

"I need to run home soon because all my winter coats are at the house."

"You should wear that dress."

"If I do, I'm going to wear this bra and not just that camisole.

"But that camisole is so sexy. What if you wear it over your bra."

"Do you really think it was sexy?"

"Extremely sexy. I'm sure your date will think so, too."

"He won't see the camisole, Matty," Annie assured him.

"How do you know? Maybe he will surprise you."

"I'm not going to go anywhere with him where he will have a chance to charm me out of my dress like you did."

"Come on. Give the guy a fighting chance, Annie. Who knows? You might like him."

She looked at him and thought, *There's no way I will like him as much as I do you, Matthew Sullivan.* She mentally flipped a coin to make her decision. "All right. I'll wear the dress."

Annie took the dress from her closet, went back into the bathroom, put on the dress and modeled it for Matt. "How do I look?" she asked as she spun around.

"Do you have to ask? I think you look very pretty. I wish I was going out with you instead of... did you ever tell me his name?"

"It's Reid. Reid Smagala and he's twenty-two."

"I remember that part. I think you should blow him off and have dinner with me."

Annie looked at her clock. "It's really too late to cancel. I don't have his number."

"Should I leave a couple condoms here in case you change your mind?"

"Thanks, they might come in handy."

"For real?"

She giggled and then said, "No! I promise I won't need them. Are you jealous of my date?"

"Should I be?" Matt asked.

"Maybe. I might decide I really like him and we might become a real couple."

"If you do, does that mean you and I can't fool around?"

Annie grinned and tapped her chin as she answered, "I'm kinda starting to like fooling around with you."

Matt walked over to Annie and put his arms around her waist as she was looking in the mirror. He kissed her neck and she turned to face him. They kissed again as Matt held her close.

"Are you going to wait two months before you see me again?" Annie asked.

"I hope not. Now go have fun with your date. Not too much fun though. I want to reserve that privilege for myself."

"You can walk me downstairs, but then you have to go, Matthew Sullivan."

"One last kiss?"

"No!" she said as she grabbed her purse and hung it on her shoulder. "You never settle for just one kiss. I've finally learned that."

"It's not my fault I find you so attractive and adorable."

Matt walked Annie downstairs, then left without one last kiss. Annie watched him go, then headed over to the fountain to meet Reid. He was waiting as promised.

"Hello, Annie."

"Hi, Reid. Have you been waiting long?"

"Just a couple of minutes."

They walked to the dining hall, got their food and found a table for two. Annie took off her jacket, sat down and hung her jacket and purse over the back of her chair.

"Wow! Do you look fantastic or what?"

"Thank you, Reid. That's very nice of you." Annie was glad now Matt suggested she wear this dress.

"How was your day? Did you have a good afternoon?" he asked.

She nearly spit out her sip of water. *Crap! Don't tell me you know about Matty.* She waited a second before saying, "The afternoon seemed to fly by. How was yours?"

"I finished classes and spent most of the afternoon at the library. I found it difficult to concentrate though. I kept looking at the clock. I confess I was anxious for dinnertime."

"That's sweet, Reid. I was going to wear jeans, but I changed my mind. I hope you don't mind."

"Not a bit. I mean you look good in jeans, but you look fantastic in that dress."

They took their time eating and getting to know more about each other.

"Do you have any brothers or sisters, Annie?"

"No, it's just me and my dad. My mother died when I was

74

five. How about you?"

"I'm the youngest of four brothers. I was what they call a 'surprise' because my parents weren't expecting any more kids. I'm ten years younger than my closest brother."

"Are your parents still alive?"

"Very much so, and they've been married for forty years. What does your father do?"

"Daddy is a SoHam detective. He works in the robbery division now."

"I guess that means I had better behave with you, huh?"

"That would be the proper way to treat any girl you date, Reid," Annie mentioned in a serious manner although she was thinking about Matt at the time.

After they finished dinner Reid wasn't ready for the date to end. Neither was Annie.

"Would you like to go somewhere else, or do you have to study?" Reid asked.

"I don't have anything important to finish tonight. Would you like to see a movie?"

"That would work for me. I'm guessing you know a place around here."

"I know the whole city pretty well. Have you got a car?"

"I've got one, but it's in the shop right now."

"That's okay. I've got a car. I don't mind driving."

Reid and Annie walked over to the Howe Hall parking area to get her car.

"I've heard Howe is a really nice dorm."

"It really is. I share a room with Erin Bezick and we get along just great."

"Is it true you have private bathrooms?" Reid asked merely out of curiosity.

"That's true and it has its pros and cons. We have to clean our own bathroom. If we had a community bathroom, we wouldn't have to clean it. We take turns cleaning it."

Annie drove to the theater and Reid bought the tickets, the popcorn and pop. They watched a romantic comedy, *Spring Is In The Air*, which ended in a typical Hollywood fashion. When they got back to Howe Hall, Reid came inside and they sat downstairs in the lounge area.

"I had a good time, Annie. I would like to see you again."

"I think I can manage to find an opening in my hectic social life to fit you in," Annie answered in jest. "Let me check my calendar." She opened her purse and checked the small calendar she carried.

"Are you busy Friday night?" he asked.

She spent several seconds perusing her calendar and then grinned. "Nope! It just so happens I have an opening for Friday night. Most unusual."

Reid looked at Annie. He liked the way she grinned and the sparkle in her brown eyes. He liked the way she twisted her hair around a finger and the way she put a finger to her mouth. She seemed innocent, but yet had a sexiness that enchanted him.

"How about dinner somewhere other than Jordan? I know a club where we could go dancing. Do you like to dance?" Reid asked.

"What girl doesn't?"

"If you tell me your number, I'll call you tomorrow. If that's all right."

She gave him the number of their dorm room phone and he entered it into his cell phone. "We could meet for dinner again if you're not busy."

"Let's see," he said as he tapped his jaw. "I think I might have an opening in my busy schedule. Say around six," he teased.

Annie laughed. "I'll see you at six, Reid."

Reid needed to leave and wanted to kiss Annie but wasn't sure if he should or not. Annie made the decision for him and kissed him briefly on his cheek.

Chapter Thirteen

"Hey, Annie, are you free for lunch today?" Elaine Novicki asked as she and Cindy saw Annie on the stairway.

"I think so. What's up?"

"Cindy and I just wanted to see you. Even though we live in the same dorm we don't get to see each other as much anymore and we miss you."

"I miss you guys, too. What time do you want to meet?" Annie asked.

"Would twelve-thirty be all right?"

"I'll see you guys then."

After her morning classes Annie dashed over to Jordan Hall, grabbed some lunch and looked around for Elaine and Cindy.

Cindy spotted her and waved to get her attention. Annie saw her and walked over.

"Annie, we saved you a spot."

"Hi, Cindy. How's Bryce doing? Where's Lainey?"

"She'll be back in a second. She's interviewing one of the cooks."

"Bryce?" Annie asked as she took a bite of her chicken salad sandwich.

"He's been busy working on a paper, so I haven't seen him for a couple days. How did your date with Reid go? What did you guys do?" Cindy asked.

"We ate dinner here, then we went to a show. We saw *Spring Is In The Air*. It was funny and kinda sappy or corny in a way, but it had a happy ending. We are meeting for dinner again tonight and going dancing on Friday."

"Sounds like you guys hit it off okay. I'm glad. I wasn't sure how he would feel about dating someone so young. His last girlfriend was older than him."

"He didn't mention any other girlfriends and I didn't ask. I suppose it doesn't matter. I can't expect a guy that old to not have a history."

"Did you hear Victoria had her baby?" Elaine asked when she sat down with her notebook. "A little girl. She didn't even want to see, or hold her, before the adoptive parents took her home. At least that's what I heard."

"That would be so hard to do," Cindy said and then sighed. "I mean you carry a baby inside you for nine months, then go through childbirth, then never see her."

"I couldn't do that!" Elaine exclaimed.

Cindy took a sip of her Dr Pepper and then said, "I don't think it bothered Victoria. She wanted to have an abortion, but her parents talked her out of it. She may regret her decision sometime down the road."

"How is Adrien? Is he looking forward to graduating?" Annie asked Elaine.

"Well, of course he is. He is still planning to go to Kansas City next year. I have thought about transferring, but Cindy won't let me."

"Lainey, you can't transfer to another college. Please say you will stay here," Annie pleaded.

"I probably will. I love Adrien and all, but he will only be gone for a couple of years. Are Mace and Erin still dating?"

Annie held up a finger as she chewed her sandwich. "They are, but they had a fight a couple nights ago and Erin told him never to call her again."

"Do you think they will get back together?" Cindy asked.

"Oh yeah! They are probably having makeup sex right now."

"Annie! How can you say that?" Cindy asked as she blushed.

"Because Erin told me not to come to the room until after one o'clock. What do you and Bryce do after a fight?" Annie asked knowing it might embarrass Cindy.

"We don't have fights, and even if we did, Bryce would certainly not be having 'makeup sex!'" Cindy was indeed embarrassed as she thought about what Annie mentioned.

"Have you run into Matt lately?" Elaine asked.

"Yeah, I saw him yesterday," Annie answered. "Lainey, did you write that story for the paper about the declining relevance of fraternities and sororities on campus?" Annie changed the subject because she was not going to talk about Matthew Sullivan—no way, no how!

"You actually read that? I'm surprised anyone ever reads the paper. We need to bring that paper out of the dark ages and write about more relevant topics. My assignment this week was to interview the cook. Boring." She faked a yawn.

"Has anyone seen Victoria or talked to her lately?" Cindy asked. "I wonder if anyone visited her in the hospital. Did she come home yet?"

"No one that I know," Elaine said. "I wonder if she's really coming to North Park next semester."

Cindy grinned. "I'll believe it when I see her on campus and carrying books around instead of a baby."

"You guys shouldn't be so hard on her. It could have happened to any one of us."

"Uh, Annie, I beg to differ." Elaine waved a finger. "You have to be having sex to get pregnant and as far as I know all three of us are still virgins. Even if we were to have sex, I think we are smart enough to take precautions."

Cindy said, "I wonder if Victoria ever found out who the father actually was."

"It was Jason Agresta," Elaine said. "Victoria admitted he was the only one she engaged in unprotected sex with."

"Where did you hear that?" Cindy asked.

Elaine took a bite of her salad and then answered, "From Rachel. She heard it from Laura Russell who got it right from Victoria."

Annie was quiet for a moment, then asked a very serious question. "Is it possible to get pregnant without actually having sex?"

Elaine and Cindy looked at Annie with surprise.

"I'm assuming you aren't talking about the Virgin Mary."

"Don't be silly! I was just wondering if it's possible," Annie asked shyly.

"I have heard about girls who were virgins getting pregnant because their boyfriends... you know... they..."

"Christ, Cindy, you can't even say it." Elaine rolled her

79

eyes as she scolded her friend. "The guy climaxes while outside and it still goes in somehow. You do understand how babies are conceived, don't you, Cindy?"

"I'm not totally ignorant of the process, Elaine!" Cindy raised her voice but then whispered, "Just because I've never had sex, like some people I know, doesn't mean I don't know how it works. I fully understand the process."

"Can we talk about something besides sex?" Annie pleaded.

"Why? Does it embarrass you, Annie? Didn't your father ever talk to you about sex?" Elaine asked.

Annie frowned at Elaine. "Yes he did and he probably did a better job than your mothers. He actually talked to me about sex and stuff a few times."

"My mother never told me anything about sex. I heard it all from my older cousin," Cindy mentioned.

Annie loaded her trash on her tray and stood up. "I gotta get to class. Maybe I'll see you guys tonight. Reid and I are meeting at six."

"See you, Annie," Cindy said. She waited for Annie to leave and then frowned at Elaine. "You don't have to act so condescending. You don't know anymore about sex than I do."

Annie met Reid for dinner and they found a table for two with a little privacy. They talked about classes, the weather, the basketball team and other items of no great importance. Then Annie brought up the subject of past relationships.

"I am twenty-two, Annie. I haven't lived in a monastery my whole life," Reid said somewhat sarcastically.

"I've never had a serious boyfriend," Annie said. "How about you?"

Reid grinned. "I've never had any boyfriends at all."

Annie stared at him without speaking.

"Okay, you might have heard some things about me from your friends," Reid said and then admitted to Annie he and his previous girlfriend lived together for a whole year.

"You actually lived with her?" Annie was incredulous.

"We shared an apartment."

"What do you mean by that?" Annie wanted him to clarify his statement. "Were you roommates? Did you each have a bedroom to yourself?"

"No, we shared a bedroom. It was a small one-bedroom flat."

"So what happened? Did you get tired of her?" Annie asked. "Did she want to get married and you wouldn't commit?"

Reid frowned at Annie. "We broke up because she left me for another guy. I found out later she had been seeing him for six months."

"I'm sorry." Annie put a finger to her mouth. "That was none of my business and it was a mean thing to say."

"It's all right," Reid said and waved a hand dismissively.

"Do you ever hear from her?"

"I still see her once in a while."

"Why?" Annie asked. "Why would you want to see an ex-girlfriend?"

"Because she's the sister of Nick Whitaker, who is a close friend—my best friend, actually."

Annie actually bit her lip. "Crap! I just stuck my foot in my mouth again, didn't I?"

Reid nodded. "Her name was Stephanie Whitaker, but now it's Stephanie Gentiluomo because she got married. She is expecting a baby. I only see her if I'm at Nick's house and she comes over to visit her parents. I don't ever see her anywhere else, Annie."

"So Nick lives at home?" Annie asked to move the conversation away from Stephanie.

"Yeah, he probably won't ever move out."

Annie wasn't sure how she felt about Reid's sexual experience now. She was a bit leery he might try something with her she wasn't ready to handle. She didn't know him well enough to completely trust him like she trusted Matt Sullivan.

Chapter Fourteen

The alarm made its annoying buzzing sound, but Annie wasn't ready to get out of bed. She hit the snooze button several times and when she finally opened her eyes to see the time, she realized class started in ten minutes. She swore at the clock, jumped out of bed and got ready in five minutes. She made it to class just barely on time. She made it through the hour but needed to talk to her father, so she called his cell phone.

"Hi, sweetie. How is my college girl today?"

"I'm fine, Daddy, but I need to talk to you."

"I'm at home. Today is my day off, but Elisabeth is working. Should I come and get you and we can have lunch?"

"Would it be okay if I just come over? I have to grab my winter coats and drop off some laundry," Annie said.

"Any way I get to see you is all right with me," he replied.

"I'll be there around noon then. I love you, Daddy."

"Love you too, Annie." He ended the call but stared at his cell phone. "I wonder what's on her mind."

Annie brought her laundry with her, walked in the front door and dropped her laundry bag. "Anyone home?"

"In the living room."

She grabbed two winter coats from the front closet and tossed them on the coat rack inside the front door. She felt a little nervous about seeing Daddy, so she walked slowly into the living room. Her father stood up and Annie jumped into his arms. She wrapped her arms around his neck and her legs around his waist and rested her head on his shoulder.

"Wow! I didn't expect this."

"I miss you so much, Daddy."

Annie was very emotional and Dad knew something was bothering her. Dad held her tight for a minute, then released her.

"I miss you, too. Now tell me what's on your mind."

"Would you mind if I have a beer?"

"Oh, it's that serious, huh? Grab one for me, too."

Annie grabbed two beers from the fridge and sat on the couch next to her father. They drank for a minute before Dad asked, "Are you ready to tell me what is upsetting you so much?"

"I have a new friend. His name is Reid Smagala and we have just started dating. I kinda like him, but I found out something about him that worries me."

Dad sipped his Sam Adams and listened quietly as Annie explained.

"He's twenty-two and a second year student."

Dad raised his eyebrows but didn't interrupt.

"Yeah, I know that's bad," Annie said. "He worked for a couple years after high school before he started college. Anyway, he had a girlfriend and they lived together for a year. They lived in a one-bedroom apartment."

"I see," Dad said.

"They broke up because she cheated on him. He was used to having sex and I'm worried he might try to pressure me into getting more serious than I'm ready for." Annie paused to catch her breath.

"Have you known him very long, Annie?"

She took a sip of her beer and then shook her head. "No, he has a class with Cindy and she set us up on a blind date kinda thing. We had dinner with the group and we went out to a show. We're supposed to go out tonight for dinner and dancing at this club."

"Can I safely assume he hasn't tried anything yet?"

"He has been a perfect gentleman so far. I did give him a quick kiss, but that's it. Is it difficult for a guy, who has been used to having sex all the time, to just stop?" Annie asked.

Dad rested his head on the back of the couch before answering. "I suppose it depends on the guy and why he stopped. When your mother passed away, I had no trouble giving up sex, but this is different."

"I get that," Annie said.

Dad looked at Annie and smiled.

"Why are you smiling?" Annie asked.

"I pity the guy who tries to take advantage of you, Annie Mercer." Dad put an arm around her shoulders and squeezed her. "He won't know what hit him. Is this Reid guy a huge football player or something?"

"No, he's just a regular guy. He's about six feet tall and about average build. He's handsome but not like a movie star. More like you."

"You're not dating him because he reminds you of me are you?"

"He's not that old, Daddy!" she said and then grinned.

Dad looked at Annie and knew there was more to tell.

"What else is on your mind, honey?"

"Will you promise not to hate me if I tell you?"

"Are you hooked on heroin again?" Dad teased.

Annie laughed. "No, I'm still off the junk." She was quiet for a moment. "It's about sex. Don't worry, I haven't done it yet! Except for the basketball team, of course."

"Goes without saying."

Annie laughed at the inside joke.

"I saw Matty Sullivan and he came up to my room." She looked at her father, but his face didn't give anything away. "We made out and I let him do some things with me. I know Matty has a reputation with girls. A well deserved reputation I might say. I know he's not ever going to be my boyfriend, but... how can I say this without upsetting you? He gets me hot! There's just something about him that makes me feel kinda tingly inside."

"You aren't the first girl to fall under the spell of a 'bad boy,' Annie. It happens a lot actually. I know Matthew can be very charming when he wants to be."

"He has always been honest with me and I trust him. He could have taken advantage of me, but he didn't. I told him I wasn't ready and he didn't try to persuade me."

"Some guys are very patient, sweetheart. Just because he didn't try one time doesn't mean it will always be that way."

Annie took another sip and then shook her head. "For some reason, I think it will. I don't think he will do anything until I am ready. I'm just worried because I have a hard time saying no to Matty. Does that make me a slut?"

"I don't think I've ever heard of a slut who was a virgin. Not counting the basketball team," he added.

84

"Oh, Daddy!" She poked him in the side.

"I understand how you feel about Matt, and I think now you understand more about how he gets you 'hot'."

Annie blushed.

"It's perfectly normal for a pretty young girl like you to have those feelings, Annie. Your mother had those same feelings for this really hot guy she knew in high school."

"For real? Did she ever do anything about those feelings?"

Dad flashed a wide smile. "You were the result of those feelings, Annie. A few years later, of course."

"Were you really hot?"

"You better believe it," Dad said and then grinned. "So many girls were after me. I had to fight them off with a stick."

"I don't think Matty has ever fought off the attentions of any girl."

"You might be right about that," Dad said. "Do you want to borrow my old boxing gloves? In case you have to fight off any other college guys."

"They might come in handy," she said and took another drink of her beer.

"Well, now I think you will be better equipped to fight him off, sweetie. What about Reid? Does he stir your emotions the same way?"

"Not so far. I think he's more like a Crock-Pot type guy."

Dad raised his eyebrows. "You want to clue me in?"

She finished her beer, set it down on the coffee table and explained, "If you put a roast in the Crock-Pot, things start off slow with low heat and they just keep building for several hours until the roast is done. Matty is like setting a marshmallow right in the bonfire. It gets real hot right away, but then turns black and falls off the stick."

"That is quite a good analogy, Annie. I guess you are learning a few things at college."

"I might learn more if I went to some classes," she joked but then asked a serious question. "Does it embarrass you to talk about sex with me?"

"It's not the easiest thing in the world to do, but it doesn't

85

embarrass me. It makes me feel good you trust me enough to talk about that kind of stuff. You could talk to your friends instead."

"I don't think I could talk to any of them about sex," Annie said.

"You can always talk to me about anything, sweetie. It doesn't matter what it is."

"Do you still love me, Daddy?"

He scratched his jaw. "No, I don't think I ever loved you."

Annie knew he was teasing. She moved onto his lap and he hugged her so tightly she couldn't breathe.

"Am I too big to sit on your lap?" she asked while keeping her eyes closed.

"I used to love it when you would sit on my lap and fall asleep. You're just a bit heavier now but it's not unbearable."

"Oh, Daddy, you're teasing me. I have to get back for a class. I'll do my laundry Sunday, I guess."

Dad let go and Annie stood up.

"I could do it for you, Annie. Unless you don't want me to. You probably have your underwear to do."

Annie checked her pocket to make sure she still had her keys. "That would be so sweet of you to do it for me and I don't care if you see my dirty unmentionables. Everything is sorted out. Do you remember...?"

Dad got up and followed her to the front hallway. "I know how to wash your unmentionables, Annie. I did it for years, remember?"

"Thanks, Daddy! I've got to run. I'll be back Sunday. I love you even if you don't love me." She grabbed her winter coats and ran out the door.

Dad walked outside, waved and hollered, "Maybe I love you a little."

Chapter Fifteen

Annie couldn't decide what to wear on her date. She tried on three outfits before settling on a navy blue skirt, a white blouse and a sweater. Reid made a reservation for seven o'clock at Ciao Bella, a fancy Italian restaurant in the 'Hill' district of SoHam. He got ready and drove to Howe Hall. He walked up the stairs and knocked on Annie and Erin's door.

"Hi, Reid. Come on in. I'll be ready in a second. Do I look okay? I wasn't sure what I should wear since we're going dancing after dinner."

"You look very nice, Annie. I like that skirt."

"Thanks. I hope it's not too out of style. It's kinda long on me."

"That doesn't matter. It looks better than if it was really short."

"Are you saying you don't like the way my legs look?" she teased.

He shook his head. "It's not that. I think you have really good looking legs. At least what I've seen of them. We should get going."

Annie noticed Reid looking around the room.

"I cleaned it up a little."

"It looks like a typical dorm room, Annie."

"Should I drive?" Annie asked.

Reid held up his keys. "I got it back from the shop. I'll drive."

Reid drove to Ciao Bella and couldn't find a parking spot closer than three blocks away.

"I don't mind walking. The fresh air is good for us."

"Are you sure, Annie? I could drop you off, then find a parking spot."

"I'd rather walk with you, Reid."

Annie held Reid's hand as they walked to the restaurant. She felt warm and cozy in her winter coat. They were seated within five minutes, placed their drink order and ordered a sampler tray of appetizers. They talked about school and ordered one of the specials for dinner. An hour later Reid paid the check and they walked back to the car.

"Are you ready for some dancing, Annie?"

"It will be fun. I haven't been dancing for some time."

They arrived at the club and spent an hour on the dance floor. Annie discovered Reid's ability as a dancer. She especially liked the way he held her as they danced to a slow song. He didn't try to hold her too close.

"Are you ready to leave, Annie? We can go if you want."

"Would you mind if we left and found a place where it's a little quieter and maybe more private?"

Reid smiled at Annie.

"I didn't mean it like that. I just want to talk to you about something important."

"We could go to the coffeehouse on campus. It's quiet there."

"Yeah, but it will be busy on a Friday night. They usually have live music. Could we just find a place and sit in the car?" Annie asked.

"You name the spot, Annie. Anywhere you feel safe is okay with me."

"I would bring you to my house, but Daddy is home today. I'm not ready for you to meet him."

"I would like to meet your father sometime. But I can wait until you're ready," he said as he held the door open for her. He even opened the car door for her.

"Could we park in the lot by the Riverwalk?" Annie asked after Reid got in and started the car. "That way we will be close to my dorm."

"If it wasn't so cold we could take a walk. I think the temperature's dropped twenty degrees from when we left."

It only took a few minutes to arrive at the Riverwalk parking area. Reid kept the car running and the heater going."

"What was wrong with your car?" Annie asked.

"They replaced the ignition switch. It wasn't as expensive as I thought it was going to be. If you get too warm, let me know."

"I"m fine now, but if I get too hot I'll let you know."

Annie blushed because she remembered what she told her father about Matty.

"What did you want to talk about? I bet I can guess."

She smoothed out her skirt as she looked out the windshield. She turned her head and looked at Reid. "I wanted to talk about your last girlfriend. Would that bother you?"

"No, I feel you have a right to know about my previous relationship."

"Relationship. Like only one."

"I've only ever had one real girlfriend, Annie. I guess I didn't tell you that before. Steph and I started dating when she was a sophomore in high school. We were together all through high school. Of course, I've known her a lot longer than that, but we were just friends then. She is Nicky's little sister."

"It must have really hurt when you discovered what she had been doing."

Reid adjusted the heat and turned down the fan speed. "I was devastated at first, but I realized we had changed and were growing apart. We made a mistake by living together. I'm happy for her now though. She met a great guy and she's going to be a great mother."

Annie looked at Reid and wasn't sure how to ask what was really on her mind.

"You really want to ask about sex, don't you?" Reid asked after a moment of silence.

"Yes, I guess I do," Annie said as she looked out the passenger door window.

"Steph has been my only lover. We first made love after going to prom. We were both a little naïve, but we were careful. After that we discovered we really liked being together. Her parents knew about our relationship and while they weren't thrilled about it, they supported our decision to move in together."

"I talked to Daddy about sex this afternoon. If you haven't guessed, I am a virgin. Daddy was always willing to answer my questions as I grew up. He wasn't the kind of parent who avoided the difficult issues. Anyway, since he was fairly young when my mother passed away, I asked if it was difficult for a guy, who was

89

used to having sex all the time, to suddenly be cut off."

"You're worried about what I might try to do. I understand that and there is the age thing. Five years is a significant difference in our ages right now."

"I'm not concerned with that, Reid. We are in college together, so we have that in common. We are both going through the same routines of studying and going to class. Partying!"

"I get the feeling you and I share the same attitude when it comes to frat parties. I like to have fun and I still have a beer now and then, but I'm not into getting wasted all the time."

"So do I. The beer I mean. I had one today with Daddy. He knows I don't drink at school though."

"It sounds to me like you have a really cool relationship with your father."

"I really do. Did I tell you Daddy and Mace Franklin's mother are dating?"

"No, you didn't mention it."

"At first it bothered me, but I'm okay with it now."

"Did your father ever get serious about anyone after your mother passed away?" Reid asked as he checked his fuel gauge.

"Nope. He didn't date at all for a few years. Elisabeth is his first serious romance since Mom."

"I'm guessing they are... lovers."

"Yeah! It was hard to get used to that at first, but they make each other happy. You can turn off the car if you need to save gas. I'm plenty warm."

He shut down the car and turned in his seat to look at her. "I'll be upfront with you, Annie. I find you very attractive. Not only that but you are smart and funny and once you get over the shyness thing, you are interesting to talk with. I will take it slow with you, but I won't hide the fact I am interested in having sex at some point."

"I told Daddy you were like a Crock-Pot guy."

Reid raised his eyebrows.

"Let me explain. I know this guy who is a real lady killer and we have made out before. He has a new girl every week it seems. I told Daddy he was like a marshmallow at a bonfire. It gets

90

real hot, then melts and falls into the fire and it's no good anymore. A person can only get so close to the fire before they get burned. I told Daddy you were like a roast in a Crock-Pot because it starts off nice and slow, then gradually heats up and when it's ready, it is very good. Does that make any sense to you?"

"It makes perfect sense. Do you really like marshmallows and bonfires?"

"You are really asking about the other guy, right?" Annie asked as she twisted her hair around a finger.

"I said you were smart."

"I've known him for a few years and I like him, but I would get sick if all I ever ate was marshmallows. Eventually, you get to the point where you never want to see a marshmallow again."

"Are you to that point, Annie?"

"I think I could very well be sick of marshmallows and never want to eat another one, ever." She knew it wasn't true as soon as she said it, but how could she tell Reid about her feelings for Matty.

Reid moved closer to Annie and she turned her face to his. They kissed very briefly.

"I think you should take me back to my dorm," she said.

He drove her back to Howe Hall, parked his car and walked her inside.

"I had a wonderful time tonight, Reid. Will you call me sometime?"

"I will," he answered. He tried to kiss her again, but she backed away.

Call me," she said as she ran over to the stairs.

Reid watched as she dashed up the stairs, then he left.

"How was your date?" Erin asked as Annie entered the room and plopped down on her bed.

"It was all right, but I kinda have a taste for a roasted marshmallow."

Chapter Sixteen

Coach Bazetich gave the guys a pep talk in the locker room before their Saturday afternoon game against Missouri Wesleyan University. Bradley College defeated the Redbirds in their last game by five points and Coach didn't want a repeat. The same five guys were starting although Kevin Murphy had a very sore shoulder. His shooting was affected, but not his passing or defense. Mace was ready to takeover as point guard to give Kevin more of a break.

The Roosevelt High gang attended the game. Elaine and Cindy arrived with their guys. Erin and Annie quit studying early so they could be at the game. Reid was going to meet Annie at the gym as soon as he finished a paper. Annie saw Matt Sullivan walk in with a girl. She didn't recognize her and Matt didn't see Annie. Diana Ahronson walked into the gym and headed to the section where the Roosevelt High alumni usually sat.

Cindy poked Elaine in the side. "Here comes Diana."

"I can see that, Cindy," Elaine said as she nudged her friend.

Diana walked up the bleacher aisle and spotted her old friends. "Hi, guys! How are you? I haven't talked to you for so long."

"How have you been, Diana? How is life in the Alpha Phi house?" Cindy asked. "We have room if you want to sit with us."

"Thank you, Cindy. I will sit with you for a moment, but I am supposed to meet some of my sorority sisters." Diana sat next to Cindy and looked around the gym.

Cindy sighed as she caught a whiff of Diana's expensive, but understated perfume.

Diana turned her head and smiled. "I like it. It's not anything like the guys' frat houses. The girls are serious about school. We have stricter rules about boys than the resident halls. How are things going in Howe Hall?"

"We like it. The only bad part is cleaning our own bathroom."

"I see you are still with Adrien and Bryce."

"Yes, are you and Damon still together?" Cindy asked.

"We are. Thank God for email. He will be home for the holidays. I can't wait to see him. I really miss him. We are going to Aspen for the Christmas holiday, but we'll be back for the New Year's Eve party."

Elaine saw Annie and Erin and stood up to wave at them. Annie led Erin up the bleachers and stood in the row in front of her friends.

"Hi, Diana. How have you been?" Annie asked as she removed her winter coat.

"Annie! It's good to see you."

"This is Erin Bezick. We're roomies. I don't know if you've met her before."

"Hi, Erin. I'm Diana. I bet you are having fun rooming with Annie."

"We get along pretty good."

"Erin is dating Mace."

"You're lucky. Mace is really handsome. I saw the last home game and he is getting better and better. Are you dating anyone, Annie? Do you ever see Matt Sullivan anymore?"

"I see Matty around occasionally, and my date will be here a little later. His name is Reid Smagala and he's twenty-two."

"Oooh! Dating an older man. Does your father know?"

"Daddy knows, but he hasn't met Reid, yet."

"That name seems familiar for some reason. I just can't place it though."

"He's from Chicago," Annie said.

Diana snapped her fingers and Cindy noticed her manicured nails and light pink polish. "I remember now. He's a friend of my cousins Nick and Stephanie. Well, they're really third cousins or something."

Annie whispered to Diana, "He told me he actually lived with Stephanie for about a year."

"Good. He told you about that. I felt really sorry for him when I heard Stephanie broke up with him. Did he tell you she's married now?"

"He told me she's married and expecting."

Diana and Annie sat together and talked about Reid until Annie saw him walking toward them.

"Here he comes now, Diana," Annie said.

Annie waved to Reid and he hurried up the bleachers to her. He smiled at Annie, then looked at Diana.

"Hi, Reid. I don't know if you remember me or not? I'm Diana Ahronson."

"Diana, I remember you. You're Stephanie's friend or cousin, right? We met a couple of times. How are you?"

"I'm good."

"If I remember correctly you were going out with Damon Barclay," Reid said as he removed his coat. He sat down next to Diana even though Annie made space for him to sit by her.

"We still are, but he's at Princeton University and I'm here."

"That must be difficult," Reid said as he stared at Diana.

"It is at times. Annie told me you were dating. I think that's great. Annie is a super girl and she's so smart."

Just then the crowd rose to their feet and roared as the Redbirds took the court.

"I should find my sorority sisters," Diana said and grabbed her purse and coat.

Cindy noticed Diana getting ready to leave, so she scooted past Annie and grabbed Diana's hand. "Diana, there's a bunch of us going out for pizza later. Would you be interested in joining us, or do you have plans with your new friends?"

"I'm not sure, Cindy. What time are you meeting?"

"We're going to meet at the Student Union at six and leave from there."

"If I can make it, I'll see you at six at the Student Union, but don't wait for me."

"I hope you can make it, Diana," Cindy said as Diana left to find her friends. Cindy sat back down and found Elaine staring at her. "What?" Cindy asked.

"Do you have to fawn over her every time you see her?" Elaine asked.

"I want her to know we're still her friends," Cindy said.

The game was soon underway and the Redbirds started off fast. Every shot they took went in. They built up an eighteen point lead at the half and extended it to thirty halfway through the second half. Coach pulled all his starters with six minutes to go. Missouri Wesleyan cut the lead to twenty-five but never closer.

At six o'clock Diana walked into the Student Union.

"She's here," Elaine said as she nudged Cindy and pointed.

Cindy smiled at Diana and ran to greet her as Diana glanced around the Student Union. "You made it! I'm so glad. You can ride with us. We're going to Beggars. Is that all right?"

"Beggars is all right with me. How many people are going?" Diana asked.

Cindy quickly counted. "There are ten of us. You make eleven. This will be fun. We would walk but it's getting rather cold."

Adrien took Elaine, Cindy, Bryce and Diana with him. Cindy insisted Diana sit in the back with her and Bryce.

"Annie, would you mind if I drive your car?" Mace asked. "Erin and I will probably leave earlier than you."

"Why should I let you borrow my car?" Annie asked.

"I'll fill the tank," Mace promised.

"Deal." She handed him the keys.

Annie rode in front with Reid. Solomon and Ashley rode in the back and, as usual, they were in their own private world. When they got to Beggar's, they split up into groups. Solomon and Ashley found a table for two along one wall. Adrien and Bryce grabbed a booth on the opposite side of the dining area.

Cindy pulled Diana by the arm. "You have to sit with us. We'll make room."

Diana nodded, looked at Annie and shrugged then followed Cindy and Elaine. Annie, Reid, Mace and Erin sat at a table next to the booth. Cindy squeezed close to Bryce to give Diana enough room to sit next to her.

"Should we order our regular or should we try something different?" Adrien asked.

"Maybe we could get two large pizzas and have our favorite toppings and something new also," Elaine suggested while reading the menu. "The chicken and pineapple pizza is supposed to be good."

"That sounds good to me. Is it all right with you, Bryce?" Cindy asked and then explained to Diana. "We like sausage, green peppers and mushrooms. That's our regular, but we can order whatever you like."

Elaine rolled her eyes then shook her head.

"Whatever you choose is okay with me. Let's order a pitcher of pop, too," Diana said.

While Elaine and Cindy were only eighteen, at least for a little longer, their relationships were more serious than Mace's or Annie's. Elaine and Adrien talked about getting married and Cindy was deeply in love with Bryce, even if she had to fight off his advances more frequently. Mace and Erin enjoyed being together, but their relationship was based solely on their physical needs. Solomon and Ashley were true soul mates and were already planning how many kids they would have. They decided to start a computer company together after they graduated in four years. Solomon wanted to earn a PHD while Ashley was going to be satisfied with a masters. Diana and Damon were basically pre-engaged and only waiting until the start of their final year to make it official. As for Reid and Annie, it was anyone's guess. It was too early to tell if the age difference will prove to be too much for Reid to handle. Annie was only seventeen and though mature in most respects, she was still a teenager and behaved like one. Especially tonight at Beggar's.

"What would you like on your pizza, Annie?" Reid asked.

"Anything is okay with me except for green olives. Black olives are all right."

"Do you like sausage or pepperoni better?"

"Pepperoni. Can we get onions, mushrooms and green peppers, too? Is that all right with you, Erin? I know Mace will eat anything."

"Hey, you know I don't like mushrooms on my pizza. Can we get olives instead?" Mace asked.

"No! I want mushrooms. A pizza just isn't complete without mushrooms," Annie insisted.

96

Annie and Mace argued back and forth about what to put on the pizza. Erin and Reid looked at them, then each other. Diana overheard them arguing and smiled because she had known Mace and Annie long enough to know they were just messing around. Cindy and Elaine ignored Mace and Annie.

"Is it just me, or do they sound like brother and sister?" Reid asked Erin.

"You got that right. They sound like junior high kids, too," she answered.

"You know we could order two pizzas, then you could each get what you like," Reid mentioned.

"We know," Annie said. "We just like to argue to see who gets their own way. He is so spoiled."

"I'm not nearly as spoiled as you, Princess Annie."

Annie stuck her tongue out at Mace.

"You better keep that in your mouth unless you want to lose it."

"Reid, will protect me from you. Won't you?"

"I think Mace might need protection from you, Annie."

Annie looked at Reid and pouted.

Elaine and Cindy were ready to leave ninety minutes later.

"Diana, would you like to come with us? I could show you our room," Cindy begged with her eyes.

"Maybe another time. I'd like to stay and talk to Reid," Diana replied. She walked over to Annie and asked, "May I join you?"

"Of course," Annie said then waved goodbye to Elaine and Cindy. "We could give you a ride back to campus if you'd like."

"I would appreciate that." Diana sat between Annie and Reid. "I haven't seen Nick or Stephanie for some time. How are they doing?"

Annie listened to Reid and Diana talk about Nick and Stephanie.

"We're taking off," Mace told Annie a few minutes later. "I'll take Solomon and Ashley back. Don't let Reid ignore you."

"It's all right," Annie said. "I like to listen. I learn stuff."

Diana tried several times to include Annie in the

97

conversation, but Reid would quickly ask Diana another question.

Thirty minutes later Diana said, "It's getting late. I have to finish reading two chapters."

"We can leave," Reid said. "I'll drop you off."

Reid dropped Diana off at the Alpha Phi house. He walked her to the door while Annie waited in the car. When he got back to the car he told Annie, "It was nice to see Diana again. She's really sweet."

"Not to mention absolutely gorgeous."

"Yeah. There is that. Are you ready to go home, Annie?"

"Not really. Mace is with Erin, so I really can't go home."

"Would you like to come over to my place?"

"Are you asking me or Diana?"

He hung his head. "I deserved that. I'm sorry."

"Apology accepted," Annie said. "You've never even told me which dorm you're in."

"I'm not in a dorm. I share an apartment with Ron Wilcher. I know him from the city. We were at Lakeshore together. He's in his last year here."

Annie thought about it for several seconds. "Okay, I would like to see your place. Is your roommate home?"

"He's probably home. He doesn't go out much."

"I don't know. Will you talk to me?" Annie asked.

"Yes, I will talk to you. Do you want to come over or...?"

"Yes."

Reid brought Annie to his apartment. It was a typical two-bedroom, one-bath unit with a small kitchen and a crowded living room. Annie noticed a TV and stereo against one wall. The coffee table in front of the cracked, brown leather couch was cluttered with pop and beer cans and partially eaten bags of chips. A Beggar's pizza box was under the table. Reid noticed Annie looking at the mess.

"Ron can be a bit of a slob at times," Reid said.

"I see," Annie said as she removed her coat and handed it to Reid who immediately hung it up in the closet.

"Hey, I heard that. Who are you talking to?" Ron walked into the living room from his bedroom. He wore a faded bathrobe over his sweatpants and stained t-shirt and held a slice of pizza in his hand.

"Annie, this is my roomie Ron. Ron, this is Annie O'Dell."

Ron set his pizza on the coffee table and wiped his hand on his bathrobe. "Hello, Annie. Reid told me a little about you," Ron said as he offered his hand. "I'm sorry for the mess. Reid is always getting after me to clean up after myself. FYI, he's a neat freak."

"Just because I clean up after myself doesn't mean I'm a fanatic," Reid said. Then to prove Ron's point, Reid cleaned up the mess on the table.

"Be careful about going into his room, Annie," Ron said.

"Why?"

Ron whispered, "He's never brought a girl over here before. He might get all excited and try to put a move on you."

"Do you think so?" Annie had a twinkle in her eye as she and Ron teased Reid.

"Don't pay any attention to this guy, Annie. You don't have to go in my room."

"But I want to see it. Are you hiding something in there you don't want me to know about?"

"I'm not hiding anything. Do you really want to see it?"

"I only want to see it, Reid. Nothing else."

"I just wanted to be sure, Annie. Come on, I'll let you in and you can check it out," Reid said as he looked back at Ron and caught him checking out Annie's bluejeans. He frowned at Ron.

Reid opened his bedroom door and stepped aside to let Annie enter. She noticed right away his room was much cleaner than her dorm room, or her room at home. She spotted the uncluttered desk and felt envious. Her eyes caught the small stereo was on top of his dresser and a computer in sleep mode. She didn't see any clothes lying on the floor and his bed was made.

"Your room is a lot neater than mine, Reid. You would be shocked at my room at home."

"It's not always this neat, Annie."

Ron stood in the doorway. "Don't believe that, Annie. He makes his bed before he gets out of it in the morning. Don't know how he does it."

99

"Will you give us a little privacy, please?" Reid asked Ron.

Ron grinned and walked away while eating another slice of pizza.

Annie walked over to Reid's bed and sat on the edge. "It seems nice and firm. Can I try it out?"

Reid looked at Annie with a grin on his face.

"I didn't mean like that," Annie said.

"Too bad. We could have some fun," Reid answered.

Annie was really beginning to enjoy Reid's sense of humor. She stood up and moved over next to Reid. "Do you have anything for a sweet, innocent, young girl to drink around here?"

"We have milk in the fridge," Ron hollered from the living room, "and cookies in the pantry."

Reid turned around and rolled his eyes. "Ron, don't you need to go back to your room and listen to some music through your headphones? Some loud music. Headphones."

"I can tell when I'm not wanted. It was nice to meet you, Annie. I hope he brings you over again. I'll tell you all his deepest secrets." Ron stood up, looked at the mess under the table and decided not to bother cleaning it up.

"I might just come over by myself sometime just so you can give me all the juicy details," Annie said.

"Has he told you about..."

"Headphones, Ron!"

"See you around, Annie O'Dell." Ron waved and headed back to his room.

"What would you like to drink, Annie?"

"Milk and cookies, please," she said as she bounced on her toes.

He looked at her to see if she meant it.

"I'm kidding. I'm not ten. Water or pop, please."

"Can of Coke okay?"

"Sure!"

Annie went back to the living room and sat on the couch. Reid cleared the mess under the coffee table and took it to the kitchen. He brought out the pop and two glasses with ice. He turned on the TV and sat next to Annie. He put his feet on the

100

coffee table and Annie noticed he took his shoes off.

"Should I take my shoes off, Reid?"

"You don't have to, but you can if you want. Anything you wanna see on TV?"

"Doesn't matter. Anything is okay. Sports are all right."

They sat and watched a rerun of *Seinfeld*. Annie moved closer to Reid.

"Are you cold, Annie?"

"Just a little."

"I've got a blanket in my room. I'll get it."

Reid brought out the blanket and covered them both.

"Thanks, Reid. This is better."

Annie snuggled closer to Reid and he put an arm around her shoulders. They laughed as Kramer was up to his usual antics. Even though they were snuggling close together, Reid didn't try anything. He didn't even kiss Annie. She got very comfortable and rested her head on Reid's shoulder. When the show ended Reid wondered if Annie was ready to go home.

"What time do you need to get back to your room?"

"I don't have a curfew. I'm not ready to leave yet. Is that okay?"

"Sure. I wasn't trying to get rid of you. You can stay as late as you want," Reid said. "Will Mace spent the whole night with Erin?"

"No. She will toss him out at some point. He's never spent the night as far as I know. Not with Erin, anyway."

"What do you mean by that? Has Mace had many girlfriends?"

"Just a couple that I know of. Trish and now Erin. I meant that Mace has spent the night with me." Annie realized how this must have sounded to Reid. She giggled. "That didn't sound right. I meant Mace has crashed at our house before. He never spent the night in my room though."

"I figured that's what you meant, Annie. You did tell me you were..."

"I really am, Reid!"

"I believe you, Annie. I'm not doubting you at all."

"Were you a virgin when you and Stephanie made love?"

"Yes. She has been my only lover."

"Oh, that's right. You told me that already. I don't mean to be nosy. Sometimes I stick my nose in places it shouldn't be. At Roosevelt I acquired a reputation as someone who could get things for people. I solved a few problems for Grandpa, who is the principal there. Some of the kids called me 'Annie O'Drew' at times."

"Maybe they should make a TV show about you, Annie. They could call it 'Annie O'Dell. World's Youngest Private Eye' or something."

"I told you I talked to Daddy about us, didn't I?"

"The slow cooker thing, right?"

"Yeah. Does it bother you I talk to Daddy about my sex... love... dating life."

"Not at all. Should it?"

"No, but if we ever reach that point where you want to go..."

"You mean if we ever have sex?"

"Yes. If that ever happened, I would probably tell Daddy about it. Not the details. Just that it happened."

"That's a relief. I'd hate to think your father would know intimate details of our sex life."

"Reid!" she said as she poked him in the side.

"Just teasing, Annie. I know we don't have anything close to a sex life together... yet!"

"Yet? Are you thinking we should start soon?"

"I don't want to rush you, Annie. You know that."

"Would a little kiss be considered a start?"

"I think that's how most people start. Can I kiss you once?"

"I would like that."

Reid kissed Annie tenderly on the mouth. She returned his kiss.

"I might be able to spare one more kiss if you want, Reid."

He kissed her again and whispered, "I think we might have just turned on the Crock-Pot, Annie O'Dell."

Chapter Seventeen

"Daddy is off this weekend. I am going to go home to do laundry, so I think it's the perfect time for you to come with me," Annie said to Reid on Wednesday night as they finished eating dinner.

"Are you going to spent the weekend at home?" Reid asked as he gathered their trays.

"I was planning to spent Saturday night at home and come back to campus Sunday evening. If you'd rather sleep in your own bed you can. I won't mind."

Reid looked at Annie with a mixture of surprise and joy on his face as he held their trays.

Annie realized how he misinterpreted what she said. "I didn't mean you would be sharing my bed. You would have to sleep on the couch if you stay overnight. It's a two-bedroom house."

"Since it isn't that far back to school, would you mind if I went back to my apartment Saturday?"

"That means you'll come with me?"

"Yes, I'll go with you and meet your father."

"Thank you, Reid. Daddy has been asking about you." She walked with him as they left the dining hall.

"Should I be ready to be interrogated?" he asked.

"Yes, but he probably won't use torture. Well, maybe a little bit."

"Sounds like fun," he said and then sighed.

Annie spent more time than ever studying during the week. Finals approached and she wanted to be ready. She finished all the papers due for her classes.

Saturday morning Reid picked up Annie and her dirty laundry at ten o'clock.

"Are you forgetting something, Reid?" she said as she stood beside his car.

"What? Do you have more laundry in your room?" he

asked as he placed her laundry in his trunk.

"No, but I haven't gotten a kiss yet."

"Oh, I'm sorry, Annie. I guess I'm just a little nervous."

Reid kissed Annie on the cheek. She sighed and rolled her eyes.

"Daddy! We're here. Where are you?"

"In the living room, monkey!"

Reid grinned because Annie seemed embarrassed.

"Does your father always call you monkey?"

"No, he doesn't normally. He used to call me that when I was little. Now he only does it if he wants to embarrass me in front of someone."

Reid followed Annie into the living room. Her father was reading a newspaper.

"Daddy, this is Reid Smagala. Reid, this is my father."

Detective O'Dell stood up to shake Reid's hand.

"It's nice to meet you, sir. Annie has told me a lot about you."

"Have a seat, Reid."

"Aren't you happy to see me, Daddy?"

"Of course I am, sweetie."

Daddy hugged Annie and kissed her cheek.

"Would you start making some coffee, Annie. I need to grill... I mean talk to Reid for a second."

"Oh, Daddy! You promised..."

"I'm just teasing, Annie—about the coffee. I plan to fully interrogate Reid. Have a seat, young man."

"Sorry, Reid. I hope you pass the lie detector test. Be careful for trick questions. Daddy is very skilled at getting confessions out of perpetrators."

Reid sat in the recliner where Detective O'Dell pointed and looked at Annie with a weak grin on his face. Annie sat on the couch next to her father. He put an arm around her shoulder and squeezed. He smiled at Reid, and Reid realized Detective O'Dell was completely wrapped around Annie's finger. His nervousness vanished.

"Annie has told me a few things about you, Reid. Why

don't you fill me in and then I'll tell you some stories about her."

"Daddy, you better not embarrass me again."

Dad put a hand to his forehead. "Oh, I forgot. You get embarrassed if I call you monkey."

"You didn't forget. You did it on purpose."

They talked until lunchtime and Reid relaxed and felt right at home. They ate a light lunch, then Annie started on her laundry. She chased Reid away when he tried to help her. She didn't want him to see her unmentionables.

"Elisabeth and I are going out for dinner tonight. Would you like to join us, Reid?" Dad asked.

"Be careful, Reid—trick question," Annie hollered from the laundry room.

"I would like that, Mr. O'Dell."

"Good. I'll treat. We are going to eat around six, if that's all right with you?"

"Six would be fine."

"Annie, I have to help Elisabeth with shopping this afternoon. Will you and Reid be all right?"

"Yes, Daddy. We will be okay."

Reid looked at Annie.

"I guess you passed. He trusts you to be alone with me."

"The security cameras are on, Annie, and a squad car will be parked out front."

Annie smiled at Reid. "Come on, I'll show you my room."

Dad hollered, "You have time to escape if you run now, Reid. I'll distract her somehow."

"She told me her room was a little messy. How bad can it be?"

"Ever hear of of a force five tornado?"

"Yes," Reid answered a bit unsure where her father was going.

"A force ten went through Annie's room."

"Don't believe him, Reid. I cleaned it up the last time I was home."

Annie showed Reid her room and he was impressed.

"I can actually see the floor, Annie. Oh no, sorry I guess

105

that's just some dirty towels," Reid teased as Dad laughed from the doorway.

Annie put her hands on her hips and pouted. "It may not be as neat as your room, Reid, but it's better than it usually is."

"I'm just teasing, Annie, I like your room. It shows more of your personality than your dorm room."

Annie looked at her father. "Reid has been in my dorm room. He picked me up to go out."

"I didn't say anything, Annie."

Dad left to pick up Elisabeth. He talked to Mace and Keyshon and explained to Keyshon why he couldn't see Annie right now. Annie took a shower and got ready to go out to dinner with her father and Elisabeth. She decided to wear a skirt and top and black tights. Reid didn't bring any other clothes.

"You look really nice, Annie."

"Thanks, Reid. Daddy called. They'll be here in a few minutes. Are you ready to go?"

"I don't have anything else to wear."

"I didn't mean that. I was asking if you were ready to have dinner with Daddy and Elisabeth."

"Sure. I mean he trusts me, right?"

"I think he likes you," Annie said.

Detective O'Dell picked up Annie and Reid and they ate dinner at Larry's Uptown Grill. They started with drinks and appetizers. Everyone ordered a beer except for Annie who had a Coke.

"So, Reid, tell me more about yourself. I know you are going to North Park."

"Yes, Mrs. Franklin."

"Please, call me Elisabeth."

"All right. Elisabeth it is."

Dad looked sternly at Reid. "You can still call me Detective O'Dell."

"Daddy! Don't tease Reid."

"Who says I'm teasing?" he said as he held out his hands with the palms up.

"It's okay, Annie. I would feel more comfortable if I don't

call your father by his first name."

Reid told Elisabeth about his family and she told him about her sons and her position at the bank.

"Another round for everyone?" Dad asked.

"I'll buy this round, Mr. O'Dell."

Reid had a little beer left in his glass. Annie looked at her father, then finished Reid's beer. Her father didn't say anything. The waitress brought another round and the appetizers. They ordered their entrees. Annie told Reid more about her friendship with Mace and Keyshon. She also drank some of her father's beer.

"If you want a beer, Annie, could you wait until we get home? You can have one but that's all."

"I just wanted to taste yours, Daddy. I don't want a whole bottle."

"Did you like it?"

"Not really. It's a little too bitter for my taste."

"Are you an expert now, Annie Mercer?" Dad asked.

"No, but I like certain beers better than others."

They finished their dinner and left Larry's around eight. Detective O'Dell dropped Reid and Annie off at the house.

"I'm going to watch a movie at Elisabeth's. I'll be home around midnight, Annie."

"Okay, Daddy. Have a good time. Tell Mace to call me tomorrow, okay."

"Sure. Are you going to stay up?"

"I'm sure we will still be up at midnight. We are used to being up late remember. We're college students and we stay up late every night to party."

"How could I have forgotten? Well, just make sure you hide the beer if the cops come."

"I'm not going to drink anything except pop," Annie said.

Mr. O'Dell returned home shortly before midnight. He checked Annie's room since he saw a light. She was sound asleep and Reid was gone. Her reading light was still on and she held a book in her hands. He took the book and set it on her dresser. He kissed her forehead lightly and whispered, "Sleep tight, my little monkey." He turned out the light as he left.

Chapter Eighteen

Finals were over by December nineteenth. Annie aced hers and was getting ready to spend the holidays at home with her father. Mace was helping Erin pack for the trip home to Nebraska. They wouldn't see each other for nearly a month.

Erin took a look around her side of the room. "I think I've got everything, Mace."

"Are you sure you don't want to take the fridge?"

"Very funny! It's only two suitcases."

"Yeah, and they each weigh a hundred pounds."

Mace was only slightly off in his estimate.

"I will miss you, Annie," Erin said as she held out her arms to hug her.

Annie hugged Erin. "I'll miss you, too. We can email each other and I'll keep an eye on Mace for you."

"I like the sound of that," Mace said.

Erin and Annie punched Mace in his side.

"I didn't mean like that, you sex maniac," Annie said. "You are so gross at times."

Mace carried Erin's bags downstairs where a taxi was waiting to take her to the airport. He kissed Erin goodbye and headed back up to Annie's room. The door was open and Mace walked in and didn't close the door.

"Are you ready to go, Annie?"

"I just need to say goodbye to Reid. He should be here any minute."

"Do I need to leave so you two can get all mushy?"

"No, I want you to stay," Annie said and then grinned. "We like an audience when we do it."

"Very funny, Annie O'Dell. I'll wait downstairs so you can kiss him."

"Don't be silly, Mace. We're just going to say goodbye."

"Who's gonna say goodbye?" Reid asked.

Annie turned to face him. "Hi, Reid. Come on in. I was just telling Mace he didn't have to go downstairs because we were going to say goodbye."

"Should I kiss Mace goodbye?" Reid asked.

"Gross! Don't even joke about that."

Reid moved close to Annie and kissed her.

"I need to get going, Annie. I'll call you as soon as I arrive. We are going to see each other before school starts again."

"I know. I want to see where you live and meet your parents and brothers."

"They are going to love you, Annie, and I think you'll like them."

"I hope so. I am kinda nervous about meeting them."

"Annie, it's not that big a deal. It's not like we're engaged or anything, but I would like them to meet the girl I'm dating."

"I know. I'll see you later. Have a nice Christmas."

Annie kissed Reid again and he left. The drive home to the Lakeview neighborhood of Chicago, where his parents lived, would take over an hour. His three older brothers would all be home for Christmas.

"Ready to go, Annie?" Mace asked.

"Just a second. I seem to be forgetting something." Annie looked around the room. "Oh yeah, I told Daddy I would bring back his CDs. Will you grab them for me? They're on top of the dresser."

Mace grabbed the discs and looked at them. He shook his head as if disapproving of the artists. "Your father needs to realize big bands are out of style."

"He likes to take Elisabeth to this place that plays old-fashioned music so they can dance."

Annie and Mace headed out and she dropped him off at his house a few minutes later. She ran inside to see Keyshon.

"Hey, little buddy! I'm home," Mace shouted.

Keyshon slowly walked into the living room. His eyes lit up when he saw Annie. "Annie! You came to see me. I've missed you."

Annie hugged Keyshon. "I couldn't drop Mace off without coming in to see my favorite little brother."

"I'm not your brother yet, Annie O'Dell. Mom hasn't married your father yet. She should before she gets pregnant."

109

"Whoa there, Keyshon! No one is getting pregnant. It's good to see you, Annie." Mrs. Franklin hugged Annie and kissed her forehead.

"Hey! What about me? Isn't anyone happy to see me?" Mace dropped his suitcase and held out his hands.

"No! We just want to see Annie O'Dell," Keyshon teased his brother.

"Of course I'm happy to see you, Mace. Oh, Annie, before I forget. Your father called and he won't be home until morning. He said you should have dinner here because there's nothing in the house to eat. With you away he doesn't cook as much. I worry about him sometime. He's eating too much fast food and it's not good for him."

"Will you stay for dinner, Annie?" Keyshon asked.

"I'll stay if I can sit next to you," Annie said.

"Okay! Come with me, Annie. I want to show you what I did in my room."

Annie went with Keyshon. He proudly showed her how he had rearranged his room.

"Do you like it, Annie? I did it all by myself."

"I like it, Keyshon. It seems bigger now."

Annie stuck around and ate dinner with everyone. She helped with the cleanup afterward.

"I should get home before it's to late. Thanks for dinner, Mrs. Franklin."

"You're welcome, sweetie. You come over anytime you get hungry."

"Do you want me to go with you, Annie?" Mace asked.

"Why? If you did, then I would just have to bring you back. What would be the point in doing that?"

"I just want to make sure you're all right."

"I'll call you tomorrow, Mace. Maybe we can go to Darby's for lunch or something."

"Annie are you still asleep? I'm home and I've got breakfast. Can I come in?" Dad asked the next morning as he walked down the hallway toward her bedroom.

"I'm not asleep anymore and you can come in, Daddy."

He stepped into her room and saw her clothes scattered about. "Good morning. How's my little angel this morning?"

Annie sat up in bed and her father sat on the edge and kissed her forehead.

"Why are you in such a good mood this morning?"

"Two reasons. First my little girl is home from college."

"Daddy! I'm only twenty minutes away."

"And secondly. We busted that auto theft ring operating on the south side. Cormac Sullivan helped us, but you can't ever let that slip."

"What did you make for breakfast?" she asked while stretching her arms over her head.

"I made some biscuits and sausage gravy. There's hash browns and scrambled eggs. Are you hungry?"

She shook her head and ran her hands through her hair. "Starving, now that I think about it."

"Well, get your butt out of bed and help me eat all this food."

Annie got up and followed her father into the kitchen. She loaded up a plate with a little of everything. She poured ketchup on her eggs and hash browns and then handed the bottle to her father. He exchanged the salt and pepper for the ketchup. They sat at the island and ate. Annie told him about finals and her classes for the coming semester. She mentioned a few details about the basketball team and shared some gossip about some of the girls from her floor. She also told him about going into Chicago to see Reid and meet his family.

"Are things more serious between you two now?" Dad asked as he loaded up his plate with a second helping of everything.

"Not really. He wants me to meet his family for some reason and he's going to show me around the city. We don't see each other everyday. We don't even talk on the phone everyday and we haven't slept together, Daddy."

"I wasn't asking about that," he said as he put two slices of bacon on a piece of wheat bread.

"You know I would tell you if that happened. Even if you don't want to hear it." She got up and filled her plate with the last of the biscuits and gravy.

"Do you need to do any Christmas shopping, Annie?"

"Nope! Not doing any this year."

"Why not? You always buy something for your grandfather and your school friends."

"Just kidding. What do you want for Christmas, Daddy?"

"I want to spent some time with my favorite girl. That's all I want, then I want to spent time with my daughter, too!"

"So I'm not your favorite girl anymore, huh?" she asked with a very serious look while she held up her fork which dripped gravy onto the island.

Dad smiled because Annie knew he was teasing her. He remembered teasing her the very same way when she was younger and how she would tease him right back. In his mind he pictured a girl of ten sitting in the same spot in her Disney princess long pajamas. They were teasing each other about a woman he dated briefly. He looked at her now and still pictured his young daughter.

"Earth to O'Dell! Planet Earth calling Daddy."

"Huh? What were you saying?" he asked as she startled him back to the present.

"You looked like you were a thousand miles away. What were you thinking about?"

"You!" he said as he patted her hand. "I was just remembering you from a few years ago, sweetie."

Annie hugged her father and kissed his cheek. "I love you, Daddy!"

"I love you more than anything in the world, Annie Mercer." He hugged her back. "I could use a new electric razor if you need any ideas for Christmas."

Chapter Nineteen

Annie woke up early on Christmas Day. She lay in bed and thought back to the first Christmas she could remember—when she was four-years-old. She jumped out of bed quickly and opened her closet door. She stood on tiptoes to reach the shelf and pulled down a large cardboard box. Inside were stuffed animals of all sizes, shapes and species. She dug through the box looking for a special animal.

"Here you are," she whispered as she pulled out a tattered brown puppy with yellow floppy ears, a black nose made out of some kind of unidentifiable fluffy material and a red tongue barely hanging on by a few threads. A tail made out of strings and two buttons for eyes completed the woeful looking puppy. All in all it was about the ugliest stuffed animal she had ever seen and the one she valued the most.

"I'm never going to put you back in this old box," Annie whispered as she hugged the little puppy, then placed her on top of the dresser.

She remembered the day she and her mother picked it out at the resale shop. It was late on Christmas Eve and the store was about to close. They were hurrying to finish their shopping and get home to see Daddy. She saw the puppy sitting alone on a shelf with nothing else around it.

"Look, Mommy. I think that puppy is lonely and needs a new home. Do you think we could take it home with us?"

Mom looked at the puppy and immediately realized why no one else had bought it. She looked at the price tag. It had been slashed from one dollar to absolutely free—and still no one had wanted it.

"I think we might be able to give it a good home."

They took the puppy to the cashier and Mom handed the lady a dollar, even though she didn't need to. As they walked outside through the swirling, falling snow, Mom asked, "What do you want to call your new puppy?"

Annie cuddled her puppy and tried to think of a name. "I think I will name her... hmmm... what should I name her, Mommy?

I can't think of anything."

Mom thought for a moment. "Maybe you could call her... Tatters."

"That's a funny name, Mommy, but I like it."

So Tatters, the last Christmas present Amy Catherine Mercer O'Dell ever bought, went home to live with Annie.

Annie dried her wet cheeks with the sleeve of her pajama top and blinked her eyes until the tears were gone. She slipped out into the hallway and peeked in his room to see if her father was still sleeping. He was. She tried to be very quiet as she made breakfast. Dad smelled the coffee and bacon and woke up.

"Merry Christmas, Annie. You're up early," he said as he walked into the kitchen. "That smells good."

Annie placed a paper towel on a plate and set the bacon on the towel. "Couldn't sleep anymore. Did you get a good night's sleep?"

"Yes," he said as he grabbed his favorite coffee cup from the wooden tree on the counter. "It was good to be able to sleep for eight hours."

"What time are we supposed to be at Grandpa's?" Annie asked.

"He wants to eat at noon. I'm supposed to pick up Elisabeth at ten. Will you bring Mace and Keyshon with you?"

"Sure. Do you remember that tomorrow I'm going to Chicago to see Reid and his family?"

"I remember. How long are you staying?" he asked and then took a sip of coffee.

She grabbed a loaf of bread from the breadbox and set it on the counter by the bacon. "Three days and nights. I'll be home Monday morning."

"I don't mind the three days. I guess it's the three nights I'm worried about."

"Oh, Daddy! I'll be okay. Reid is not going to try anything at his parents house."

"Doesn't mean I won't worry about you."

"I know. You will always worry about me."

"And don't you forget it, young lady," he said as he kissed

the top of her head and rubbed her back.

By eleven-thirty everyone arrived at Grandpa's house in the country. Grandpa Liam didn't put up a Christmas tree, but he made a big dinner. As soon as she walked in the door, Annie could smell the ham and sweet potatoes cooking in the oven. They exchanged more gifts before sitting at the dining room table to eat. It was different this year because of Elisabeth's and the boys' presence. Annie thought it felt more like a family than the previous year when it had only been Grandpa, Daddy and herself. Although Annie had been friends with Mace and Keyshon for many years, she still had trouble thinking of Mace as a stepbrother—if that ever happened.

As they were sitting at the table eating it started to snow.

Annie pointed outside. "Look, guys, it's snowing again."

"Annie, do you think we can go sledding on the big hill?" Keyshon asked excitedly.

"Would you like that?"

"Yes, and maybe we can build a snowman too."

Soon the flakes were coming down so fast that Annie could barely see the barn. With three inches already on the ground there would be enough snow for sledding. Behind the barn was a hill and on the other side of the hill was a creek. When the creek froze, you could sled down the hill and all the way across the creek.

"Grandpa, is it all right if we go sledding on the hill?"

"Of course you can, Annie. Just be careful because the creek's not frozen yet."

"Do you need help with the dishes?" Annie asked as she carried some dishes into the kitchen. "I don't mind helping."

"Your father and I will take care of that Annie. You have some fun. Maybe we will come out and watch after we finish cleaning the kitchen," Elisabeth told her.

"There are two sleds in the barn, Annie. Do you need help getting them down from the loft?" Grandpa asked.

"I can get them down, Mr. O'Dell."

"Thanks, Mace. Be careful. Annie gets carried away sometimes. I'd hate for her to land in the creek. The water is close to freezing."

"We will be careful," Mace said.

Annie and Mace bundled up and Annie helped Keyshon. Mace got the sleds from the loft and they walked up the hill.

"Doesn't it look so beautiful now, Mace. I love the way the snow covers everything," Annie said sentimentally.

Yeah, it looks great. I'll race you to the bottom." Mace could care less about how everything looked. He simply used the snow for his enjoyment.

Mace took off on his sled while Annie and Keyshon were a little slower getting started. Mace waited at the bottom to make sure Annie and Keyshon didn't go into the creek. They stopped in plenty of time. Mace carried both sleds up the hill while Annie and Keyshon started throwing snowballs at each other. A half hour later they were still having fun as Grandpa, Keith and Elisabeth watched from the top of the hill. Mace was throwing snowballs at Annie, and Keyshon was throwing snow at Mace. Mace chased Annie around trying to hit her with a snowball. He caught her and tackled her to the ground.

Keyshon came over to check on her. "Are you okay, Annie? Did Mace hurt you?"

"I'm fine, Keyshon. Mace didn't hurt me. We are having fun."

"You should get off of Annie, Mace. You might squash her. Let's go down the hill again."

"Okay, Keyshon." Mace stood up and then helped Annie to her feet. "Lets go down the hill again."

"I want to go by myself," Keyshon said while picking up one of the sleds. "On the sled by myself. Annie can go on your sled, Mace."

"Okay, but be careful, Buddy. Remember the creek isn't frozen."

"I know. I'll stop before the creek. I don't want to get wet."

Annie and Mace shared one sled and Keyshon used the other. They took off down the hill. Keyshon made it to the bottom with no trouble. Annie and Mace however hit a hidden rock and flew off the sled. Mace landed on Annie and knocked the wind out of her.

Keyshon hurried over to check on Annie again. "Are you hurt bad, Annie? Can you talk?"

"I'm all right, Keyshon. Mace just landed on me funny," Annie said between deep breaths.

"We should go back to the house. I want to build a snowman with you, Annie."

"That will be fun, Keyshon. I've had enough sledding."

Mace carried the sleds back up the hill.

"Are you all right, sweetie?" Dad asked.

"I'm fine, Daddy. Mace just knocked the wind out of me. I didn't hurt anything. We're going back to the house. Keyshon wants to build a snowman."

They tromped through the snow as they headed back to the house. Annie and Keyshon stayed outside to build a snowman while everyone else went inside. It didn't take long for Annie and Keyshon to build a large snowman. Annie found a couple sticks for his arms and Keyshon found small rocks for his eyes and mouth. They stood back and admired their creation.

"I think he looks like Mace. What do you think, Keyshon?"

"I think you're right, Annie. He looks like Mace—big and fat!"

"Should we go inside and tell him?"

"Yeah, I'm getting cold."

Annie took Keyshon's hand and they went back in the house as Keith and Elisabeth watched.

"Mace! Annie and I built a snowman and it looks just like you. Big and fat with skinny arms."

"So you think I'm big and fat, huh, little brother?"

Mace grabbed Keyshon and picked him up over his shoulder.

"I'm kidding! You're not fat."

"Okay, I'll let you go."

"Annie thinks you're big and fat and I agree with her," Keyshon teased as he laughed.

117

Chapter Twenty

Before she went to bed Christmas night, Annie started to pack her suitcase. Dad walked down the hall to her room after he heard her slamming the drawers of her dresser and swearing at something or someone.

"Are you all right?" he asked as he stood in the doorway to her room.

"I'm trying to get packed for tomorrow, but I can't find a special top I wanted to bring. I thought it was in one of these drawers, but I can't find it."

She looked at her father, who had a big grin on his face. She threw a t-shirt at him. "Okay, so I should clean up my room more often."

"Tell me what this top looks like and I'll help you look."

"Well, it's..." Annie described the top and a couple minutes later...

"Is this it, sweetie?" Daddy held up a top he found under her bed.

"Yes! That's it. Where did you find it?" she asked as she grabbed it out of his hand.

"It was under the bed. Are you sure you want to take it? Maybe you should wash it first."

"I did wash it earlier this week, but I forgot to put it away."

Dad smiled and she stuck out her tongue at him.

That night she tossed and turned in bed as she struggled to fall asleep. Although she wouldn't admit it to her father, she was nervous about going into Chicago to meet Reid's family. She finally fell asleep around two. The annoying alarm clock woke her up at seven-thirty with its loud buzzing. She had packed most of her suitcase the night before so it didn't take too long to finish. She showered, got dressed and added her toiletries bag to her suitcase.

"I'm ready to go, Daddy. The train leaves at nine so we need to get going."

Dad set down his magazine. "Did you call Reid to make sure he will be there to pick you up?"

"Yes, and he will meet me at the station. I have my new cell phone and I know his address just in case something happens."

"You will call me when you get to his parents' house, right?"

"I promise, Daddy," Annie sighed. "I will be okay. You don't have to worry, but I love the fact you will."

"Come on. I might change the locks while you are gone," he teased.

"Is Elisabeth spending the night tonight?"

"That's none of your business, young lady."

"I saw you change the sheets, Daddy. I know she's coming over and I don't mind. Just be careful. I'm too old to have a baby brother."

Dad smacked Annie's bottom playfully. "I know this isn't right, but you need to do as I say and not as I do."

"I will behave."

Dad took Annie to the station and hugged her and gave her a kiss.

"Call me when you get there, or else I will call Sgt. Thomas to go looking for you."

"I will call," Annie said as she rolled her eyes.

Annie boarded the train and arrived in the city in less than an hour. She looked for Reid and saw him with another man. He hurried to her and kissed her cheek. He took her suitcase and Annie carried her backpack. She called her father as they walked to the car.

"I'm here already and Reid is with me."

"Okay, Annie. Thanks for calling and have a good time. I love you."

"I love you, too, Daddy." She paused, then added, "Daddy, I'm a little scared to meet his family."

"You don't need to worry, sweetheart. They will adore you, and if for some reason they don't... well... then... you can consider them all insane."

"Oh, Daddy. You always know exactly what to say to make me feel better," she said and then wound her hair around a finger, but she didn't feel afraid any more.

119

Reid introduced the man with him. "This is John my oldest brother. This is Annie O'Dell."

"Hello, Annie. How was your ride?"

"It went quick and the driver didn't get lost at all."

Reid looked at John. "Told you she had a sense of humor."

John patted Reid on the back. "I knew she would, little brother. She is dating you after all."

They got to the car and Reid put her suitcase in the trunk. Then he got in the front with his brother. Annie opened the rear passenger door and sat in back.

John looked over his shoulder at Annie. "Reid tells me you are a freshman at North Park. How do you like it so far?"

"I'm having a good time. I'm taking a full load of classes, but I enjoy the challenge."

After that Annie was rather quiet for the rest of the trip to Reid's home. John and Reid talked about school.

They arrived and Reid carried Annie's suitcase up the front sidewalk. "Are you ready to meet the parents?"

"If I say no, will you hate me?"

"No, I won't hate you. I was nervous when you brought me home to meet your father and that turned out all right."

"In that case I'm as ready as I will ever be."

They walked up the front steps and entered the house.

"Mom and Dad! We're home."

His parents were in the living room. His father read his paper while his mother watched TV.

"This is Annie O'Dell, my friend from North Park. Annie, Mom and Dad."

Hello, Annie. It's nice to meet you. Reid has been telling us all about you. Come and sit down. How was the train ride?"

"It was fine."

Reid knew Annie well enough to know she was being shy and quiet.

"Maybe I should take Annie upstairs and show her where she will be sleeping. We'll be back in a few minutes."

Reid took Annie upstairs and his parents waited until she was out of the room.

"Frank, did Reid say how old she is? She looks too young to be in college."

Frank turned a page of his newspaper. "I thought he said she is seventeen. She doesn't even look that old."

"John, did Reid say anything to you about her age?" Mrs. Smagala asked.

"No, Mom. He just said they go to school together."

"Did he mean college or is she in high school?"

Mr. Smagala set his paper down. "She's in college, Nancy. He told us that before. Don't make a big deal about her age. They're just friends. He even introduced her as a friend."

Upstairs, Reid showed Annie where she would be staying.

"This is Tom and Bob's old room. Mom fixed it up after they left. Different bed and dresser. Stuff like that. They will be here tonight for dinner with their wives and my nephews. John and his wife live in Denver. She couldn't get away because of work, so John flew in by himself for a couple of days."

"How old is John?"

"He's thirty-seven, Robert is thirty-four and Thomas is thirty-two. They each have one boy, and they live in Uptown. Robert is a teacher and Thomas is a dentist. He might try to look at your teeth, but don't let him."

"Are you going to show me your room?" Annie asked as she set her backpack on the bed.

"Sure, it's across the hall. Come on in."

Reid showed Annie his room and it was just as neat as his apartment—maybe even neater. Annie sat on the bed and motioned for Reid to sit next to her.

"What's on your mind? Are you still nervous?"

"Kinda," Annie answered. "When you introduced me to your parents, you said I was your friend. Is that all I am to you?"

"I didn't mean to say that. You know you are more than just a friend."

"Your mother looked at me like I was a little kid. I felt almost tongue-tied. They probably think I'm stupid or something."

"Do you believe my parents think so little of me that I would bring home a stupid girl. Give me some credit and don't be

121

afraid to talk to them. They won't bite. My father will just do his normal stuff, but Mom will want to talk to you."

Reid and Annie went back downstairs to the living room. Annie began to feel more at ease as they talked about how she and Reid met. By lunchtime Annie was completely over her shyness. She and Reid went for a walk around the neighborhood.

"This is where Nick lives. He's my friend..."

"I remember. He's Stephanie's brother."

"Would you mind if we stop and see if Nick's home?"

"I don't mind."

They walked up the sidewalk and rang the bell. Nick answered and invited them in.

"Nick, this is Annie. My 'girlfriend.' Annie, my best friend, Nick Whitaker."

"Nice to meet you, Annie."

"Reid, is that you?"

Annie heard a voice from somewhere in the house.

"Steph? Is that you?"

Stephanie walked out to greet Reid. She gave him a hug and a kiss on the mouth.

"I didn't know you were home, Steph. You look good."

"I look as big as a house, Reid."

"This is Annie O'Dell."

"Hi, Annie! That name rings a bell for some reason."

"Not sure why," Annie shrugged. "I know your cousin Diana Ahronson. We went to high school together and now we're both at North Park."

"That's where I heard your name before. Is your father a detective or something?"

"Daddy is a detective in the SoHam robbery division."

Reid and Annie stayed and visited for an hour. Annie didn't meet the parents because they were both at work.

"We should get together this weekend, Reid. Maybe hit the bars," Nick said.

"Yeah, we can do that. Is Avanna home from school yet?" Reid asked.

"She got back two days ago. We were together last night,"

Nick said and then looked at Annie and wondered if she and Reid were lovers.

"I'll call you. Say bye to Steph for me."

On the way back to Reid's house, Annie held his hand.

"You called me your girlfriend when you introduced me to Nick. Thank you."

"He might think we are lovers since I introduced you like that. Does that bother you?"

"No, I will let him think we are lovers. He probably thinks you are in danger of being arrested for statutory rape though. Maybe you shouldn't tell any more people how old I am."

"I didn't know Stephanie was home or else I wouldn't have stopped."

"It's okay. She's very pretty and tall, too. Does she always kiss you on the mouth whenever you see her?"

"Oh, that. Don't pay any attention to that. That's just how Steph is. Doesn't mean anything," Reid said.

"She has really long legs."

"Annie, what are you thinking?"

"I was just thinking about how you and Stephanie are about the same size and I am so much shorter. She is so... well built."

"Annie, are you worried that if we become lovers, not saying we ever will, but if we do, are you worried I will compare you to Stephanie?"

"Maybe that did cross my mind."

"I wish I could answer that, but since I've never been with anyone other than Steph, I don't know the answer."

"Well, I'm not going to think about it anymore. Let's have fun while I'm here. I want you to show me around the city."

"I'll show you some really cool places, Annie. There are some places I can't take you."

"I know," she said as she grinned. "No children allowed."

"Are you ready to face the whole family tonight at dinner? It can be a bit overwhelming when we're all together."

"Yes! I'm ready to face the inquisition."

Chapter Twenty-One

"Do you want me to go over it again?" Reid asked as he and Annie sat on the edge of his bed.

"Please, just one more time."

Reid was showing pictures of his brothers and their families to Annie.

"This is Robert and his wife is...?"

"Sarah and their son is Bobby."

"Right. So this is?"

"Thomas and his wife Denise and Isaac."

"You got it right. You are so smart."

"What was John's wife's name again?" she asked.

"Let's just stick to who will be here and not worry about who isn't." Reid seemed reluctant to talk much about his oldest brother. "Are you ready to go downstairs?"

"As ready as I'm gonna be," Annie said.

"Will you be okay if I introduce you as my friend again? I don't want them to pester you about our relationship and believe me they will."

"I don't mind. Your parents think we are just friends."

Reid took Annie in his arms and kissed her. She returned the kiss. They went downstairs to face the family.

"Took you long enough to get down here, little brother. What were you guys doing so long?" Robert teased Reid.

"Stop that, Robert. I'm sure Reid wasn't doing anything with his young friend. Are you going to introduce us, Reid?" Sarah asked.

"Okay, this is Annie O'Dell. Annie, I want you to meet the rest of the family..."

He introduced everyone to Annie and she remembered their names. His brothers talked to Reid about his young friend while Annie helped the women get dinner on the table.

"Where did you meet Annie? How old is she, anyway?" Robert asked.

"She's seventeen and I met her at the dining hall at school. A friend of hers is in one of my classes and she set us up."

"Like a blind date?" John asked.

"Yeah, we ate dinner with a group of people and she was so shy, but she kept stealing glances at me. We talked, then we started going out."

"Do Mom and Dad know you are lovers?" Thomas asked.

"We aren't lovers," Reid insisted.

"That's it. Plead innocent," Thomas said. "I heard you took Annie over to the Whitakers and Steph was there. How did that go?"

"It went well. Stephanie kissed me on the mouth though."

"She kisses everybody like that," Robert said. "Did you tell Amy that?"

"Annie! Her name is Annie. Not Amy and yes, I told her that was Steph's way with everyone."

In the dining room Annie was talking to Sarah about college.

"Do you have any idea what your major will be?" Sarah asked.

"I haven't decided for sure but I think I might choose Education. I think I would like to teach handicapped kids—young ones. My friend has a younger brother with Down Syndrome and he's the sweetest kid. I would love to work with kids like Keyshon."

"Robert teaches Biology and I teach second grade. I thought about teaching handicapped kids, but I just don't have the patience. It's difficult enough working with normal second graders. If you have the desire and skills required to teach kids with Down Syndrome, I have the utmost respect for you."

Finally, dinner was ready and the family gathered in the large dining room to eat. Annie sat quietly with Reid and listened to everyone. It seemed as if there were a hundred conversations going on at the same time. Somehow everyone managed to be understood. Having dinner with such a large family was totally foreign to Annie. Reid squeezed her hand at times to reassure her this was normal for his family. After everyone was stuffed and the table cleared, Annie offered to help in the kitchen.

"That's very kind of you, Annie dear, but you go be with

125

Reid and his brothers. The three of us can handle this. We're used to it."

Annie put a finger to her mouth. "If you're sure you don't need any help..."

"Go have some fun," Mrs. Smagala said as she waved a hand. "And don't let his brothers tease you too much. They have never seen Reid with any girlfriend other than Steph."

"We're just friends..."

"You can fool my husband, but I see the way Reid looks at you. Don't worry, sweetheart, I won't tell him."

Annie smiled and went out to the living room with the guys. They were in a heated discussion about sports. Yet somehow they managed to keep an eye on the little guys who were playing with each other.

"The White Sox are going to win the World Series before the Cubs even win a pennant!" Robert exclaimed.

Thomas shook his head. "You are out of your freakin' mind."

Annie sat next to Reid and listened. The guys kept discussing baseball.

"Annie, are you a sports fan at all?" John asked.

"I don't follow baseball much, but I like basketball. My friend Mace Franklin plays for North Park."

"Yeah, he's a freshman and he starts. I've seen him play and he's really good," Reid added.

"I heard North Park is pretty good this year. They might even win their conference and get into the tournament," Robert said.

"Stranger things have happened," Reid replied.

"Yeah, like the Cubs getting to a World Series. That would be like the strangest thing ever in the history of the world," Thomas said emphatically.

The brothers were back to baseball. Even Mr. Smagala got in on the discussion.

"Issac!" Thomas hollered. "You have to share with Bobby. Let him have the ball for a while. You have to take turns."

Thomas disciplined his son, then went right back to the

126

discussion without missing a beat. Annie enjoyed listening to the four brothers argue. The sibling rivalry and the brotherly love between them was obvious, even as they yelled at each other.

Reid looked at Annie and smiled. "Ah, the joys of a large family."

"I like it, Reid."

Isaac started to fight as Bobby took his toy away. Robert and Thomas stepped in and handled the situation.

"How about it, Isaac and Bobby? Would you like to go with Grandpa and get some ice cream?" Mr. Smagala asked.

Both kids were happy again as Grandpa took them out to the kitchen.

"So, Annie, tell us about your family. Do you have any brothers or sisters?" Robert asked.

"No, I'm an only child. My Mom passed away when I was five and Daddy has raised me by himself. I have a grandfather who has helped. He is actually the principal of the high school where I went."

"I'm sorry about your mother, Annie. That must have been difficult," Thomas said.

"It was, but I was still little so I didn't understand everything."

Around nine o'clock Robert and Thomas took their families home. It took twenty minutes for the goodbyes and hugs.

When they were out the door, Mr. Smagala sat in his recliner. "I am beat. When you guys get together, it wears me out listening to you. As soon as I regain my strength, I'm going to bed. Nancy, are you ready for bed?"

"I will be up after the news, Frank. You know that."

"Mom always watches the news before going upstairs. Dad knows it, but he always asks anyway," Reid explained.

Frank stood up. "You guys can stay up as late as you want. You won't bother me."

Reid laughed and then smiled at Annie. "What Dad means is he snores so loud he wouldn't hear a train if it came through the living room."

"Good night everyone," Frank said and then pointed at his

youngest son. "You might snore, too, Reid. Ever think of that?"

"Night, Dad. See you in the morning."

The news ended and Mom Smagala told them, "I don't know why I bother watching the news every night. All it does is rile me up. Can you believe how many stupid people there are in the world? Oh, well. I'm going to bed. See you kids in the morning." She turned to leave, but then added, "Annie, I put clean sheets on the bed and Reid can show you where everything is—blankets, towels, whatever. I'll see you in the morning, dear."

"Good night, Mrs. Smagala."

At midnight John told Reid and Annie good night and headed upstairs.

"Are you ready for bed, Annie?"

She nodded. "Yes. I am kinda tired."

"Let me check the doors and we can go up."

Reid made sure the doors were locked and he and Annie headed upstairs.

"The bathroom is right here, Annie. I know I showed you earlier. Mom keeps that little light on for Dad so he can see. He has trouble at night sometimes. If you need any more blankets they are in the closet here. You can close the door or keep it open whichever you are used to. If you need more..."

"Reid," she whispered loudly with her hands on her hips.

"Yeah, Annie."

"I'm not a baby. I'm not afraid of the dark and if I get cold during the night I will come and cuddle with you."

Reid looked at Annie with surprise, then he grinned and said, "I get it now. You're kidding. Good night, Annie. See you in the morning. It's Saturday so Mom and Dad will be home. They usually get up early and make breakfast. You can sleep as late as you want though."

"Reid!"

"Yeah."

"Just shut up and kiss me good night before I fall asleep."

Reid kissed Annie good night and she went to bed—with the door closed.

Chapter Twenty-Two

Frank and Nancy Smagala got out of bed at six o'clock and got ready to face the day. Frank went out to get a newspaper and donuts. Nancy made coffee and turned on the TV to watch the morning news. Frank drank his coffee, read his newspaper and ate his donuts. The house was quiet except for the TV. Reid woke up at seven and went downstairs. John got up a minute later.

"There is coffee and some donuts in the kitchen. If you want anything else, let me know."

"Thanks, Mom."

Reid and John went into the kitchen and returned with coffee and donuts.

"Is your little friend still asleep?" Dad asked.

Reid shrugged. "I guess so. I didn't look in her room."

"She's really cute, son. I know she is rather young, but have you ever asked her for a date?" Dad asked. "You have to quit thinking about Stephanie."

Mom looked at Frank, then at Reid and whispered, "He can be so dense sometimes."

"Why am I dense? She is cute and Reid should find a new girlfriend. Stephanie is married with a baby on the way. He's not getting any younger. You and I were already married at his age."

"Yes, Dad. I will find a new girlfriend sometime."

Reid winked at his mother.

Annie woke up and looked at the clock. "Oh crap! It's nine o'clock. I didn't mean to sleep so late." She jumped out of bed and put on a long sweatshirt over the tank top and shorts she slept in. "Double crap! Reid's parents will think I sleep all day." She ran her hands through her hair and raced downstairs. She saw everyone in the living room. "I'm sorry I stayed in bed so long. I guess I was more tired than I realized."

Mom Smagala smiled at her. "That's all right, dear. We have four boys and when they were teenagers they would sleep until noon if we let them."

Annie noticed Mr. Smagala and John were looking at her legs. She realized they couldn't tell she wore shorts under the sweatshirt. "I should go put some pants on." Annie realized this gave them the impression she wasn't wearing anything under her sweatshirt. She hurried upstairs and Reid followed.

"Are you okay, Annie?" he asked at the top of the stairs.

She turned to face him. "Just embarrassed. I think your father thinks I wasn't wearing anything under my sweatshirt. I've got shorts on, see."

Reid looked at her shorts. "I see that. Dad is just not used to having a pretty young teenage girl in the house. That's all."

"Thank you, Reid." Annie slipped into her bedroom.

Reid walked downstairs and explained, "Annie got embarrassed because she thinks you... she had shorts on under her sweatshirt, but you couldn't see them."

"She shouldn't be embarrassed. She has nice legs," Dad said without looking up from his newspaper.

"Frank! Why were you looking at her legs? She is only seventeen."

Frank set down his paper, tilted his head and said, "I was looking because I thought I would mention it to Reid. Maybe he and Annie could go on a date when she is older if he doesn't find a new girlfriend before then. That's all."

Mom shrugged her shoulders and rolled her eyes.

Annie showered, dressed, came back downstairs and sat by Reid in the living room.

"Are you hungry, Annie? We've got a couple donuts left. Do you drink coffee?" Reid asked.

"Sometimes, but I don't need any this morning. I will eat a donut though."

"Come on back to the kitchen with me. We can have a little privacy there. If you want anything else to eat let me know. We could even go out. There's a little place down the street."

"The donuts will be enough for me. Thanks, Reid."

"What do you want to do today? I talked to Nick earlier and he wants to go out tonight. I told him I would ask you. You could meet Avanna. She's really fun to hang out with."

"That sounds like fun. Could we go to a museum or somewhere like that this afternoon?"

"Whatever you want to do is okay with me, Annie."

Reid took Annie to a local deli for lunch, then to the Macy Museum. Annie hadn't been there since a fifth grade field trip. They spent three hours exploring the various exhibits, then walked over to the Sherman Aquarium. After an hour there, they headed back. Annie was hungry so they stopped and grabbed two pretzels and pop to share. When they got back to the house, it was empty.

"Mom and Dad are at mass. They usually go on Saturday night. They might have forced John to go with," Reid said.

Annie took off her coat and hung it on a hook by the back door. "Last night I got the impression you didn't want to talk about John. Is there anything wrong? Do you and John not get along?"

Reid shook his head. "It's not that, Annie. We get along all right. I never knew him that well as a kid though. He was married by the time I was three. He's like an uncle in some ways."

Annie listened patiently as Reid talked about John.

"Mom and Dad don't know it yet, but John and Kathleen have separated. It doesn't look good for their marriage."

"That's too bad. Do they have any kids? Did you already tell me?"

"They've got three kids. Jeff is, let me think, he's eighteen already. He's older than you, Annie. I've got a nephew older than my girlfriend."

Annie did not look amused.

"Mary Margaret must be fifteen and Michael twelve or thirteen. John and Kathleen got married as soon as they graduated. She was pregnant as you might have guessed."

"That's a real shame. It must be hard on the kids."

"Jeff is away at college so it's easier on him, but Mary Margaret is very upset with her father right now. John told me she won't even talk to him."

"I hope they can work out their problems. I imagine it's better for kids to have both parents living together."

"I'm sorry, Annie. I forgot about your mother," Reid said and then hugged Annie for a moment. "Mom doesn't normally cook on Saturday night. We can grab something here or go out. Do you still want to meet up with Nick and Avanna later?"

"Yeah, that should be fun."

"We might have a problem getting you into the club," Reid said as he rubbed his jaw.

Annie grinned at him. "I think I have a way around that."

"What? How?" Reid asked.

Annie reached into her pocket, pulled out her ID and handed it to Reid.

He examined it carefully. "Is this real? It looks totally real."

"It is real."

"How did you get this? No, wait, I don't want to know," he said waving a hand. "Does your father know about this?"

"Daddy knows. He knows I won't use it to just go out drinking, but it has come in useful a number of times."

Reid smiled. "This is a new side of you, Annie. I never would have suspected it."

"What should I wear tonight? I brought a dress just in case I needed one."

"Wear the dress. You look so pretty in a dress."

Annie glared at him.

"I mean you look even prettier. You always look pretty no matter what you're wearing."

She laughed. "Reid, you should know by now I don't care about that. I don't worry about whether I look pretty or not. I am who I am. Take it or leave it."

After a light dinner at a nearby restaurant, Reid and Annie walked over to the Whitaker house to meet Nick and Avanna. Stephanie was still home and she opened the door. Once again she greeted Reid by kissing him on the mouth. This time it didn't bother Annie.

"Come on in. Nicky should be ready soon. He's upstairs with Avanna. Have a seat. Do you want anything to drink?"

"No thanks, Steph. We're fine. How are you doing?"

She sighed. "I can't wait to have my baby. He's kicking all the time now."

"So you know you're having a boy. Do you have a name picked out?" Reid asked.

"Not yet. We have it narrowed down to three though."

Nick dashed into the room followed by his girlfriend. "Hi, guys! Are you ready to have some fun?"

"Hi, Avanna," Reid said and then turned to face Annie, who was standing behind him. He put an arm around her shoulders and nudged her forward. "This is Annie. Annie, may I present Miss Avanna Bellamy."

"Hi, Annie. Nicky told me you and Reid go to North Park."

"Yes, this is my first year there."

"I'm in my last year at Tennessee. I can't wait until I'm finished," she said and then moved closer to Nick. "Where are we going tonight, Nicky? I want to dance until the sun comes up!"

"I thought we could go to Club Zephyr. You like that place and it's relatively close," Nick suggested.

"What time does it open?" Reid asked.

"It doesn't open until nine so we've got time to have a few drinks, get something to eat. Whatever you want, Reid."

"We can do that, but Annie and I don't drink that much," Reid said.

"Since when? I understand about Annie since she is underage, but when did you stop drinking?" Avanna asked.

"I didn't say I stopped totally. Just that I don't drink as much as I used to. I don't see the point of getting wasted."

"Good for you, Reid. I'm happy for you," Avanna said and then kissed his cheek.

Nick smiled and added, "Annie, you must be a good influence on my old friend."

"Actually, I stopped even before I met Annie, but you're right, Nick. She is a good influence."

"Are you guys finished with your bonding or whatever you call it?" Avanna asked. "I'm hungry. I'm going to have fun tonight and I will have a few drinks. You guys can drink or not. It doesn't matter to me."

"Should we call a cab or you wanna walk?" Nick asked.

"Let's walk. It's not too cold out. We can catch the bus and grab some food down at Chex and Balances."

Fifteen minutes later they were at the bar. They ordered some appetizers and drinks. Annie's ID was not even questioned.

Annie needed to use the restroom so she excused herself.

"So, Reid, how old is Annie really?" Avanna asked as soon as Annie left the table.

Reid turned his head to look in the direction Annie had gone. "Seventeen, but she'll be eighteen at the end of May."

"Reid, you're really robbing the cradle. I hope you are careful. She is jailbait, you know."

"Annie may only be seventeen, Avanna, but she is very mature in more ways than you might think."

Avanna grinned. "Are you talking sexually, Reid?"

"That's none of your business, Avanna."

"Hey, you guys! Knock it off. If Reid wants to date a younger girl, that's his business." Nick intervened.

"There must be some older girls at that college. Why one so young?" Avanna asked.

"We met on a blind date and I'm starting to really like her."

"She's a lot different than Steph as far as her body goes. Is she better in bed than Steph?" Avanna asked. "Don't give me that 'none of my business' crap either. I want an answer."

"You may not believe it, but we haven't reached that point in our relationship yet," Reid admitted.

"Hi, Annie! We were wondering if you had gotten lost." Nick stood up as she returned.

"It was just busy in there. You know how it is with the ladies room. Oh, maybe you don't."

"I know what you're talking about, Annie."

They hung around Chex and Balances until nine, then walked up the street to Club Zephyr. They were allowed to go in right away. They were seated at a table with some privacy and treated as if they were VIPs.

"Avanna's father is kind of a celebrity," Reid explained.

"I know who Mitchell Bellamy is. I've seen most of his movies. You guys didn't say anything before, why?" Annie asked.

"Avanna doesn't like everyone to know who her father is. She doesn't like to draw attention to herself. We've been here before so they make sure we are left alone."

Everyone ordered something to drink. Annie ordered

bottled water for now. She drank one beer at the bar and didn't want to have another one until later. She had set a limit of three for the whole night. By ten o'clock the club was packed with people of all types—from local residents of the area to people with tons of money to blow. Annie even spotted a few celebrities she recognized from TV and movies. The DJ kept the music pumping and the dance floor was filled with people swirling and grooving to the pulsating beat of the club music. Annie danced with Reid, then they switched. Reid and Avanna danced and Nick danced with Annie. Nick and Annie went back to the table to talk while Reid and Avanna kept dancing.

"You are a good dancer, Annie."

"I don't have a clue what to do. I just move around to the beat."

"I was watching you with Reid. You dance well together. Like that *Dirty Dancing* movie."

"Oh, you watched that, huh?"

"Yeah, sorry if that embarrasses you."

"No, I should have worn tights or something though."

"What do you think of Avanna?" Nick asked. "Don't be afraid to speak your mind."

Annie stared at Reid and Avanna as they danced. "She seems a little spoiled, I suppose. She's very pretty and I get the feeling she is used to getting whatever she wants."

"Very astute observation. Reid told me you were very smart. He was right about that, but he underestimated your looks."

"I know I'm not gorgeous or anything."

"Maybe not like a movie star glamorous, but you are very attractive. You have such expressive eyes and you're just so natural. I bet you look just perfect as soon as you wake up in the morning. You have a sexiness about you that can't be faked or done with makeup."

"Thank you, Nick. I think."

"I meant it as a compliment, Annie, and I'm not trying to make a move on you. I wouldn't do that to you, or Reid. He's my best friend."

"Even after he and Stephanie split up?" Annie asked and

135

then took a drink of her water.

"He and Steph were too young when they started having sex, but what could I do?" He shrugged. "I love my sister and I love Reid, too. They split up and it was probably the right move. Steph found the right guy for her and maybe Reid has as well."

"I'm too young to think about a long term relationship."

"Too young to think about sex?" Nick asked.

"Not too young to think about it, but maybe too young to do it. Too much info?"

"No, do you wanna dance some more?"

"In a minute. I want to ask you about Avanna. Have you known her long?"

"All my life. Avanna's parents split when she was two and she has lived with her mother all these years. They live next door to me."

"So you and Avanna have grown up together, huh?"

"Reid, too. He has known her just as long. They were never involved if you're wondering about that. We have done a lot of things together, the three of us. Drinking our parents' beer when we were twelve, trying cigarettes. Most of the things kids try to be cool. We even went skinny dipping a few times."

"Really?" Annie's eyes sparkled.

"Yeah, we used to go to my parents place in Wisconsin. They have a cabin on a small lake and we used to go swimming all the time. When we were in junior high school we started skinny dipping."

"I've learned something new about Reid."

"I hope that doesn't bother you, Annie. I mean there was really nothing between Avanna and Reid sexually. Well, I guess that's not totally true. I did catch them making out one time, but that was a long time ago. Now he treats her more like a sister."

"What about you and Avanna?"

"We have a different kind of relationship. We sleep together. We have for a few years, but we go out with other people. Avanna is very careful about dating though. She doesn't get involved with other guys."

"She has you for that."

"Yeah, I'm her safety valve. Come on! Let's dance."

Nick and Annie wound their way through some people as they headed back to the dance floor. Reid and Avanna passed them on their way back to the table.

"Avanna wants to take a break, Annie," Reid said. "Do you want me to dance with you? I will if you let me have a break first."

"Why don't you take a break first while I dance with Nicky? I don't want to wear you out."

Annie smiled at Reid as Nick took her hand and led her onto the dance floor. The DJ slowed down the tempo and Nick and Annie danced close. They faced each other as Nick pulled her close to his body. They slow danced for a couple of minutes, then Nick took her hand.

"Will you come with me, Annie? I want to show you something."

"Okay, where are we going?"

"I'll show you. You'll be amazed."

Annie followed Nick as he led the way through a door guarded by a bouncer, who let them pass. Nick led Annie up some stairs behind the DJ's stage. They opened another door and entered a small dark room. Annie could see the lights of the club and feel the throb of the sound system but it was very quiet in the room. Nick was still holding her hand and they walked to the window.

"This is a two way mirror, Annie. We can see out, but if anyone looks up here all they see is the mirror and the lights of the club."

"I saw the mirror when I was dancing with Reid. Do you bring Avanna up here?"

"Sometimes, if we want to just dance by ourselves, we come up here. As you can tell it is quiet enough to have a conversation without having to scream to be heard. Do you want to dance some more?"

"You are a very good dancer, Nicky."

"Thank you, Annie. I've taken lessons. Avanna and I like to go ballroom dancing when we can. She wants to teach dancing after she graduates." He placed his hands on her waist.

Annie put her hands on Nick's chest and looked up at him.

137

"Do you and Avanna ever think about marriage, or is that none of my business?"

"We have discussed it, but she doesn't see herself as a wife. At least not in the foreseeable future." Nick answered as he pulled Annie closer and they moved their hips in time with the thumping, but muffled, bass of the music.

"Have you had a lot of different lovers, Nicky?"

"Whoa!" Nick froze. "Where did that come from?"

"Sometimes I just say what I'm thinking without filtering it."

"I don't know what you mean by a lot, but I'll tell you and you can tell me if that's a lot. I've been with five different girls. Does that make me a bad boy or something?"

"How funny you use that term. There is this guy at school that has a reputation as a 'bad boy' and I've been kind of a friend of his for years."

"A friend?" Nick asked as they began dancing again.

"Just a friend. I mean we aren't lovers," she said and then thought about the day in her dorm room. "I talked to Daddy about him and told him how this boy gets me... excited."

Nick stopped dancing and asked, "You told your father?"

"I talk to Daddy about everything. Daddy told me sometimes girls are attracted to bad boys even when they know it's wrong."

"And you're attracted to bad boys. Is that what you are telling me?"

They started dancing again.

"Not all of them, just this one. I told Reid about him. I told Reid I wasn't going to see him anymore."

Nick put his hands on Annie's shoulders as he looked into her eyes. "Would you be upset if I kiss you, Annie?"

"Are you trying to seduce me, Nicky?" she asked as she put a finger to her mouth.

"No, I'm sorry. I shouldn't have asked that. I guess it was the beer clouding my judgment. That and the fact that we are dancing like this."

Annie backed away. "I'm sorry if I gave you the wrong

impression, Nicky. I like dancing with you, but I don't want to kiss you."

"I'm sorry, Annie. I apologize. Do you want to go back and find Reid and Avanna?"

"Maybe we should. He will wonder what has happened to me. Nicky?" She looked up at him.

"Yes, Annie. What is it?"

"Thank you for being a gentleman. I suppose you could have kissed me without asking."

"Annie, you are so sweet—sexy, too. But you are such a sweet girl. I would feel like an ass if I took advantage of you. Let's go find Reid. If you want to come back up here with him, just let me know. That bouncer is my distant cousin and his grandfather and one of his uncles own this place. Deaglan and Cormac Sullivan..."

"Did you say Cormac Sullivan?" Annie asked as she grabbed Nick's hand.

"Yeah, why?"

"Do you know a guy named Matthew Sullivan?"

"Sure, he's a distant relative. Twenty times removed, or whatever, I think. I've met Matt. Oh, I forgot you are from SoHam. Do you know the Sullivan family?"

"Yes. I went to school with Matty."

Nick looked at Annie and it dawned on him. "Does Reid know it was Matty?"

"I just told him a little bit about what happened, but I never mentioned Matthew's name."

"I won't either. Let's go find those guys."

Annie and Nick rejoined Reid and Avanna.

"I took Annie up to the room. I just wanted her to see the view from there."

"What did you think about it, Annie? Pretty sweet, huh?" Reid asked.

"It was so easy to talk in that room."

They hung around for another hour, then called it a night. They grabbed a taxi back to Nick's house. They went next door to Avanna's place since her mother was at work. They each drank

139

another beer and sat in the living room and talked. Annie thought about the three friends swimming together. She didn't feel jealous since it was obvious Reid and Avanna were just friends. It was two o'clock before Annie and Reid left. They walked back to Reid's house since it was close and the neighborhood was safe.

"I had a good time tonight, Reid. I like your friends. Nicky was really nice to me and Avanna is really special."

"Did I tell you how long I've known Avanna?"

"Nicky told me you guys have all been friends since you were little kids. You've grown up together and done everything together."

"Not quite everything, Annie." Reid grinned.

"I didn't mean that, Reid. Nicky told me there was never anything sexual between you and Avanna."

"I've kissed Avanna and we've made out a few times but nothing more than that. Did he tell you anything else?"

"You mean the skinny dipping?"

Reid looked at Annie wondering if she was upset, but she was smiling.

"Doesn't bother me in the least. Would it bother you if I went swimming with other guys?"

"Swimming or skinny dipping?"

"I guess skinny dipping. I've been swimming with friends of course. Would it upset you if I went skinny dipping with you and Nicky and Avanna, too?"

"Would you really do that?"

"Who knows? Maybe someday when we are farther along in our relationship."

Reid held her hand as they walked. They slipped in the front door and quietly make their way upstairs. Annie could hear Reid's father snoring and grinned.

"Good night, Annie. I'll see you in the morning."

"Night, Reid. Thanks again for tonight. It was fun."

Reid kissed Annie quickly and they slipped into their rooms.

Chapter Twenty-Three

Annie heard a knock on the door, then footsteps. She opened her eyes to see Reid standing next to the bed.

"Hi, sleepyhead. Mom made me come in and check on you. She was worried."

"Why? What time is it?" Annie asked and then turned onto her back.

"Eleven thirty," Reid said and then grinned.

"Crap!" Annie pulled the cover over her head. "I'm sorry. You parents must think all I do is sleep."

"I told them what time we got in last night. They understand. Did you sleep all right?"

Annie popped her head out from under the cover. "Yeah, but I seem to remember dreaming about swimming with a bunch of guys."

"Really? How strange. Do you remember anything else about the dream?" Reid grinned.

"I remember you were there and you weren't wearing any swim trunks."

"Maybe we should talk more about this dream later. Are you hungry? Mom wants to know if you want anything now because we won't be eating until around one thirty. My brothers and families will be coming over. A family tradition kinda thing."

"I'm not starving. Are there any donuts or bagels or anything?"

"My father always has donuts in the house on the weekends. There might be a couple left if you hurry downstairs."

"Should I get dressed, or can I just put on my sweatshirt like yesterday?"

"You can just slip on your sweatshirt. Mom and Dad won't mind. John will like seeing your legs again. He's separated remember."

"That's gross! He's got a daughter almost as old as me."

Annie got out of bed and slipped her sweatshirt on over her head as Reid watched. They went downstairs and Annie smiled sleepily at Reid's parents.

"Reid told us how late you were out. Did you get enough sleep, Annie?" Mom Smagala asked.

"Yes, thank you for understanding. Daddy would have dragged me out of bed at eight o'clock. He would have told me if I went to bed at a decent time I wouldn't sleep so late."

"Sounds like your father is pretty strict with you."

"He is! I'm not complaining. I love my father and I try to behave. We were just having so much fun last night."

Annie sat in the kitchen with Reid's parents as Reid ran upstairs.

"We need to run to the store for a few things. Is there anything special you would like for dinner, Annie? I usually make a roast on Sunday."

"That sounds delicious. I don't need anything special. Whatever you are having is okay with me."

Reid's parents left and Annie was sitting alone as John walked in the kitchen. He had been outside talking on his phone. He sat down and sighed.

"I don't mean to pry, but Reid told me about your situation. Are you all right?"

"Yeah, I'm fine. I finally got Mary Margaret to talk to me, at least. She wouldn't even talk to me until today."

"Reid told me you have a son older than me."

"Jeff is eighteen. I guess I didn't even think about him being older than you. He sure doesn't act as mature as you. Did you have fun last night?"

"It was exciting. We stopped at a bar, then went to Club Zephyr."

John wondered how Annie managed to get into the club but didn't ask. He couldn't help but look at Annie's legs.

She stood up so John didn't see too much. "I should go shower and get ready for this afternoon."

"Talk to you later, Annie," John said as he looked out the back door window.

By one thirty the whole family had arrived and dinner was just about ready. Annie felt more comfortable with the family today. She played with the grandkids. The two boys thought of

142

Annie as just a kid herself. Reid had to come to Annie's rescue because the boys were trying to tickle her.

"Hey, what are you guys doing to my Annie?"

"We're tickling her, Uncle Reid. We were chasing her and we caught her so now we get to tickle her."

"Be careful with her. She's just a girl and not as tough as you boys."

"We won't hurt her."

Annie played with the boys until dinner was ready. Nancy hollered to let everyone know it was time to eat. Reid went into the living room to see if Annie needed to be rescued. She was on her back on the couch with Isaac straddling her trying to tickle her some more. Bobby was trying to tie her shoelaces together.

"Do you need any help, Annie?"

"Yes, I surrendered, but these boys keep telling me they don't take any prisoners. I think they want to scalp me or something."

"All right, guys! Leave Annie alone now. I want to play with her. It's time to eat anyway."

The boys stopped torturing Annie and Reid sat on the couch with her. She sat up and Reid kissed her as the boys watched wide-eyed. The boys ran into the dining room and announced to everyone, "Uncle Reid kissed that girl on the couch!"

"That's all right, Isaac. He can kiss her if he wants," Thomas said.

"Where is Aunt Stephanie?" Isaac asked. "Uncle Reid should be kissing her. We want to play with Annie."

"Was Reid really kissing Annie?" Grandpa Frank asked the boys.

"Yeah, he was, Grandpa, and she kissed him, too."

Grandpa Frank looked at Grandma Nancy. "I told you he should take that girl on a date. If she let him kiss her, maybe she will go on another date with him. Maybe they can be more than friends when she gets older."

Grandma Nancy sighed. "You're right as usual, Frank."

Annie and Reid walked into the dining room and Frank smiled at Annie, then at Reid. Annie blushed a little as she sat across from Reid and between Isaac and Bobby. After dinner the boys asked Annie to play.

"What do you want to play? Are you going to tickle me again?" Annie asked.

Isaac grabbed her hand and pulled. "We won't tickle you. We want to build a fort."

Bobby grabbed her other hand. "We'll show you how to build a fort."

Annie looked over her shoulder at Reid and smiled. "Maybe I can play with you later."

"Come on, Annie. This will be fun."

When Reid came downstairs later, he saw a fort by the couch. "Is anyone here?"

Isaac stuck his head out and said, "We're playing with Annie. She's our prisoner."

"Help! Help!" Annie whispered. "I'm being held hostage by the bad guys."

"Be quiet, prisoner, or I will have to tie you up," Bobby said.

Reid laughed, got his knees and peered into the fort. "Can I play with Annie now? I want a turn, too. You boys need to learn how to share."

"All right! You can play with her for a while, Uncle Reid. Are you gonna kiss her again?" Isaac asked.

"Do you mind if I kiss Annie a few times?"

"Go ahead if you want. We won't tell Aunt Stephanie if you give us each a dollar," Bobby said as he grinned.

"Get out of here. I'm gonna kiss Annie and I don't care who you tell. So there."

Chapter Twenty-Four

"Are your brothers leaving?" Annie asked later that afternoon.

"Yeah," Reid answered. "Robert and Thomas are going home, but John is meeting up with some old friends from high school. It's just us and my parents here."

Annie and Reid sat on the living room couch to watch TV. Reid's father took a nap in his chair while his mother talked on the phone with her sister. Reid kissed Annie, but she was afraid to kiss him back with his parents nearby. Nick and Avanna stopped by to see Reid and Annie around four.

"Hi, guys! Are you doing anything tonight or this afternoon?" Avanna asked.

"We don't have any plans yet," Reid said and then looked at Annie. "What do you have in mind?"

"We want to go out again. Somewhere we can have some privacy. My mother is home and getting on my case. We want you guys to go with us so we can say we weren't alone and not have to lie."

"Why is your mother getting on your case all of a sudden?" Reid asked.

"She's upset because she is worried about the media attention we might attract."

"I don't get it. The media has never bothered you before. Why would they start now?"

"I don't know for sure, but Mom is worried about something. Can we just go somewhere? The four of us."

"Sure, Avanna. Let me tell Mom we're leaving."

Nick pulled some keys out of his pocket. "I've got my car today, Reid. We can leave the city if we want."

Reid waited until Mom ended her call and said, "We're going to go with Nick and Avanna. Nicky's got his car so we're going to take off, maybe head out of the city. I've got my keys and my cell phone. Call me if you need, but don't wait up for us."

"Okay, Reid. Have a good time. I'll see you in the morning if not tonight."

The four of them piled into Nick's car and headed east. They picked up Lake Shore Drive and headed south. Annie stared at the lake and the buildings. Nick drove and Reid sat in the front with him. Avanna found it amusing to see Annie gawking at the scenery like a tourist from the sticks.

"How do you like it at North Park? Did you ever think of going away to college?"

"I never really thought about going anywhere else. I wanted to be close to Daddy and my Grandpa. They're the only family I have."

"It sounds like you and your father have a really good relationship. I fight with my mom more and more these days. I just had to get away today."

"Do you ever see your father?"

"Once in a while. He keeps in touch by email and an occasional call. Hey, Nicky, can we take 55 and get out of the city? Let's go to Grandma's house."

"Is she home?" Nick asked. "I thought she was in Florida."

"She is, but I have a key and the security code. Gram won't mind if we hang out there."

Nick drove to South Hinsdale where Avanna's grandmother lived when she was not in Florida.

"Grandma has this big old house and she lives there by herself. She spends most of the winter in Florida and has a caretaker who comes by twice a week to clean the place and make sure everything is okay. There's an indoor pool and a hot tub, or Jacuzzi thing. Grandma knows I stop by once in a while so she keeps the pool going year round. We can go swimming and have some fun."

"I don't have a suit with me," Annie said.

"Do you have colored underwear on by any chance?" Avanna asked.

Annie was slightly embarrassed but answered, "Yes, I do."

"Then if we can't find something that fits you better, you could swim in just your undies."

"I won't go skinny dipping!" Annie insisted.

"You won't have to, Annie. If nothing else you can wear a

146

pair of my shorts. I keep some clothes in my bedroom. I call it my room because it's where I have always slept when I stayed with Grandma."

It didn't take long to get to Grandma's house. Nick pulled into the driveway and up to the security gate. Avanna told him the code. They drove alongside the house to the parking area behind the house.

"This place is ginormous," Annie said while staring.

"That wing over there is the pool," Avanna explained.

Annie got out of the car and spun around. "I love this place. Look at all the trees. That's got to be the biggest garage I've ever seen."

Reid grabbed her hand. "Come on, Annie. Let's go inside."

They entered through the back door with Avanna's key and she punched in the code to shut down the alarm. Avanna showed Annie around the place while the guys checked out the pool. They caught up with the girls as they were coming back downstairs.

"The water is nice and warm and the Jacuzzi is heating up," Nick said.

"Excellent! Let's go swimming. Come with me, Annie, and I'll see if I can find something for you to wear."

"Reid and I will be in the pool. Don't take all day."

"We will be there when we are ready," Avanna said.

Avanna took Annie to her room and searched through her clothes for something Annie could wear.

"What are you going to wear, Avanna?" Annie asked.

"I always have my bathing suit with me."

"Is it a one piece or a two piece?"

Avanna smiled. "It's more like a no piece, Annie."

Annie got the picture.

"Will that bother you? You know Reid has seen me before. If it bothers you, I will wear my underwear."

"You can wear what you usually wear, or what you don't wear. It won't bother me as long as Reid doesn't mind."

"He never pays any attention. It's not a big deal to him."

Avanna kept looking and found something. "Aha! I think this will work." Avanna held up a pair of running shorts with an elastic waistband. "Try these on, Annie. They should fit."

Annie slipped off her jeans and tried on the shorts. They fit okay, but were just a little loose. "They will work. Thanks, Avanna."

"What about a top?"

"I'm going to be brave and just wear my bra. It's blue so I don't think anything will show. Will you let me know if you can see anything?"

"Sure, Annie. Can I ask you something personal?"

"Okay."

"Has Reid ever seen you undressed?"

"No, we've never done anything like that yet.

"Will it embarrass you if he sees you in your bra?"

Annie giggled. "I don't think so. Not as long as my bra stays where it's supposed to."

"I'm going to get ready."

"I think I'll go on down to the pool if you don't mind."

"Do you know where it is?" Avanna asked.

"I'll just listen for the guys. If I get lost I'll just wander around. I'll be like a ghost forever searching for the pool."

Annie went downstairs and found the pool without any trouble.

"Annie, are you coming in?" Reid asked. "The water's nice and warm."

Annie looked at the men. "Are you guys wearing your boxers?"

"We are for now," Nick answered with a grin.

Avanna walked into the pool area wearing a white robe. She didn't waste any time as she slipped off her robe and dove into the pool. Annie took off her shoes and socks, then removed her top. The guys didn't any attention to her as they swam laps. Annie got in the water and realized it was colder than the guys let on. Reid swam over to Annie and realized she was shivering.

"You'll get used to it in a minute. Once you start swimming around it's not too bad."

Nick and Avanna swam over to join Reid and Annie. The guys didn't pay any attention to the fact Avanna was naked.

148

"Are you a good swimmer, Annie?" Nick asked. "I'll do laps with you if you want to get warmed up."

"I'm a pretty good swimmer. I should be able to keep up with you, Nicky."

Nick and Annie started doing laps up and down the pool. Avanna floated around on her back. Reid did a couple of laps, then joined Avanna. They talked about school and her father.

"Are you warmed up now?" Nick asked.

"It's better now," Annie replied with her head just above the water. She deliberately avoided looking at Reid and Avanna.

"Wanna race?" Nick asked.

"Sure," Annie answered. "One full lap. Down and back."

"Okay, should we make it interesting and make a bet?" Nick asked.

"What do you have in mind?" Annie asked.

Nick thought about it. "Loser buys diner tonight."

"Okay by me," Annie said.

"I can think of a better bet than that. One with much higher stakes," Avanna mentioned with a smile.

"What would that be, Avanna?" Nick asked.

"Loser loses their clothes. That will provide incentive. You guys want to see Annie naked and she doesn't want to let you."

"I lose both ways!" Annie exclaimed. "If I win then I have to see these guys naked."

"That's not always a bad thing, Annie," Avanna smirked at the guys. "And anyway, I've seen them both naked and there's not a lot to see."

Both guys caught Avanna and dunked her in the water.

Annie decided to take the bet. "Okay I'll do it. Who is going to be the starter?"

"I will," Reid said "I'll count down from three, then yell go. Avanna will make sure you both touch the other end and I'll be the judge at the finish line. Okay?"

Annie and Nick agreed and swam to the end of the pool. Nick helped Annie get out. They got into position and Reid began the countdown.

"Instead of counting I'm going to say ready, set, go. Take

off on go! All set. Ready! Set! Go!!!!"

Annie reacted. She dove into the water and took off. Nick smiled at Reid and waited a couple of seconds before he dove in. He took his time and Annie reached the other end of the pool about a length ahead of Nick. Annie made an awkward turn while Nick expertly turned over and used his feet to propel himself forward. Nick then took off for real and easily beat Annie to the other end. He was already out of the pool when Annie touched home. She looked up and Nick and Reid were both smiling at her. They reached out a hand and lifted her out of the pool. Avanna emerged from the pool at the other end, put on her robe and walked around to join the guys.

"I guess I won the bet, Annie. Do you agree?" Nick asked. "Now it's time to pay up."

"Crap!" She swore as she hugged herself to cover her chest. "Reid, I'm sorry. I don't want you to see me naked yet."

"Come on, Annie. A bet is a bet," Reid said while staring at her legs. "What have you got to hide, child?"

Nick looked at Avanna and whispered, "He's pushing her buttons, huh?"

"I'm not a child." Annie tugged Avanna's shorts down and stepped out of them. She looked at Reid and was about to unhook her bra when both guys stopped her.

"You don't have to do that, Annie," Reid said. "You were set up."

"What do you mean?" she asked holding the shorts in front of her.

Reid explained, "Nick was state champ in the 100 meter freestyle in high school. He could have won without using his arms."

"You stinkers! I should be declared the winner by default. I should make you guys drop your boxers!"

"They will if you want them to, Annie," Avanna said.

"No! I don't want to see."

Annie put the shorts back on as the guys laughed.

"You are such a good sport, Annie. I'll buy dinner for everyone tonight," Nick offered.

"Good! I want something really expensive."

"Were you really going to take off your bra?" Reid asked.

"You wouldn't even have noticed, Reid! You were so busy looking at Avanna."

"I was not," he pleaded. "Not all the time at least. Anyway, Avanna is with Nick."

"Come on. Let's get dressed so we can go eat," Avanna said.

"We have to dry our boxers first. We don't have anything to change into."

Avanna laughed. "You could go commando."

"I don't think so, Avanna."

"Why not, Reid? Haven't you ever done that before?"

He shook his head. "No, not that I can remember."

"Annie and I are going upstairs to change. We'll meet you in ten minutes."

Avanna and Annie went up to her room. Avanna removed her robe and pulled clean underwear out of her dresser. Annie slipped out of her wet clothes, dried off and put on her shirt and jeans as Avanna watched.

"Are you going to dry your underwear, Annie?"

"I don't mind going commando for a while. I'll toss my clothes in the dryer. We are coming back here after we eat, right?" Annie asked.

"Sure. We can send the guys to Papa Palumbo's and have them bring it back here to eat. That would be even better. Let's go tell the guys."

"Avanna, before we do that. Do I look all right?"

"You look fine why. You look cute with your hair all wet."

"I mean do I look okay without my bra?"

"I don't think Reid or Nicky will complain," Avanna said after looking at Annie. "They can't see through your shirt. Let's go tell the guys our plan."

Annie followed Avanna downstairs. The guys were still waiting for their boxers to dry. Annie tossed her underwear in the dryer, too. Reid looked at her.

"Are you going commando, Annie?"

She grinned. "I am for now."

"Come on, guys, we want you to go to Papa Palumbo's and bring the food back here. You can surely go through the drive up without your boxers and they'll be dry when we get back. Annie is brave enough to go commando."

Reid and Nick looked at each other, then at Annie. She used her arms to cover her chest.

"All right," Nick said. "What do you want?"

"I'm not sure," Avanna said.

The guys rolled their eyes and they all got in the car to go since no one knew for sure what they wanted. Nick drove to Papa Palumbo's and they ordered a ton of food. When they got back to the house, the guys checked to see if their boxers were dry and they were.

"Are you going to put your underwear on, Annie?" Reid asked.

"Maybe later. I want you to think about me as you eat."

They sat in the breakfast area to eat. Annie stared out the window at the snow covered landscape.

"I'm going to be sick," Nick moaned as he wiped some mustard off of his chin. "I'm stuffed."

"You should be, Nicky! Two jumbo dogs, fries and a chili dog," Avanna said.

Reid had been looking at Annie the whole time they were eating.

"For crying out loud, Reid," Avanna shouted. "You would think you've never seen a girl before. Annie is braless not topless! Quit staring at her. You aren't going to see through her shirt no matter how hard you stare."

Annie grinned as Avanna scolded Reid.

They stayed at the house until eleven at night before they returned to the city. Nick dropped Reid and Annie off.

"It was a pleasure to meet you, Annie. It was a fun weekend. I hope we can do it again sometime. You have my email address and my number, right?" Avanna asked.

"Got 'em! Thanks, Avanna. Good night."

"Bye, Annie. See you again soon, I hope," Nick said.

"Bye, Nicky! Thanks for everything."

Everyone was asleep when Reid and Annie walked into the house. They sat in the living room in the dark for awhile.

"I had so much fun today, Annie."

"So did I. Nicky and Avanna are a lot of fun to be with."

"You didn't seem to be bothered when Avanna was swimming," Reid whispered.

"I wasn't jealous because you saw her. Were you disappointed I didn't go swimming like Avanna?"

"Yes and no, I want to see you like that, Annie. I would be lying if I told you I didn't, but I wasn't going to pressure you. Besides I didn't think you would do it with Nicky there. I think it's a very personal thing for you."

"I don't think I would have done it even if it was just the two of us. If we are to that point in our relationship the next time we see them, I would go skinny dipping in front of Avanna and Nicky."

"Nicky really likes you. Not as a girlfriend, but as a friend, even though he did put his hands on your butt. He wasn't doing that in a sexual way."

"What do you mean? When did he have his hands on my butt?"

"When you were getting out of the pool. He helped you get out by putting his hands on you and pushing."

"I didn't even know it, Reid. I'm sorry."

"You don't have to be sorry, Annie. I'm not jealous."

"Do you want to do what Nicky did?"

Reid smiled but Annie couldn't tell in the dark.

"Never mind! I know the answer."

Reid kissed Annie. She returned the kiss but then wiggled out of his arms and stepped back.

"Was I going too fast?" Reid asked.

"If we don't go to bed soon I will.... I meant go to sleep. We're not going to bed together."

"I know, Annie. Let's get to bed. You have to catch the train in the morning."

153

In the morning Reid took Annie to the station. Reid waited with her and kissed her goodbye just before she boarded the train.

"Call me. I will miss you until school starts again."

"I'll call, Reid. Thanks for the great weekend."

An hour later Annie stepped off the train in SoHam and called her father.

"Daddy, I'm at the train station. Are you picking me up?"

"I'm on my way. I got stuck at the office, but I will be there in a few minutes."

"I could call Mace if you want."

"No, I want to pick you up, Annie. Just wait inside and I'll be there ASAP."

"Okay. I'll wait inside by the front windows so I can see you pull up. You won't have to come inside that way."

Annie's father arrived after a few minutes. She ran outside, threw her suitcase and backpack in the trunk and got in the car.

"Hi, Daddy! Did you miss me?"

"Were you gone, sweetie?" he replied and she giggled.

"Can we stop and get something to eat on the way home? I'm starving!"

"Sure, anyplace in particular?"

"Just the nearest fast food place. I need a burger."

Dad saw a Burger Bob's and went through the drive-up lane. They took the food home to eat.

"So how did everything go with Reid? Did you meet his whole family?"

"Pretty much and even some of his friends. His family gets together for dinner just about every weekend, except for his oldest brother John. He lives in Denver, but he was in town for the holiday."

"Do they have a nice house? Are there a lot of rooms?"

"You can just ask, Daddy. You don't have to try to be coy with me."

"Okay, whose room did you sleep in?" he asked and then popped a fry into his mouth.

"I slept in the room that belonged to his brothers Robert and Thomas. They are both married with their own families. The

154

house is big and Reid's parents are sweet."

Annie told her father more about her time with Reid and talked about Nicky and Avanna and meeting Stephanie. She even mentioned swimming.

"Where did you go swimming? I didn't know you were planning to do that."

"I didn't know we were going to, either. Avanna's grandmother has this huge house in South Hinsdale. She's in Florida right now, but Avanna had a key. There's an indoor pool and a Jacuzzi so the four of us went over there."

Annie realized what her father was wondering.

"I didn't have my bathing suit, Daddy."

"Annie! Don't tell me..."

"No! I didn't do that. I borrowed some shorts from Avanna and wore those and my underwear. It was blue so no one could see anything."

"Did everyone else have bathing suits or trunks?"

Annie stared at her father without answering.

"Okay, don't tell me. I don't need to know. You are old enough to make your own decisions about some things."

"I love you, Daddy, and you know you can trust me."

"I know, sweetheart. I trust you."

"Yeah, I know. It's the guys you don't trust."

"It's just part of being a father. I'm glad you're home now. I missed you."

"How was your time with Elisabeth?" Annie asked.

"We had a good time together. We... Oh, you're trying to make a point, huh?"

She held up a hand. "That's all right. I don't need the details."

"I'm going to get some sleep, Annie. Wake me up by five so we can have dinner together. I don't have to work tonight."

"Okay. I need to do some laundry. I'll try not to wake you."

155

Chapter Twenty-Five

"Are you still planning to go to the Barclay's New Year's Eve party tonight, Annie," Mace asked as they were eating lunch at Darby's.

"I'm not sure. Reid is busy with his family in the city. Lainey and Cindy are going with their guys," Annie answered. "They have a party every year, but I hate to miss it. I've never been invited before."

Mace took a bite of his burger and said, "I'd like to go, but Erin's still in Nebraska. Hey, girl. We could go together. How would you feel about that?"

Annie set her Coke down. "I suppose I will have to drive if we do."

"That's a good idea. Thanks for volunteering."

"Are you ever going to get your own car?" she asked as she rolled her eyes. "And stop talking with your mouth full. It's gross."

"Why? You have a car and there are buses. Just consider it my contribution to help clean up the air."

"Why do I even consider you a friend?"

Mace laughed. "Because I am so sexy."

Just as in the past, most of the guests were college-age, or younger, with no alcohol being served. The dress code specified the party as formal. The same DJ provided the music again this year. He specialized in music suitable for ballroom dancing. Annie parked her car and she and Mace followed the brick-paved path to the front door.

"I've never been to a house with a paved parking lot before," Mace commented.

Annie poked him in the side. "This isn't a house, you doofus. It's an estate."

They handed their invitations to the staff at the front door and walked inside. Some "hostesses" took their coats, gave Mace two receipts and placed them in what Annie assumed to be a large walk-in closet.

"Did you see the look I got from that one dude?" Mace asked. "I thought he was going to call the cops on me."

156

"You've got an over active imagination. You aren't the only 'dude' here." She used air quotes to let Mace know what she meant.

"Have you ever been here before, Annie?"

"Oh, sure. Damon and I hang out a lot," Annie answered facetiously. "When would I have ever been here?"

"Geez, Annie, I was just asking. You don't have to bite my head off."

They meandered through the large public rooms on the first floor and admired the art work and antiques spread everywhere.

"Do you think that's a real Picasso?" Mace asked as he stared at a painting.

"Yep! I've seen pictures of it in art books. I can't remember what it's called, but it's real."

They continued to wander around as they looked for their friends.

"I don't see Lainey or Cindy. Do you?" Annie asked.

Mace glanced around and shook his head. "Haven't seen either of them. Would you like to dance, Annie?" Mace asked.

"Sure! Who should I dance with?" she teased.

"I was hoping you would dance with me, but maybe you could dance with that guy over there."

"Who?"

"The guy standing in the corner in the red suit."

Annie poked Mace in the side. "That's a Santa Claus statue, you dope."

"Well, then dance with me."

"Fine."

Annie and Mace laughed because they enjoyed dancing together.

"Have I told you how pretty you look in that fancy dress?" Mace asked as they danced to a Frank Sinatra song.

"No... I'm waiting for the punch line."

"No joking. I think you look very pretty tonight."

"Thank you, Mace. You look handsome in that suit. As uncomfortable as hell, but very handsome," she said.

"Have you talked to Reid lately?"

"He called this afternoon. He was going to his brother's

house tonight with Nicky and Avanna. They were going to cut out early and go dancing."

"Would you rather be with Reid?" Mace asked as he spun her in a circle.

"Would you rather be with Erin?" she responded.

"I see what you mean. We are still friends, Annie."

"We'll always be friends, Mace. You know that. We might even be more if Daddy marries your mom."

"Do you ever hear them talking about marriage?" Mace asked as he pulled Annie close enough to smell the strawberry shampoo in her hair.

"No, not really. I haven't brought the subject up lately. Have you?"

"No, Keyshon is always asking though. He thinks if they get married you will move in with him."

"That might not be a bad idea. I could make him clean up the room, so I don't have to."

"That's sick."

Later, Annie talked to Damon Barclay and Diana Ahronson about their long distance relationship.

"Damon being able to fly home as often as he does certainly makes it easier," Diana said.

"Hi, Annie. I'm glad you came," Damon said as he smiled at her. "Are you still seeing Reid Smagala? Diana told me you were dating him."

"We are dating, but it's not real serious like you and Diana." She looked into his dark eyes. "How do you like Princeton, Damon?"

"I like it, but I would rather be with Diana. If my father had gone to North Park instead, I wouldn't be so far away."

"I understand how you feel."

Cindy and Bryce arrived late just before eleven.

"Cindy, were have you guys been?" Elaine asked. "Adrian and I were getting worried."

"So were we," Annie said.

"Bryce had an accident on the way here," Cindy explained.

"Are you guys all right? Was anyone hurt?" Adrien asked.

"Only the deer that ran out in front of me." Bryce laughed. "Oh, and the car. I think it's totaled."

"How did you get here? Are you going to need a ride home?" Elaine asked.

"We got a ride from the officer who stopped. Can we hitch a ride home with you guys?" Cindy asked.

"Sure. We're not going to stay as late as last year. Probably leave around two," Elaine said as she looked at Adrien.

"Hey, look!" Annie pointed. "There's Derrick Keasling with someone new. Wow! Is she gorgeous or what?"

"I thought they were still in Aspen. There's Kristen with Christopher Braun," Cindy said.

Elaine said, "I guess they came back early. I wanna talk to Kristen."

Cindy and Elaine left the guys to talk to Kristen.

"Hi, Kristen."

"Hi, Lainey. Hi, Cindy. How is life at North Park?"

"We love it! We thought you were still in Aspen. Did you leave early for some reason?"

"Not really. We planned to be back for the party."

Annie watched her friends talking with Kristen. "Mace, I want to go see Kristen. Will you be all right without me?"

"It will be a struggle, but I'll survive somehow."

Annie stuck her tongue out at Mace and headed over to talk to her girlfriends. Mace found other girls willing to dance.

Hi, Annie. How have you been? I saw you dancing with Mace. Are you here together?" Kristen asked.

"We came to the party together, but just as friends."

Annie filled Kristen in on the latest news.

"Wow! An older man, Annie. What did your father say?"

"He likes Reid, but we aren't real serious yet or anything. Is there anything new going on at Roosevelt?"

"Do you remember my friend, Emmy Colasanti?"

"Sure. I heard she was being harassed by Todd Delaney. Is that true?"

"She was, but my cousin Tony Bertucci put a stop to it. Tony and Emmy are dating now."

"Really? Emmy is so tiny compared to him."

"They are in love. Emmy is graduating early."

"Is she planning to go to college. She must be, she's so smart. Is she coming to North Park?"

"She's going to work full-time and take classes at Paul Frank. She doesn't have the money for North Park," Kristen said and then put a hand to her mouth. "Please don't tell anyone I said that, Annie. It might embarrass Emmy. She doesn't want any help from her parents or anyone. She wants to put herself through college."

"She will do it. I'm sure if anyone can, it would be her."

Annie and Kristen kept talking and Annie noticed Derrick's date.

"Who is that with Derrick?"

"Her name is Amber Quinlan. They met at college. Isn't she beautiful?"

"She's not any prettier than you, Kristen."

"Take a closer look, Annie," Kristen said with a smile.

Annie looked at Amber again and giggled.

"See anything?" Kristen asked.

"Okay, she is a little bigger than us."

"That's one way to put it, Annie."

Later, Derrick and Amber happened to see Annie and Mace sitting at a table. They sat with them and talked about school for a few minutes.

"Would you like to dance, Annie?" Derrick asked. "Amber wants to take a break."

"Sure! I'd love to dance with you, Derrick."

Derrick and Annie danced to a couple of songs, then returned to Mace and Amber. Midnight quickly approached. The couples gathered together for a toast to the new year. Mace took Annie's hand and as the countdown reached zero, they kissed quickly.

"You are still a good kisser, Mace. I know you wish you were kissing Erin instead of me."

"And you wish I was Reid."

"Happy New Year, Mace."

160

"Happy New Year, Annie O'Dell. I hope you have an even better year than the last one."

"Do you think your mom and Daddy are kissing right about now?" Annie asked. "Should I even worry about that?"

"Doubtful. They are probably sound asleep."

"Who was watching Keyshon tonight?" Annie asked.

"He's spending the night with your grandfather."

"Grandpa didn't tell me that."

"They have been spending more time together. Keyshon really likes your grandpa."

Annie was ready to leave around one o'clock. She and Mace said good night to their friends and headed back to the O'Dell house.

"Does your father know I'm crashing here tonight?" Mace asked as he tossed his suit coat at the couch. ripped off his tie and unbuttoned his collar.

"I told him it was a possibility."

"What did he say?"

"He just told me to have a good time at the party. He knows the Barclays won't serve alcohol at the party, so he's not worried about me drinking and driving. I didn't know how late we were going to stay though. Are you going to call Erin?"

"I would, but we talked earlier today and she said she wasn't going to stay up any later than normal. Her parents go to bed early."

"Did you tell her about the party?" Annie placed Mace's suit coat on a hanger and put it in the front closet.

"Yeah, I told her, and I told her I was going with you. She didn't seem to mind although she did make me promise to kiss you on the mouth as I recall."

Mace moved close to Annie as he pretended to kiss her.

"Stay away from me, you horny pervert. We're almost related now."

Mace laughed as he pulled Annie onto the couch with him.

"It's a good thing being related isn't retroactive if you know what I mean."

"I know what you mean and we aren't doing that again.

161

You have Erin and I have Reid."

"Are you and Reid doing..."

Annie smacked Mace on his arm. "You know I haven't. Why do you keep teasing me about that?"

"Just because I can. You know I still love you."

"As a sister!"

"A sister with benefits maybe?" he raised his eyebrows as he asked.

Annie shook her head. "In your dreams. The only benefit you are getting is that I will let you live."

"That's better than the alternative."

Annie kissed Mace on the cheek, then got up.

"I'm going to bed, Mace. See you in the morning."

"Night, Annie."

"You know where the blankets are. Do you need a pillow?"

"Can I have one of yours?"

"There is a spare pillow in the closet with the blankets. You can't have one of mine."

"I had a good time tonight, Annie."

"So did I, Mace. Night."

Chapter Twenty-Six

With the second semester only a week away, Annie was getting anxious. She also wanted to see Reid again. They talked on the phone nearly every day, but Annie wanted to see him in person. Annie was alone in the house cleaning up the kitchen Monday morning when she heard a knock on the door. She looked in the direction of the front door. *Who can that be? It better not be someone trying to sell something.* She tossed her paper towel toward the trashcan, walked out of the kitchen, down the hall, looked through the sidelight and her heart started beating faster. She smiled and opened the door.

"Matty! What are you doing here?"

"Can I come in, Annie? I want to talk to you." He stuffed his hands deep into the pockets of his coat. "I'm sorry for just showing up, but it's kinda important."

"Sure, come on in. Daddy isn't home, but you can come in as long as you behave." She opened the heavy wooden door all the way and stood back.

"I will, Annie. You don't have to be afraid of me. I wouldn't ever hurt you," Matt said as he opened the storm door, wiped his shoes on the welcome mat and stepped inside.

Annie looked up at him. "I'm not afraid of you, Matty. I know you wouldn't do anything to hurt me. Do you want something to drink? Coke or a Dr Pepper?"

"A Coke would be fine."

Annie got two Cokes from the fridge. Matt followed her into the kitchen, looked around, saw the paper towel on the floor and put it in the trashcan. She and Matt sat next to each other at the island in the kitchen.

"Are you ready for school to start? I am," Annie said.

They talked about school and fathers for a time.

"Daddy and Elisabeth are still dating," Annie said.

"That's nice," Matt said without any emotion.

"Okay, what's on your mind?" Annie asked as she noticed Matt clenching and then opening his fists. "You aren't in trouble, are you? Are the cops looking for you? If so, this would be a good place to hide."

"I might be, Annie." He waved a hand. "Not cop trouble."

"For real? Why? What did you do?"

He took a deep breath and then exhaled slowly. "I've been seeing this girl from school. Joni McAllister. She's a senior and she's pregnant."

"Oh," Annie said without betraying the hurt in her heart. "That is serious. Is she sure? Are you sure?"

"She's sure. She took one of those early pregnancy tests and it was positive so she went to her doctor and he confirmed it."

"Matty, don't get upset with my question, but are you sure it's your baby?"

"Yes, she hasn't been with anyone else."

"Is there any chance she's lying? People lie all the time."

He shook his head. "No, Annie, if you knew her you would understand. She never lies about anything."

"What are you going to do, Matty?"

"I don't know, Annie." He stared at the ceiling before looking at Annie. "I don't want to get married, but I know Joni won't get an abortion. I don't think she will give the baby up for adoption like Victoria. I guess the only option is to become a father."

Annie grinned and said, "I think that's going to happen no matter what. Even if she gives the baby up for adoption, you will still be the biological father."

Matt and Annie sat quietly for a few moments as they drank their pop.

"Can I have a beer, Annie?"

"Yeah, go ahead." She pointed to the fridge. "I guess this calls for more than pop."

"Do you want one?"

"No. Too early for me, but you can have one."

Matt got the beer from the fridge and sat back down.

Annie put her elbow on the island, rested her chin in her hand, stared at Matt and asked, "How could this have happened?"

Matt looked at Annie and smiled.

She saw the smile and smacked his hand. "I know how it

happened, Matthew. I'm not totally unaware of where babies come from. Didn't you use protection?" she asked and then took a sip of her pop.

"Most of the time. Joni was on the pill although she did change her prescription. I guess I should have been more careful, or maybe one of the condoms must have broke."

"What do you mean it broke?"

"It happens, Annie. Sometimes they break or have a hole in them."

"I didn't know that. I thought they always worked."

"You would know more if you were having sex, but since you aren't..."

"How do you know I'm not having sex?" she asked as she poked his side. 'Maybe I decided it was time to lose my virginity."

"Because I know you, Annie O'Dell. Just because you are going out with Reid doesn't mean you are sleeping with him."

Her voice rose in pitch as she asked, "How do you know about Reid?"

"I talked to Randy Braun, and he heard it from Cindy. Word gets around, Annie. SoHam isn't that big a city."

"I suppose so," she said. "Oh, I met a friend of Reid's who is related to you somehow— Nick Whitaker. Do you know him?"

"I've met him a couple times, but I don't really know him."

Annie told Matt about staying in Chicago with Reid and meeting his family.

"Reid and I went out to a club with him and another friend. Avanna Bellamy. We had fun."

"Have you and Reid made out at least?" Matt asked.

"We have made out a little—just kissing though."

"So you haven't gone as far with any other guy as you did with me, huh?" he asked while staring into her brown eyes.

"No, I haven't, Matty. Does that make you happy?"

Matt looked at Annie and smiled. He remembered the times they made out.

"Yeah, in a way, Annie. I'm glad no one else has seen you the way I have."

"Screw you, Matthew!" Annie kicked his shin.

"I'm sorry. I think Reid will want to do more than just a little making out before too much longer."

"Mace saw me! Remember? He and Erin walked in on us."

Matt set his beer down and raised his eyebrows. "He might have seen you, but not the way I did and you know it."

"Do you even remember what I looked like Matty? You've been with so many other girls. How could you remember me?"

"I'll always remember you, Annie. You are special. You're not like all those other girls. They don't mean anything to me."

"What about Joni? Doesn't she mean anything to you?"

"Yeah, I suppose so, but if she wasn't pregnant I would just move on to someone else. You mean more to me than they do."

"That's just because you haven't slept with me yet, Matthew Sullivan. If we had already had sex, you wouldn't be thinking about me."

He shook his head emphatically. "You're wrong about that, Annie. Even after we have sex, I will still be thinking about you."

"How can I ever believe that, Matty?" she asked. "And I caught what you said. You are pretty sure of yourself, huh?"

"Have I ever lied to you, Annie? Ever?"

They turned to face each other and their knees bumped together. They stared at each other for a moment without speaking. She moved her knee until she felt his leg against her jeans.

"Have I?" he asked as he touched her knees.

"Not that I know of. Daddy said once that you were just being patient and just because you didn't take advantage of me once doesn't mean the next time will be the same. He helped me understand why I feel the way I do about you."

Matt finished his beer. "How do you feel about me, Annie? Do you still feel the same as before?"

"I am older and wiser now. I understand why I am so attracted to you. It doesn't mean that it's any easier to resist you. Especially when you try to be so charming and treat me like I really mean something to you."

"You do mean something to me, Annie. Even if we never make love." He waved his hand. "Even if I never get to kiss you again, you mean something to me."

Annie looked at Matt, and he looked into her eyes. He moved closer and put his hands on her shoulders.

"Oh, Matty! Please don't kiss me right now. I wouldn't be able to resist you even after what you did to Joni. Maybe because of what has happened."

"I won't kiss you, Annie, because I know I wouldn't want to stop today. I should leave. Will you promise not to tell anyone yet." He stood up and ran a hand through her hair.

"Of course, Matty. I won't say anything to anyone. Not even Daddy. I'll tell him you stopped by to talk, but I won't tell him why."

"Thanks. Do you still have the same email and phone number?"

"Yes, same ones. You can call me if you need to talk to someone, Matt. I'm still your friend."

"You might be my only friend, Annie O'Dell," he whispered.

Matt walked out of the kitchen and Annie followed him to the door. He kissed her cheek as he left. Annie closed the door, leaned back against it, crossed her arms over her chest and closed her eyes. She thought of Reid and wished he caused her heart to flutter and made her knees grow weak the same way Matthew Sullivan did.

Chapter Twenty-Seven

The dorms reopened on the tenth and the hallways buzzed with the activity of students returning from the holidays. Erin Bezick arrived on Sunday and Mace helped carry her suitcases back to the room she shared with Annie O'Dell.

"What have you got in here? Bricks?" he asked as he dropped the suitcases next to her bed. "They weigh a ton."

Erin grinned. "Books. I brought some books with me. Why? Are you getting weaker?"

"No, I thought all you took home was some clothes."

"I have an extra suitcase now."

There was one new student from Roosevelt High living in Howe Hall this semester. Victoria Madison had given up her baby for adoption. She occupied a room on the second floor a few doors away from Rachel Lowery. Victoria's roommate was Leila Fanaka from Milwaukee. Victoria and Leila met and soon discovered one thing in common—sex! They both loved to have sex. Victoria told Leila about the baby and Leila confessed she aborted a pregnancy two years ago.

Reid Smagala moved back to his apartment on Sunday afternoon. His roommate Ron Wilcher stayed in the apartment throughout the holidays. He only went home for two days at Christmas. His parents were divorced and his father now lived in Australia. His mother, who still lived in Chicago, had a new man in her life and Ron didn't get along with him. Reid unpacked and called Annie.

"I'm here and settled in. Are you ready for me to come and get you?"

"I'm ready," Annie said. "Daddy hurt his ribs at work chasing some kid so he can't lift anything right now."

"I'll be over ASAP."

Reid arrived at the O'Dell home in less than twenty minutes. Annie opened the door and he kissed her cheek.

Not exactly the greeting I hoped for. Annie thought as she looked up at Reid.

Dad walked up behind Annie and offered a hand to Reid.

"Hi, Reid. Thanks for helping Annie. I appreciate it. I never should have been chasing that kid. It wasn't worth it."

Reid shook hands. "I don't mind helping, Mr. O'Dell."

Reid took her suitcases out to her car and came back inside. "You've got more stuff than last semester, Annie."

"More clothes and a few books. Sorry it's so heavy."

Annie hugged her father and she and Reid left for North Park.

Reid carried the two large suitcases up to the third floor. Annie giggled because she didn't tell him about the service elevator.

Erin was already visiting Mace in his room. They hadn't seen each other for a month and were making for lost time.

"Are you hungry, Annie?" Reid asked. "Wanna grab a burger somewhere or do you have to unpack right away?"

"I can unpack later. I'm kinda hungry. I haven't eaten since breakfast. Can we go to The Hungry Lion?"

"What's that?" Reid asked.

"A place I like to visit once in a while," she answered softly.

Annie had only been there three times before, but she thought Matt might be working tonight.

"We can go wherever you want. Avanna and Nicky said to say hi."

"How are they doing?"

"They're doing okay. Avanna went back to Knoxville and Nicky is still at DePaul."

Reid drove to the restaurant and they were seated in a corner booth. Annie didn't see Matty at first, but after a minute she saw him talking to one of the waitresses. He saw Annie with Reid and smiled at her. She smiled back and he pointed to the restrooms.

"I'll be right back, Reid. I need to use the restroom."

Reid looked around the restaurant. "It looks like an Irish pub. Should I order a pop for you and an appetizer?"

"Dr Pepper, please, and how about the loaded potato skins to start," she answered without looking at the menu."

"Okay." Reid opened his menu and listened to the music

169

playing above him.

Annie walked over to the restroom located in a hallway out of sight of their table.

"Hi, Annie," Matt said as he touched her arm from behind. "Why are you here? Is that Reid with you?"

Annie turned to face Matt and smiled up at him. "Yes, it's Reid. Why are you asking? I thought you knew him."

Matt shook his head as he rubbed her arm. "No, I've never met him. I only knew you were dating a guy named Reid."

"Well, what do you think?"

"He's good looking, Annie. Does he excite you the way I do?" he asked as he pulled on the fine hair on her arm.

"How can you ask me that, Matty?" She pulled her arm away. "How are things with you and Joni?"

"She's still pregnant," he whispered. "I still haven't told anyone but you."

"Are you going to marry her?"

"I told you I wouldn't. I'll support the baby, but I won't get married."

Annie looked over her shoulder. "I should get back to Reid. Call me soon, Matty."

"I will. We should get together and talk sometime, Annie. Just talk."

"Okay, Matty. I really need to get back."

Annie turned to go, but Matt stopped her. He held her shoulders and kissed her on the mouth. She returned the kiss. Matt released her and Annie went back to her table. Her heart raced as she sat down.

"Do you know what you want to eat, Annie?" Reid asked.

"I want a burger with bacon and pepperjack cheese and a drink of your beer," she answered and hoped he couldn't tell how fast her heart was racing.

"I'll get the same thing. Should we split some fries?"

"Okay."

Annie kept looking for Matthew but didn't see him again. She and Reid placed their order and talked.

"John and Kathleen have decided to try again. She let him

170

move back in the house, but he's sleeping on the couch for now."

"That's a start at least. Everyone else okay?"

"Mom told me Dad keeps asking if you are really in college. He's worried you might be too young."

"Too young for what?" Annie asked and then frowned. "Why does everyone I know think I'm too young? I'm not a child. I knew this girl at Roosevelt High who had a baby when she was fifteen. She was old enough to have the baby and she decided to keep her."

Reid waited for her to finish venting and then said, "For me. Too young for me. He knows I want a relationship like I had with Stephanie and he thinks you might be too young for that."

"I'm too young to move in with you. We both know that."

"I know and I would never ask you to do that. At least not now. Who knows what might happen in a couple of years."

"Reid, I can't imagine what's going to happen next week let alone two years from now," she said as she shook the ketchup container vigorously.

"Annie, I don't want to get into a fight over this. I was just telling you what Dad said. Let's just forget about it, okay?"

"I don't want to fight either. How's your burger?" she asked as she added extra ketchup to her burger.

"It's just right. Do you want a fry?"

Annie nodded her head and Reid fed her a french fry.

"I'm still upset about what you said, Reid."

"What? The part about moving in together or something else?"

"The moving in together. I've got three and a half years of school left and I'm not going to lose my focus."

"Christ, Annie! Let it go. I never should have said anything. I'm not going to ask you to move in with me anytime soon."

"The answer would be no if you did. In fact I might live at home after this year. It would be less expensive."

"But you'd still be going to North Park, right?" he asked.

"Yes, I don't plan to transfer anywhere else."

They finished eating and Reid paid the check.

171

"Do you need some money for the tip?" Annie asked. "I have some singles."

Reid shook his head. "No need. I got this."

He took Annie back to Howe Hall, parked the car and followed her upstairs. They stood outside her door for a moment and stared at each other.

"Are you going to talk to me, Annie, or are you still mad?" Reid asked.

"I'm not mad. Thanks for helping me today and for dinner. I'll see you later." She dug her key out of her purse.

"Okay. You're welcome for everything, Annie."

Reid leaned over and tried to kiss her, but Annie turned her head. Reid kissed her cheek and walked away.

"You can call me later if you want," Annie said then slipped into her room. She closed the door and leaned back against it. *I know you're upset with me, but I didn't want you to kiss me just now.* She tossed her purse in the direction of her bed, sighed and plopped onto her back. She thought about the difference between kissing Reid and Matt. *I'm not sure which I liked better. The slow steady buildup of Reid's kisses or the fiery flames of Matt Sullivan. Who am I kidding? I know who I want to kiss me.*

Chapter Twenty-Eight

Two weeks of classes had gone by and the Roosevelt grads were getting together for dinner on Friday in the Jordan Dining Hall at six. Elaine and Cindy grabbed a table for the whole group while Bryce and Adrien talked. Mace and Erin arrived holding hands. Solomon and Ashley were still in their own world although something seemed different now. Rachel Lowery and Diana Ahronson stopped by to say hi. Victoria and Leila joined the group. Randy and Christopher Braun saw everyone and came over to eat. They sat with Victoria and Leila and convinced the girls to double date Saturday night. Annie finally arrived with Reid.

"Sorry we're late, guys. We stopped at the Student Union. How is everyone doing?"

"Annie, did you hear about the administration building?" Elaine asked.

"No, what happened?"

Elaine explained, "Someone broke into the main office and stole some petty cash. Maybe you can check into it."

"I can't, Lainey. My sleuthing days are past. It's not like back at Roosevelt where I had access to everything."

"Hey, Reid. Are you guys doing anything tonight?" Mace asked.

"Not that I know of, Mace. You wanna do something?"

"Yeah. We should go somewhere and do something. It's a Friday night and I don't have to be anywhere until noon tomorrow."

"What time is the game tomorrow?" Annie asked.

"It's starts at three. Coach relented and told us we could stay out till midnight tonight and no room checks. I think he's getting soft. Damian told me that a few years ago players had to be in bed by nine the night before a game."

"Alone?" Victoria asked.

"Damian didn't say," Mace answered as he glared at her.

"Can Leila and I join you if you go out somewhere tonight, Mace?" Victoria asked.

"It's all right with me as long as Erin doesn't mind. Do you mind, Erin?" Mace said hoping Erin would object.

"No, I wanna go somewhere though. I've been stuck in the room all week studying."

"They have live music at the coffeehouse tonight. It's just a guy with his guitar, but he's pretty good," Reid informed them.

"Boring! There's gotta be a better place to go than that. Let's stop by the frat houses. There's always something going on there on Fridays," Victoria suggested.

After dinner Leila and Victoria hurried back to their dorm.

"We'll be ready in a half hour. Should we meet downstairs?" Victoria asked.

"Why don't you meet us in our room, Victoria. Annie and I need to change."

Annie talked to Erin in private for a moment, then told Victoria, "Maybe we should just meet downstairs, Victoria. Say at 7:30."

"Okay. We'll see you then."

Mace and Reid were already waiting when Leila and Victoria made their way downstairs. They were both wearing short dresses and the guys noticed. Annie and Erin decided to wear dresses, too. They wanted to surprise Mace and Reid by dressing up instead of wearing old jeans. Annie and Erin came downstairs a few minutes after Leila and Victoria and saw the guys talking to Leila and Victoria.

"We're ready to go. Whose car are we taking?" Erin asked.

"I thought we would walk. We can't all fit in one car. Let's just walk," Reid suggested.

Annie looked at Reid and he could tell she was upset.

"Fine! Come on, Erin, let's get our coats. I don't want to freeze to death." Annie turned around and stomped away.

"We need to get our coats, too. We'll be right back, boys. Don't go anywhere," Victoria said as she put a hand on Reid's chest and actually batted her eyes.

The girls got their coats and they walked over to the street where all the frat houses were located. As they approached the Beta house, they heard the music from inside.

"Let's check this out." Victoria ran to the door.

Everyone followed her inside. The loud pulsating music shook the place. Groups of college students drinking beer out of plastic cups crowded into the house. Mace and Erin gravitated to where the music played and started dancing. Annie stared at Reid and did not talk to him.

"Annie, why are you mad at me? Did I do something wrong?"

"You were flirting with Victoria in the dorm. I saw you touch her arm."

"Maybe she tried to flirt with me, but I didn't flirt back. She's pretty and all, but you told me about her. I'm not interested in her. I like you, Annie."

Annie looked at Reid and sighed.

"Don't mind me tonight, Reid. It's just... it's that time of the month and I am being too emotional. I'm sorry for the way I've been acting. Will you forgive me?"

"Of course I will," Reid said as he rubbed her back. "Do you want something to drink?"

"Just pop! I don't want any beer tonight, but you can have some. I don't mind if you have fun."

Reid went to find some pop for Annie.

Victoria walked over to Annie with a huge grin on her face. "Hey, Annie. Reid is cute. Is he any good in bed?"

"I don't know, Victoria! We haven't had sex yet." *Not that I would tell you if we did.*

"You haven't? What are you waiting for? Oh, you're still doing it with Matt, huh? Matt is really good in bed. Isn't he?"

Annie glared at Victoria. "What makes you think I'm sleeping with Matthew? Did he say something about us?"

"He didn't say anything. I thought everyone knew though."

"I haven't slept with Matty, either," Annie said.

"Come on, Annie. I know better than that."

"I really haven't slept with him, Victoria!"

"You should! He's really good in bed, better than most guys. Of course, he's had a lot of experience."

"Maybe I'm not ready to sleep with anyone, Victoria. Did you ever think about that? Maybe I want to wait."

"How long? Do you want to wait until you're married? How perfectly quaint. Is Reid willing to wait for you? Is he a virgin, too?"

"No, he's not!"

"Not what? Willing to wait, or he's not a virgin. Which is it?"

"He lived with his girlfriend for a year so he's probably more experienced than Matty."

"I doubt that. Matty has been with a lot of girls. You should take advantage of his experience. He could teach you a lot. If you want, I could teach Reid a few things. He seemed to be interested in me."

"Just stay away from him, Victoria!"

"I won't make any promises I can't keep, or don't want to keep," Victoria said with a smile.

Annie stormed away from Victoria. She found her coat and left the frat house. Reid held a plastic cup of pop for Annie, but couldn't find her. He looked all over the house without any luck. He finally saw Erin and Mace sitting in a recliner.

"Erin, have you seen Annie? I can't find her."

"We haven't seen her, Reid," Erin said. "Is she with Victoria and Leila?"

"I don't know," he said as he was jostled by someone from behind. The pop spilled over the edge of the cup onto the carpet. Reid glanced down and saw several other stains as he walked away.

Reid found Victoria and Leila talking to two of the frat guys, grabbed her arm and said, "I can't find Annie. Have you seen her, Victoria?"

"Yeah, we were talking and she got upset and left. She grabbed her coat and took off."

"Did she say where she was going?" Reid asked angrily as he handed the pop to one of the guys. "Here! Take this."

The guy smiled and took a sip, then he spit it out onto the floor. "That's not beer!"

Victoria touched the buttons of Reid's shirt as she smiled. "No, she stormed out like a bat out of hell. She might be going to look for Matty."

Reid looked at Victoria's hand and brushed it away. "Who's Matty?"

"Matty Sullivan. Hasn't Annie ever told you about her loverboy Matty?"

"Not by name. Thanks, Victoria, for being such a good friend."

"Sure," she said as she smiled again. Victoria didn't realize Reid was being sarcastic. "Would you like to dance or maybe something else, Reid? I can show you a better time than Annie O'Dell."

"Maybe another time, Victoria. Right now I think I'll try to find Annie."

Victoria gave up on Reid and turned her attention back to the frat guys.

Reid tried calling Annie's cell phone, but it went straight to voicemail. He left a message, hurried over to Howe Hall and ran up to her room. He knocked on the door, but no one answered. He knocked louder and called out her name, but still no one answered. He tried her phone again with no luck. He raced down the stairs to wait in the lounge area.

Annie ran out of the frat house in tears. She was so upset that she didn't know whether to cry or punch someone. She ran all the way to her dorm but didn't go inside. She pulled her phone out of her purse and called Matt. "Where are you, Matty?" she asked without giving him a chance to say hello.

"You may not believe it, but I'm actually at the library studying. Why? Are you okay, Annie?"

"No, I'm not."

"Where are you? Do you need me to come and get you? Did you and Reid have a fight?"

"We did earlier, but that's not why I'm upset now. Do you have your car with you?"

"Yeah, it's in the lot behind the library. I can come and get you if you tell me where you are?"

"I'm on my way to the library. I'll be there in a couple minutes. Where exactly are you? I'll meet you there."

"I'll meet you by the front doors, Annie. Just inside the front doors."

Two minutes later Annie saw Matt inside the library. She ran to him and he hugged her. She started to cry again as Matt held her close.

"It's okay, Annie. I'm here. You can cry if you want."

Matt held her until she stopped.

"Can we go somewhere, Matty?" she asked as she looked up at him. "I need to talk to you."

He used his thumbs to dry her tears. "We can go wherever you want, Annie. Come on, we can leave through the back door."

Matt and Annie left through the back door and walked to his car.

"Can we go to the Riverwalk? I need to talk to you."

"If that's where you want to go, I'll take you there."

It only took a couple of minutes to get to the Riverwalk parking area. There were several other cars there, but Annie didn't mind.

Matt parked under a light, turned off the car and twisted in his seat. "Now tell me what happened, Annie. If Reid did anything to hurt you, I will beat the hell out of him."

"No, Matty!" Annie shook her head. "It wasn't Reid."

"Who? Not Mace!?"

"No, of course not. Mace would never hurt me. Let me tell you what happened from the beginning." Annie spent the next few minutes explaining everything to Matt. He listened patiently without interrupting. "So that's why I'm upset. I suppose it wouldn't bother me so much if it wasn't this time of the month."

"It's all right to be upset, Annie. I know some girls are real emotional when they... have their periods."

"I had such high hopes for tonight. Reid and I were going to have time to be alone. We weren't going to do anything because of... you know. But I put on this dress for him and all."

"It may not be what you want to hear right now, Annie, but you look very pretty in that dress," Matt said tenderly with a smile.

"Thank you, Matty. Reid didn't say anything about it at all."

"Maybe he was just waiting until later when you were alone. I want you to know I never told Victoria Madison anything about what we've done, Annie. Not her or anyone else. It's none of their business."

"She was so mean to me and she flirted with Reid just to annoy me."

"That's Victoria for you. She flirts with everyone. It's just a game to her. I admit I'm not any better, Annie. I've been with too many girls I didn't even like. I just wanted to date them because they were pretty."

"You've always been good to me, Matty. You could have had sex with me if you wanted."

"I told you before why I didn't, Annie. You are someone I care about. It seems backward, doesn't it? The girls I don't care about are the ones I try to have sex with and the girl I care most about, I don't. Go figure!"

"You really care about me, Matty? Are you saying you love me?"

For a moment he didn't say anything as he looked into her eyes.

"I suppose I do in a way, Annie O'Dell. I know we would be good together if we went that way. You turn me on just as much as I do you. Did I ever tell you that before?"

"No, do I really?"

"You better believe it!"

Matt leaned over and kissed her cheek.

"Do you feel better now, Annie?"

"Yes, can you take me home now, please."

"Whatever you want, Annie."

Matt took Annie back to Howe Hall. They parked the car and Matt went inside with her. Reid was sitting where he could see the front door. He saw Annie and Matt as they entered. He jumped up and ran over to her.

"Annie, are you okay? Where have you been? I was worried. You didn't answer your phone."

"I'm all right, Reid. I'm sorry I ran off without telling you, but I was so upset."

179

Matt stood behind Annie as she talked to Reid.

"Victoria said some things to me that upset me. I grabbed my coat and took off. Oh, this is Matty Sullivan, by the way. Matt, this is Reid Smagala."

Matt and Reid shook hands.

"I called Matty because I needed to talk to him about some of the things Victoria said. I met him at the library. We went to the Riverwalk and sat in his car and talked."

"I'm just glad you're okay, Annie."

Matt touched her shoulder. "I should go, Annie. You and Reid probably want to be alone."

She turned around and hugged Matt while Reid watched. "Thank you for being a friend, Matty."

"Thanks for taking care of Annie, Matt," Reid said.

"It's not a problem, Reid. Annie is my friend. She may be my only true friend. It was nice to meet you. I'll talk to you later, Annie. Call me."

"Night, Matty. Thanks for being there."

Reid listened to the emotion in Annie's voice as she talked to Matt. He could tell she and Matt shared a strong bond, but didn't know if it was because of any physical intimacy. He checked his cell phone and noticed he missed a call from Victoria Madison.

Matt took off and Annie and Reid went up to her room. Annie sat on her bed and Reid turned the chair from her desk around so he could face her.

"I meant to tell you earlier, but I didn't get a chance. You look very pretty tonight, Annie."

Annie had a tear in her eye as she reached out to hug Reid.

"Thank you, Reid. That means a lot to me tonight. In case you haven't figured it out yet, Matty is the..."

"I know who he is, Annie. You don't have to explain anything. He seems like a good friend."

"He is a good friend," Annie stressed the point. "I know he's a player with the girls, but he has always been a friend to me." Annie looked at Reid and confessed, "Sometimes he has been more than just a friend. I didn't lie when I said I was a virgin though. I still am."

180

"Annie, you don't have to tell me anything about you and Matt. If you can get past the fact Steph and I lived together, then I can live with whatever you and Matt have done."

"I haven't eaten any marshmallows lately," she said.

"I'm happy to hear that."

"I need to tell you the bonfire is still there. I have just been trying to stay far enough away to not get burned."

"That's a good idea, Annie."

"I would ask you to stay for awhile, Reid, but this is not a good time."

He looked at her for a moment. "Ah, I get it. I should go home."

Annie walked Reid to the door and he kissed her good night. As he hurried down the stairs he dialed a number on his cell phone. After the third ring he heard Victoria answer.

"Are you still at the party?" Reid asked.

"I moved to a different house. It's quieter here, but I still want to party."

"I might be able to help you out," he said.

Chapter Twenty-Nine

"Daniel, I think we need to..."

"What is it, Liam? Are you all right?" Mr. Kemmerick asked as he stood up. "You don't look so good."

"I don't feel so good. I think maybe you should call 9-1-1."

Mr. Kemmerick immediately dialed 9-1-1 and then helped Principal O'Dell into a chair. The ambulance arrived at Roosevelt High in two minutes and in ten minutes Principal Liam O'Dell was on his way to the hospital. The paramedics worked quickly and efficiently. Since it was during the third period, most students and teachers were in their classrooms. The ambulance came and left without disrupting classes. Mr. Kemmerick searched for Detective O'Dell's cell phone number on his computer. Keith answered on the third ring.

"Hello, Dan. Anything wrong?" he asked while reading a file on a suspect.

"Keith, I have some bad news for you. Liam was just taken to the hospital in an ambulance."

"What happened?" He dropped the file onto his desk and grabbed his keys.

"It appears to be his heart. The paramedics got here really quick and he seems to be doing all right. They said he was stable."

"Do you know if they're taking him to St. Bart's?"

"Yes. They should be there in a few minutes. I'm sorry, Keith."

"I appreciate the call, Dan." He threw on his coat while walking out of the office.

"I'll tell the staff, but I won't make an announcement to the students."

"Thanks, I'll call you back as soon as I know anything," Keith said.

Detective O'Dell made it to St. Bart's two minutes after the ambulance. He rushed into the ER and saw the paramedics who brought in his father. They saw Keith and met him.

"He's going to be all right, Detective. We were able to keep him stable. His vitals are all right. It appears he probably suffered a mild heart attack. Dr. Grant Biran is with him now. I'm almost sure they will admit him and it will take a while. You should just wait out here. Dr. Biran will come and talk to you as soon as he can."

"Thanks, Jim. Thanks, Yolanda. I appreciate you guys."

"Thanks, Detective," Jim said and they shook hands. "He's a tough old bird. He'll be giving the nurses hell by tomorrow."

Jim and Yolanda left to fill out some paperwork. Detective O'Dell pulled out his cell phone. He thought for a moment and made a decision. He called Elisabeth.

"Hi. I'm sorry to bother you at work, but Liam is in the hospital. He's had a heart attack."

"Oh, Keith! Is he all right? I mean is he going to be all right?"

"It wasn't real serious according to the paramedics who brought him in."

"Do you want me to come over to the hospital? Is he at St. Bart's?"

"Yeah. I need to call Annie. Could you call Mace and see if he knows where Annie is right now. This is what I would like to do..." Detective O'Dell explained everything to Elisabeth.

"His phone is ringing now, Keith," Elisabeth said to him as she called Mace on her work phone.

"Hey, Mom! What's up?" Mace asked.

"Mace, I need you to do something for me."

"Sure, is there something wrong? You sound serious. Is Keyshon okay?"

"He's fine but Grandpa Liam is in the hospital. Do you know where Annie is?"

"Sure! She's in her Lit class. They should be just about done."

"Can you go over there and be with her. Keith is going to call her and tell her. He would appreciate it if you were there with her when he called."

"I'm on my way there now. Just hang on and I'll tell you when I see her."

Mace ran to Lancashire Hall. He knew the room where Annie's class met. The class had just ended and Mace saw Annie with two other girls.

"I see her, Mom. Tell Detective O'Dell I'm with her."

Mace ended the call, walked over to Annie and she saw him. Mace smiled and tried not to look upset.

"Hey, Mace! What's up? Did you want to see me?"

"Yeah, I did."

At that moment Annie's phone rang. She reached into her backpack and saw it was her father calling. She held up a finger. "It's Daddy. I should probably answer."

Mace nodded his head and moved behind Annie. He put his hands on her shoulders.

"Hi, Daddy! Did I leave my Psych book at home? I couldn't find it in my room."

"I think I saw it on the kitchen island, sweetie. Is Mace there with you?"

"Yeah, he's right here." She looked over her shoulder at Mace and could tell something was not right. "Daddy, are you all right? Is there something wrong? Why does Mace look like a hound dog with bad news?"

Dad took a deep breath. "Grandpa is in the hospital. He wasn't feeling well at school so they brought him to St. Bart's."

Mace was close enough to hear Detective O'Dell as he talked to Annie. He tightened his grip on Annie.

"Why did they take him to St. Bart's? Is Grandpa okay?" she asked.

"He might have a problem with his heart, Annie."

Mace could feel Annie trembling and held on to her.

"He's stable now according to the paramedics who brought him in. They are sure he will be admitted. I wanted to tell you as soon as I could. Mace can drive you over here, sweetie. I'll meet you in the ER."

"Okay, Daddy."

Her father could tell Annie was crying and was glad Mace was with her. Annie hung up and turned to face Mace. She leaned against his chest and sobbed. Mace put a hand on her back and the other on her hair as he held her close.

"He's going to be all right, Annie. He'll be all right," Mace

184

said a couple of times.

Annie straightened up and wiped her face with her hand. "Will you take me to St. Bart's?"

"Yes," Mace said as he took her backpack. "I'll carry this for you. Do you have your keys?"

"They're in my pocket," she answered.

They left Lancashire Hall and hurried over to the Howe Hall parking area to get Annie's car. Annie didn't say a word as they ran to her car. She tossed the keys to Mace and they took off.

"Did Daddy tell you to find me and be with me?"

"He called Mom and she called me, but, yeah, he wanted to make sure I was with you before he called."

"Thanks, Mace. You're always there for me."

"I try to be, Annie. Your father knows how much you love Grandpa Liam and he knew how you would react."

After Mace and Annie arrived at St. Bart's and parked the car, they ran into the ER. Annie looked to the right and Mace to the left.

"There's your father, Annie!" Mace pointed.

They ran over to where he was talking to a doctor.

"We're here, Daddy! How is Grandpa?"

Annie hugged her father and he held onto her shoulders.

"Dr. Biran was just explaining everything to me. Grandpa will be in intensive care just as soon as they can get him up there. We can see him now, but just for a couple of minutes."

Dr. Biran led them to the curtained area where Grandpa was resting on a gurney.

He saw Keith, Annie and Mace and waved a hand. "I told them I'm okay, but they won't listen. Can you talk some sense into them? They want to keep me here for a few hours. You guys didn't need to rush over here."

Keith looked at his father and shook his head. "You are a stubborn old man. You're going to stay here until the doctors say you are okay."

"Hospitals are for sick people."

"Grandpa!" Annie exclaimed. "You don't look good. You look kinda grayish."

"Oh, come here, Annie girl." He held out his arms.

Annie moved next to his bed and Mace was right behind her holding her as she cried.

"There now, child. You don't need to be crying. I'm not going anywhere just yet. Except maybe to one of them rooms upstairs where I can bother all the pretty nurses."

Annie held his hand. "You better not pester the nurses. They are busy with other patients. I'll stay with you and take care of you."

The doctor came back in and said, "We're going to take Principal O'Dell upstairs in a couple of minutes. Did I mention I graduated from Roosevelt myself?"

"I thought you looked familiar. Biran. I remember that name now. You were class valedictorian in... sorry I don't remember the year."

"Class of '82."

A porter arrived to move Grandpa upstairs twenty minutes later.

"Now you have to do exactly what I say, Principal O'Dell," he said as he smiled at Liam. "Do you remember me?"

Grandpa looked at for for a moment, then a flash of recognition flashed across his face.

"I remember you now. You graduated about six years ago. Kolin Hawley, right?"

"That's me."

"If I remember correctly, you played football and wanted to become a doctor. How's that working out for you?"

"I earned my degree from North Park and I'm in my second year at Rush Medical School in the city. I work here part-time to help pay the bills."

Grandpa was moved to intensive care. Keith, Annie and Mace headed upstairs to a waiting area for the intensive care patients.

Elisabeth arrived a half hour later.

"How is he, Keith?" she asked as she kissed him on the cheek.

"He seems to be doing all right. He was trying to make us

186

think nothing happened. He claims he is ready to go home."

Elisabeth turned to Annie. "Are you okay?"

Annie stood next to Mace and held tightly onto his hand without appearing to realize it. It was obvious she had been crying. "I'm all right. Does Keyshon know?"

"I didn't tell him anything yet. Mrs. Casilio will watch him after school just like always. I told Barbara not to tell him anything yet."

They sat down to wait. An hour later Keith was allowed to see him. Grandpa looked tired and went to sleep. Keith waited several minutes and then went back to the waiting room.

Annie jumped up as her father entered. "How is he?"

"He's sleeping, sweetie. You and Mace should go get something to eat. You must be hungry."

"I'm not hungry, but I am thirsty. Do you need anything, Daddy?"

"I could use a Coke or something."

"Okay. Do you want anything, Mom?"

"I'll share your father's, Annie. Thanks."

Annie and Mace headed out to find a vending machine. Elisabeth looked at Keith and smiled.

He smiled back. "She called you Mom. She's never called you Mom before to the best of my knowledge."

"She probably didn't even realize it, Keith."

"I think she did."

Mace and Annie found a vending machine and bought drinks for everyone.

"Annie, do you realize what you called my mother?" Mace asked.

"I called her Mom. Does that bother you, Mace? She and Daddy could get married one of these days."

"Not at all, Annie. Not at all," he said as he grinned.

Keith made everyone go home around ten o'clock while he stayed overnight. Mace took Annie back to her dorm room and stayed with her until midnight.

"How is Grandpa doing?" Annie asked when her father

called the next morning.

"He seems to be resting all right. They woke him up several times during the night. They're taking him downstairs for some tests in a few minutes. I want you to go to your classes today, Annie. You can visit Grandpa after you are finished. If anything changes, I'll call you.

"Promise, Daddy?"

"I promise, Annie."

Grandpa stayed in the hospital for five days before going home. Annie came to see him every day after classes.

Matt called Annie on Wednesday. "I just heard about your grandfather. How's he doing?"

"He's doing better. I'm going to St. Bart's after my class." She hesitated a moment and asked, "Would you like to go with me?"

"Sure," he said. "This will be a first. I have to go see Principal O'Dell and I'm not in trouble."

Keith brought his father home on Saturday afternoon. Annie was already at the farm.

"I don't know what all the fuss was about. I feel fine and I'm not going to let you treat me like an invalid," he said while pointing a finger at Keith and Annie.

"Grandpa, the doctors said you can't go back to work for two months."

"Bah! What do they know."

"What are you thinking about, Grandpa?" Annie asked later. "You haven't touched your food."

"I'm sorry, sweetie. I don't have much of an appetite. Can I tell you something?"

"Sure, what's up?"

"I've made up my mind. I'm going to retire at the end of the year. I've got other priorities now and I want to be around to see my favorite granddaughter finish college."

"You know I'm your only granddaughter, right? But that's still sweet."

Chapter Thirty

"Erin, did you see the *Chronicle*? There's an article about the basketball team." Annie sat on her bed reading the school paper.

Erin walked out of the bathroom with a towel around her wet hair. "Can you read it to me? Does it mention Mace?"

"He's mentioned once," Annie said. "I'll read the highlights."

"Give me a second to get ready for bed first."

Annie waited until Erin climbed under the covers. "Here goes. The final game of the regular season will determine the conference basketball champion. North Park is hosting the Columbus Voyagers. Each team has one loss in the conference. The Voyagers defeated North Park earlier in Columbus. With Arnett Robinson healthy, the Redbirds are deeper with his ability to come off the bench and spark the offense. He shares time at small forward with Darrion Cunningham, who is a better defender, but not much of a scoring threat." Annie stopped and shook her head. "Darrion won't like that."

"No, but Mace said it's true," Erin said as she turned onto her side to face Annie. "Is there more?"

"Yeah. Where was I?" Annie found her place and continued, "The combination of Kevin Murphy and Mace Franklin at the guard spots has proven to be the best in the conference." Annie rolled her eyes. "Don't let Mace see this. Anyway, it says Damian Gibson and Javarius Mays are almost unstoppable on the interior. With a record of 22-3, the Redbirds have enjoyed their best season in over sixty years."

"Who wrote the article?" Erin asked.

Annie checked and said, "Tommy Hernandez. He's in one of my classes."

The gym overflowed on Tuesday night as the two teams got ready to decide the conference title. The students stomped on the bleachers as they waited impatiently for the team to take the court. Annie and all her friends sat together. Annie even purchased tickets for Matt Sullivan and Joni McAllister.

"There they are, Reid," Annie said as she grabbed his arm and pointed. "Be nice, okay."

"I'll be civil, Annie. I'm not going to be his best friend, but I will be civil because he is your friend."

Annie waved to Matt and he saw her. He and Joni made their way to their seats.

"Hi, guys. Ready for the big game?" Annie asked.

"Annie, this is Joni. This is Annie and her friend Reid."

Annie and Joni smiled and exchanged pleasantries. Reid and Matt nodded at each other. Annie and Joni sat next to each other with the guys on either side.

"Have you been to many of the games, Joni?"

"I've been to a few. I've been working a lot and finishing up my degree. So between that and getting ready for the baby I haven't had much free time. Matthew told me you went to Roosevelt together."

"Yes, we've known each other for several years."

"Matt told me you are his only real friend."

"He's got other friends, I'm sure. How are you and the baby doing?" Annie asked as she looked at Joni's stomach.

"We're doing fine. We found out we're having a girl."

"Oh that's perfect," Annie cooed. "If I ever have a family I want a girl first."

Annie reached over and touched Matt's arm to get his attention.

"Congratulations, Matty. Just think! A little girl."

"Yeah, can you picture me as a daddy with a daughter?"

"Yeah, I can. I think you'll make a good father, Matty."

Reid touched Annie's arm. "I think the players are about ready to come out of the locker room. Are you going to scream at Mace?"

"Maybe I shouldn't. It might scare the baby," Annie said.

The game began and the Redbirds started off fast by hitting their first five shots. They built up a double digit lead after five minutes and kept it for the whole game. As the buzzer sounded to end the game, Annie looked up at the scoreboard. The final score shone in bright lights—78-63—in favor of North Park. The Redbirds were going to the NCAA tournament for the first time in their history. They didn't know who or where they would be playing, but they were in the big dance.

The entire team and all the coaches gathered together in the locker room on Sunday evening to watch the unveiling of the brackets for the NCAA tournament. When the team learned they would be playing the Michigan Wolverines in Indianapolis on Thursday afternoon they rose to their feet and began to holler.

Annie and Erin skipped a class on Wednesday to see the team off.

"Just relax and try to think of this as just another game," Annie said to Mace as he got ready to board the bus.

"What do you mean? I'm as chill as I could be," Mace said as he listened to some tunes on his Discman.

"We will be cheering for you guys," Erin said and then kissed Mace.

Coach Bazetich herded everyone onto the bus. Annie and Erin, along with over a hundred other students cheered until the bus disappeared from sight.

On Thursday afternoon, in the biggest upset of the day, little North Park College defeated the mighty Michigan Wolverines by eight points. Mace led the team with seventeen points and enjoyed his best shooting day of the year. He only missed one shot the whole game. Everyone who started scored in double figures— even Kevin Murphy. He hit all six free throws at the end of the game to finish with ten points. The Redbirds dominated the rebounding stats. That and Michigan's inability to make free throws cost them the game.

Mace called Erin as soon as he could.

"I can't believe you won," Erin shouted into the phone which she placed on speaker mode.

"Why?" Mace asked. "I knew we would win as soon as we took the court. I could tell they were uptight and nervous. We have better athletes than a lot of the teams in the tournament."

"Are you getting a big head?" Annie asked. "You just won one game. There are plenty of teams left who want to win it all."

"We're not getting cocky, but we feel we can play with any team in the country," Mace said.

"Where are you staying?" Annie asked.

Mace shrugged and answered, "Not sure. Oh, wait. It's a rundown joint called the Super Oasis Travel Court."

"Are you making that up?" Annie asked.

"He is. I can tell," Erin said. "Where are you really staying?"

"It's the Westin something or other. The school splurged. I could get used to living in a place like this."

"Yeah, you better keep winning or else it's back to Humphrey Hall for you," Annie teased.

On Saturday the team faced the Louisville University Cardinals, still in Indianapolis. This time Cinderella lost. The Redbirds were no match for the more talented Cardinals. They lost by nineteen points 88-69; the most points scored against them all year. Coach Bazetich was pleased with his team's effort throughout the game. He realized they were simply up against a superior team. With a final record of 24-4, it was an excellent year for North Park College. Coach knew he would have to replace Damian Gibson, but he had an inside track on a player who might fill the void. Kevin Murphy was honored as the team's MVP. His leadership would be hard to replace, but Coach felt he already had the right guy for that job—Mace Franklin.

Chapter Thirty-One

March 27 was the last day of classes before spring break. Most of the out of town students headed for home, but some of them headed for Florida. A few of the SoHam kids made plans to head for the warm sunshine and friendly beaches of Daytona Beach. Annie heard about the plans of some of her friends, but expressed no interest in joining them.

Elaine and Adrien took a trip to Kansas City to find an apartment for Adrien after he graduated.

"I really think you should transfer and join me," Adrien said as they approached Kansas City.

"Which college would I attend?" Elaine asked. "I can't go to the seminary like you."

"Well, the University of Kansas has a campus in Overland Heights and the University of Missouri has one of their campuses right in Kansas City."

Elaine shook her head. "Those schools are too big. I'm more comfortable at a smaller university."

"I'm sure there are smaller colleges in the area. We could do some research when we arrive."

"Are you forgetting something, Adrien?"

"What's that?"

"What we discussed at the holidays. The only way I will even consider transferring is if we are married."

"Did you mention that to your parents?" he asked. "Our exit is coming up in five miles."

"I haven't come right out and told them, but I'm pretty sure they assume we will get married."

Cindy and Bryce stayed at the Mackens home for the first week of break to keep an eye on Cindy's thirteen-year-old sister Maddy while their parents were on vacation. Cindy decided to have sex with Bryce over the break and did not expect any interference. However, Cindy's plan hit a roadblock when her older brother Marshall came home unexpectedly for his spring break.

"What are you doing here?" Cindy hollered when she saw

her brother. "I thought you were going to spend your break with Dania. You didn't break up did you?"

"No, we didn't break up and before you even ask, Mom did not ask me to come home to keep an eye on you and Bryce."

"Why would I think that? How did you know Bryce was staying here?"

"I didn't until now. Where is he, anyway?" Marshall asked as he plopped down on the living room couch.

"You're so mean," Cindy said after realizing she gave her secret away. "He just ran to the store to get something for dinner tonight. Where are you going to sleep?"

"In my room, of course."

"Then where is Bryce supposed to sleep?" Cindy asked with her hands on her hips.

"Come on! Don't pretend with me, Cin. I know he was going to sleep in your room after Maddy goes to bed. What time does Maddy get home from school?"

Cindy frowned. "A little before three. She will be happy to see you."

"Good at least one of my sisters will be happy."

"I'm happy to see you, Marshall. I just didn't know you were coming home. Do you think Mom and Dad would mind if Bryce sleeps in their room?"

"I'm sure they would rather he slept in their room than in yours. Have you guys..."

"No! And I wouldn't tell you if we had."

Marshall grinned. "But you were planning to this week. I can tell."

"I hate you!" Cindy blushed because Marshall was right. "Even if we were and I'm not saying we were, we can't now."

"I'm not planning on being here all day, every day. I'm got friends to visit and things to do. You will have your privacy."

Marshall got up, walked into the kitchen and opened the fridge looking for something to drink. Cindy followed him. Just then Bryce walked in the back door.

"Hello, Bryce. What's for dinner?" Marshall asked.

Bryce set the two bags of groceries on the counter and

looked at Cindy. "Hi, Marshall. I didn't know you were coming home."

"Neither did Cindy," Marshall said and then laughed.

Cindy walked over and put her hand on Bryce's arm. "It's okay. Marshall won't be here all the time. We can still have our privacy."

"You didn't tell him..."

"She didn't have to, Bryce. I know my sister is growing up and don't worry, I won't say a word to anyone."

"Great! This is just great," Bryce exclaimed sarcastically.

Cindy glared at her brother.

Adrien and Elaine checked into their room in Kansas City.

"Where are we going to eat?" Elaine asked while checking out the bed. "I'm famished."

"Kansas City is famous for barbecue and there's a place called Arthur Edwards Smokehouse Bar-B-Q that is outstanding."

"Have you eaten there before?"

He nodded. "I found it the last time I was in town."

"Sounds good to me," Elaine said.

They freshened up and headed to the restaurant.

"Did you like it?" Adrien asked after they finished.

Elaine wiped her mouth on a napkin and nodded. "I really like the sauce."

"Do you have room for dessert?"

She took a deep breath, exhaled and said, "Not really. You can order something if you want."

"Maybe tomorrow."

He paid the check.

"Are we ready to go?" Elaine asked. She drank the last of her pop and started to get up.

"Not quite yet, Lainey. I need to ask you something first," Adrien said as he reached into his pocket and pulled out a jewel case.

Elaine put a hand to her mouth.

"Lainey, will you..."

They spent their first night together as an engaged couple.

Elaine called Cindy in the morning to tell her the news.

"He actually proposed in the restaurant!?" Cindy squealed.

"Yes!" Elaine exclaimed. "And I said yes. You should see my ring, Cin. It's so beautiful. I can't wait to show you."

"Did you... you know?"

"It was so romantic. Did you and Bryce?"

"No! Marshall came home and ruined everything. Can you believe it? He showed up yesterday afternoon out of the blue."

"What are you and Bryce going to do?"

"Marshall promised he would leave us alone during the day."

"Does he know what you are going to do?"

"He guessed, Lainey," Cindy said and then sighed. "We didn't tell him. He's not stupid you know."

"I'll talk to you later, Cindy. I gotta go."

"Bye, Lainey. I can't wait to see your ring."

When Marshall returned that evening, just before dinner, he took one look at Cindy, who was sitting on the couch reading a *Bride* magazine and he knew.

"What?" Cindy asked while still reading her magazine.

"Are you all right, Cin?" Marshall asked as he stood in front of her.

"Yes, I'm okay. How can you tell? It doesn't show, does it?"

"I can see it in your eyes. They have a new sparkle to them. Where's Bryce?"

"You won't tell..."

"Never! I swear it."

Cindy grinned. "He had to go to work."

Chapter Thirty-Two

Annie spent the first week of break at the farm helping Grandpa recover from his heart attack. Reid spent his days working but called her a couple of times at night.

Nick Whitaker called Thursday evening. "Hey, Reid, what are you and Annie doing this weekend? You are still dating Annie right, or did you break up with her?"

Reid shrugged then said, "I think we are are still dating, but I haven't seen her as often lately. She's been staying at her grandfather's house and helping him. He had a heart attack."

"Right, I remember you telling me about that. I hope he's all right. Anyway, Avanna wanted me to tell you she's having another party this Saturday and wanted to see you. You can bring Annie, or that other girl, if you want. Was her name Victoria? Anyway, there will be some available unattached females at the party if you want to check them out."

"Is it at her Grandma's?"

"Yep! Another one like last time. Grandma is home from Florida and will be there. Avanna has invited about twenty kids from high school and some of her college friends will be there. Her brother and his girlfriend are in town," Nick mentioned knowing that would please Reid.

"Drew and Leslie are in town? Where are they staying?"

"With his grandmother at the house. Do you think you can make it?" Nick asked.

"I'll talk to Annie and let you know tonight. If she can't go, I will just come alone."

"I'll tell Avanna to save a room for you. That's all right isn't it?"

"Yeah, sure. I'll call you back after I talk to Annie." Reid thought about it for several minutes. *I could ask Victoria. She likes to party.* He dialed Victoria, but she didn't answer. He hung up without leaving a message. Then he called Annie. "Hi! I just got a call from Nicky. Avanna is having a party at her Grandma's this Saturday and we're invited. Interested?"

"Yeah! I was thinking of calling you. Daddy and Mom are

staying with Grandpa this weekend so I can have some free time."

"Mom? Who do you mean by Mom?"

"Oh, I started calling Mrs. Franklin, Mom. I'll ask Daddy if it's okay and call you right back."

Reid didn't tell Annie about staying overnight. Annie called her father and asked permission.

"It would be good for you to get away and have some fun, Annie. You are on vacation after all."

Annie called Reid back. "I can go. What should I bring?"

"Bring a bikini if you have one. Jeans and tops, of course, or maybe that yellow sundress I saw in your closet."

"Why do you want me to bring that dress?" Annie asked as she opened her closet.

"I want to see how it looks on you."

"Okay," she said as she held the dress up. "What time are we going to leave?"

"I'll pick you up at noon Saturday. Is that all right?"

"I'll be ready."

"Are you ready to go?" Reid asked as he met Annie at her house on Saturday.

"I'm all packed. It will be so much fun to see Nicky and Avanna again."

"I know they're looking forward to seeing you, Annie."

Forty-five minutes later they arrived at Avanna's grandmother's home.

"It's so good to see you again," Avanna said as she hugged Annie. "Hi, Reid. Come on, Annie. I'll introduce you to Grandma. Nicky, will you show Reid his room?"

"Sure. Hi, Annie. It's good to see you again."

"You, too, Nicky."

Nick gave Annie a hug, then he and Reid went upstairs with the bags.

"So how are things going with Annie?" Nick asked. "You guys must be doing okay since you'll be sharing a room."

"Actually... I haven't told her yet," Reid admitted. "She might be expecting to go home later."

198

"What? Why? You're planning to stay, aren't you?"

"Yeah, I don't want to drive back to SoHam in the middle of the night," Reid said. "She'll be okay with it. I can always sleep downstairs on the couch or something."

Nicky shook his head. "Did you tell her anything about this party, Reid?"

"Not really. I did tell her to bring her bikini so we can go swimming."

Downstairs in the family room, Avanna introduced Annie to her grandmother. "Gram, this is Annie O'Dell. She is Reid's little friend."

"Hello, dear. It's always good to meet Avanna's friends."

"Hey, Avanna!"

Annie turned around as she heard another voice.

"Hi! I'm Drew Bellamy. Avanna's brother. I'm actually just a half-brother. We have different mothers. I live out in California with our father and this is Leslie."

Annie didn't say a word as she stared at Leslie Alexander.

"This is Reid's friend," Avanna said. "Annie O'Dell."

"Have you known Avanna very long?" Drew asked.

"We met earlier this year. Reid brought me up here to spent a weekend."

Annie stole glances at Leslie, but didn't talk to her. Nick and Reid came back downstairs and saw Drew and Leslie.

"Hey, guys! It's good to see you. How are things out in fantasyland?"

"Hi, Nicky! Hi, Reid! Things are just peachy in paradise. Leslie signed up to do the sequel to *The Masked Stranger*. She got a higher percentage this time as well as her usual fee. It took quite a bit of negotiating this time because of the nudity clause. They wanted more than Leslie and I were willing to give them."

"How much more could they want?" Reid asked. "She was naked in the original."

"Time," Drew said. "We negotiate how much time she can be naked on screen."

"Oh, I didn't know that."

"What is it like to do a love scene, Leslie?" Annie asked.

"Believe me it's nothing like real life. It's hard work and there are guys working around you. If I never have to do another one, it will be too soon."

Annie grinned. "I watched *Show Me The Money* just so I could see Tommy Cruz's butt."

Drew laughed. "Annie, I hate to burst your bubble, but that was a butt-double."

"What do you mean?" Annie asked.

"It wasn't really Tommy Cruz's butt. It was another actor hired just to show his butt."

Annie sighed with disappointment.

"I saw that movie too, Annie, and I don't care whose butt it was. It was gorgeous," Avanna said as she put an arm around Annie's shoulder.

They all laughed. Avanna, Leslie and Annie went into the kitchen and drank tea with Grandma. The guys went downstairs to play pool.

Nick sank a ball in the corner and said, "You really should tell Annie about the room, Reid."

"I will. I'll take her up there after we finish playing pool."

"Hey, Annie, you got a minute?" Reid asked later.

"Sure, what's up?"

"I want to take you upstairs to show you the room and I want to talk to you about tonight."

She tilted her head. "What room?"

"Well, I told Nick I would spend the night. We will be partying pretty late and I don't want to drive back if I've had anything to drink."

"Okay, that kinda makes sense, but I didn't tell Daddy I would be spending the night."

"Could you call him and let him know?"

"I might not be able to reach him, but I'll try later."

Reid led Annie upstairs and into the room where he would be staying.

"I put our stuff in here," Reid said.

"This is really nice, Reid," Annie said as she checked it out. "I could live here all the time. It's got a huge bathroom and I love

200

this closet. Where will you stay?"

"We need to talk about that, Annie." Reid pulled her over to the bed and they sat on the edge. "Avanna thinks we are more than just friends now and she put us both in this room."

"What do you mean? There are more rooms up here."

"Yes, but there are other couples who are going to stay overnight in the other rooms. I meant to tell you earlier, but I didn't. I'm sorry. I can sleep on a couch downstairs. I never should have agreed to what Avanna decided."

Annie clenched her jaw and frowned at Reid. "Why did you assume I would go along with this? We haven't seen each other as much lately. I should make you take me home."

"I'm sorry, Annie. I wasn't thinking straight."

Annie looked around at the room.

"It's such a nice room and there's plenty of room. Maybe Avanna has a sleeping bag somewhere you could borrow. If not, well, there are several couches downstairs."

Reid took a deep breath, then said, "I suppose that would be best. I should have told Avanna the truth about us. She assumed we were sleeping together already."

Annie shook her head. "No way we are sharing the bed. That's not going to happen."

"There's something else I need to tell you."

"What? You can tell me, Reid."

"It's about the party. There will be lots of food and alcohol. You will probably be the only underage person here. I know you might have a beer or two and that's okay. Avanna will have music playing all throughout the downstairs. Couples will be dancing and some will probably go swimming."

"That sounds like fun. I brought my bikini. I'll show it to you later if you want to see it."

"I want to see it, Annie," he said. "Are you really going to make me sleep on a couch?"

She tried to kick Reid's shin but missed. "Absolutely! Were you just hoping I would go along with sharing a room so you could see me naked and get me into bed with you?"

He looked down at her. "I'm sorry. I should have told you I

was crashing overnight. Are you upset about that?"

"Christ, Reid!" she said as she poked him in the chest. "Yeah, I guess I am upset. I think you better find that couch now. You aren't going to share this room with me."

"I'm sorry, Annie."

She took a deep breath and then poked him again. "Did you bring me here so you could get me drunk and screw me?"

"I guess I kinda blew it. I'm so sorry. I should have told you everything from the start. Will you forgive me?"

She shook her head, took a deep breath and exhaled forcefully. "I suppose I will get over it."

He tried to kiss her, but she put a hand on his chest and kept him at a distance.

"You can't kiss me now. How much time do we have before the party starts?"

"A couple of hours. Why?"

"Well, I need to shower and change but that won't take two hours. Maybe I should take a nap."

He yawned. "I could use some shut-eye, too."

"Are you sleepy, Reid?"

He grinned. "Well, now that you mention it, I could use a nap."

"She turned him around. "There's the door. I'm sure you can find a comfy couch somewhere."

"But, Annie," he protested.

"No, buts," she said. "And I mean that literally." She pointed to the door.

"Fine, I'll go downstairs and talk to Nicky and Drew."

Annie lay on her back and tossed and turned for a few minutes. *I can't believe he expected to share a room with me.*

Reid came back upstairs at six and knocked on the door.

"Who's there?" she asked.

"It's me. Is it safe to come in?"

You can come in. I'm dressed."

He entered slowly. "It's ten after six and I need to get ready. You're wearing jeans, huh?"

She walked toward the closet. "Do you still want me to

202

wear that dress? I should wear jeans."

"I would like to see how it looks on you." He moved behind her.

"On me or off of me?" Annie asked and frowned.

"You can keep it on," he said and then swatted her bottom.

She turned and pushed him away with enough force to make him lose his balance. "Stop that! You can use the bathroom to change."

"It won't take me long to get ready. Will you wait for me?"

"I'll wait right here. I don't want to go downstairs by myself."

Reid showered and five minutes later reappeared wearing just his boxers. Annie lay on the bed reading a book she found on the nightstand. She glanced at Reid as he got dressed.

"Well, how do I look?" he asked.

She set down the book and checked him out. "You look rather handsome. I've never seen you with a tie on before."

"I thought I would wear one even if you're not wearing your dress."

They headed downstairs and Annie looked at the guests.

"Are you trying to spot another movie star?" Reid asked.

"No!" She poked him in the ribs with some authority. "Do you know all of these people?"

"Just about. Some of them are high school friends and others are Avanna's friends from college. I don't know them."

"How many people are here? Do you have any idea?"

"I didn't count them, Annie, but I would guess there are probably thirty people including us."

Nick saw them and walked over. "Hey, guys. Where have you been? Avanna's been looking for you. She wants to introduce you to her new roommates. Will you dance with me later?"

"Of course, Nicky."

"I'll pick out a slow song and we can hold each other close and see if I can make Reid jealous."

Annie giggled as she looked at Reid. "That sounds like fun."

"Are you making a move on Annie?" Reid asked.

Nick put an arm around her. "Not yet, but maybe later, I will. Come on, we gotta find Avanna."

They made their way through the crowded room to the kitchen.

"There you are. I want to introduce you to my new roommates, Reid. Come with me."

Avanna took Reid's hand and Annie followed.

"Reid, may I introduce Charlene Hittinger of Atlanta, Kim Isfeld of Memphis and Jenny Kobrovsky of Philadelphia. This is my old friend Reid Smagala. Oh, how rude of me I forgot Reid's little friend. This is Annie O'Dell."

Reid smiled. "Ladies, it's my pleasure to meet you."

Avanna took Annie's arm and pulled her away. "Annie, let me introduce you to some of the other guests."

Annie thought Avanna was trying to get her away from Reid so her roommates could flirt with him. She looked back at Reid and he was surrounded by Avanna's friends.

"Hey, Nicky, would you introduce Annie to some of the guests, please. I need to talk to Leslie."

Annie was confused by Avanna's attitude toward her now.

Nick sensed her discomfort and said, "Don't pay any attention to Avanna right now, Annie. She gets really nervous when she throws a party like this. She'll be back to normal soon enough."

"I felt like she was trying to separate me from Reid so her friends could pick over him like vultures."

Nick laughed. "You are absolutely right, Annie. Those three are vultures, but they're looking for a husband instead of dead meat. Of course if they find a husband, he will soon be dead meat. Do you want something to drink, Annie?"

"I need a beer, Nicky, and something to eat."

"Come with me, my little one. I will take care of you," Nick teased in a sexy voice.

"I like the sound of that," Annie replied as Nick pulled her away from the crowd.

They found some peace and quiet in the kitchen and Nick got a beer from the fridge for Annie. She sat on the counter where there was an empty space. He handed her a slice of pizza, which had just arrived.

"Will this do for now?"

"Thank you, Nicky."

"Are you okay with your room upstairs?" he asked as he leaned against the counter next to her.

"If you're asking if I'm all right sharing a room with Reid, no. I'm not okay with that. I never would have agreed to it had I known beforehand. He didn't even tell me he would be crashing here tonight," Annie said.

"You are special, Annie O'Dell. You can be rather captivating and charming. If you weren't Reid's girlfriend, I would be very tempted to use my charm to try and seduce you myself." Nick kissed Annie's cheek.

"You are so sweet, Nicky. I don't mean that as an insult. You are handsome and sexy. I admire how you and Reid are such good friends. Do you think he will be able to resist the vultures?"

"I'm sure he is trying to escape at this very moment."

At that moment the kitchen door opened and in walked Reid seemingly no worse for wear. "Oh, there you guys are. I was looking for you, Annie."

"Nicky brought me in here because I wanted something to eat and a beer. How did you escape the vultures?"

"I introduced them to some high school buddies who were totally smitten by their good looks—the poor suckers!"

"I told Annie that Avanna was not herself right now."

"I'm sorry, Annie. I should have warned you. Avanna is rather insecure about these parties and wants to make sure everyone is having a good time. She didn't mean to slight you."

"It's okay. As long as I have my two guys with me, I'll be all right."

"Two guys, huh?" Reid lifted his eyebrows. "Were you putting a move on Annie, Nick?"

"I tried my best, but she resisted."

"I know you don't believe him, Reid. He's been so sweet to me. Oh, sorry, Nicky. I mean he has been trying to seduce me and you rescued me just in time. I was just about to surrender my body to him right here in the kitchen. You rescued me. You're my hero!"

Nick shook his head. "You guys are so weird. I need to go see who else needs rescuing from the vultures. Don't spent the whole party in here and don't drink too many beers, Annie. I want you to be sober when I dance with you later. Sober so I can seduce you properly."

Nick kissed her cheek again and left.

"If you weren't with me, Annie, I do believe my good buddy, Nicky, would make a move on you."

"He told me that earlier," Annie said and then took a bite of her pizza.

"He really likes you, Annie. He told me I was very lucky to have met you." Reid looked into her eyes. "I'm sorry about earlier. Will you forgive me?"

"You're forgiven. Should we go mingle with the other guests?" Annie asked as she jumped down from the countertop.

"In a minute. First I need to kiss you."

Reid was kissing Annie when Avanna walked in.

"Oh, Annie! I'm so sorry for how I treated you earlier. Forgive me?"

"I forgive you. Reid and Nicky explained everything."

Avanna moved close to Annie.

"Reid, would you move out of the way so I can hug Annie. You can kiss her all you want later tonight." Avanna hugged Annie and kissed her. "I shouldn't get so nervous about these parties, but I do. I know that's no reason for me to have treated you the way I did. I'm sorry, Annie. Are we still friends?"

"It's all right. I understand and we are still friends."

"Good! Now you guys need to get out of the kitchen and have fun. You can make out later."

Reid looked at Annie. She shook her head and whispered, "Ain't gonna happen."

Chapter Thirty-Three

Annie walked beside Reid as they left the kitchen. They immediately ran into someone Reid knew.

"Reid, how are you? I haven't seen you for a couple of years."

"Hi, Allan. It's been a while, huh? You doing all right?"

"Yeah. I graduated last year and I'm working at the bank for my father."

"This is my friend, Annie O'Dell, from college. Annie, this is Allan Goldstein. We were high school friends."

"Nice to meet you, Allan," Annie said.

Reid and Annie mingled and he introduced her to his old friends. Most of whose names she instantly forgot as they did hers. A variety of food covered the table and buffet in the dining room and guests helped themselves. Plenty of beer, water and even some soft drinks were on ice in the kitchen and pool area. Music played on built-in speakers throughout the house. Some of the guests were dancing in the large family room.

"Do you think all these people will stay all night?" Annie asked Reid.

"Not all of them." Reid shook his head. "Avanna has arranged for the people she wants to spent the night to have rooms upstairs. Some of the guests might hang around til morning and crash down here. Not all of them will go swimming later either."

"Are we going to go swimming?"

"I'll leave the final decision to you, Annie, but I'd like to."

"I'll see how it goes, Reid."

By eight o'clock some of the guests had made their way to the pool. Reid and Annie were in the kitchen talking to Nick and Avanna.

"Reid, let's see how crowded the pool is. If it's too crowded, I'd rather wait till later."

"It's going to be rather full right now, Annie," he answered.

"How crowded?"

"I saw at least twenty people headed that way," Avanna answered.

"I say we go swimming. How about it, Reid? I think Avanna's roommates are in the pool," Nicky said.

"Then I'm definitely not going. Annie will get upset if I go swimming with them around."

"No, I won't. You can talk to them and let them flirt with you just as long as you stay with me tonight."

Reid, Nick and Avanna stared at Annie.

"I didn't mean it like that! We are not sharing a room, guys. I'm definitely not going to have sex tonight. You can deal with that anyway you want."

"Are you sure, Annie?"

"Yes, Avanna! I'm not ready yet. I know I want my first time to be special and getting drunk at a party, then getting laid is not my idea of something special. No offense!" She waved her hands. "If you guys want to go swimming now, I don't mind. I'm going back to the family room and take a break."

"I'll see you later, Annie."

"Okay, Reid. Have a good time," Annie said the sarcasm escaping Reid.

Annie headed to the family room while Reid, Nick and Avanna moved to the pool. Annie saw Leslie and Drew and walked over to talk to them. She listened as they talked about movies for a few minutes, then left. She heard someone in the living room and discovered it was Avanna's grandmother. Annie talked to her for a few minutes about the house and Avanna's father.

"I need to excuse myself, Annie. I'm tired, so I think I'll go to my room. You have some fun tonight. You're only young once."

"I will. I just don't feel comfortable in a crowd sometimes."

"You mean you didn't want to go swimming with a bunch of boys staring at you. That's understandable and nothing to be ashamed about. Avanna has no guilt about something like that. It doesn't make her a bad person. Maybe I'll see you in the morning, Annie."

"Good night... I don't know what I should call you," Annie said.

"My name is Ava—Ava Bellamy. You can call me that."

"Were you a movie star, too?"

"That was a very long time ago, dear. I can barely remember what it was like."

Ava hugged her, then went to her private bedroom suite on the first floor. Annie grabbed another beer and drank it quickly. She walked around, then wandered into the pool area. She looked around for Reid. She saw Nick and Avanna sitting beside the pool. She kept looking and saw Reid in the pool with the 'vultures.' The roommates sat on the edge of the pool with their feet in the water while Reid floated in the water in front of them. She watched for a moment, then looked at Nicky. He waved at her. Annie turned around and left. She wasn't too upset with Reid, but a little disappointed. She headed upstairs to her room. She lay on her back on the bed and thought about Grandpa. She reached for her cell phone. She flipped it open and thought about calling Matt. She sighed and closed her phone forgetting to call her father. She fell asleep because of the beer and only woke up because she heard a loud knock on the door.

"Come in," Annie said.

"Annie, are you all right?" Nick walked over and sat on the edge of the bed. "I wondered what happened to you."

"I'm okay, Nicky. I guess I fell asleep. I've been taking care of Grandpa and not getting much sleep. What time is it?" Annie asked as she sat up.

"It's ten-thirty."

"Do you know where Reid is?"

"I saw him just before I came up here. He and Avanna and her roommates and Drew and Leslie were all in the media room watching movies. Do you want to watch with him?"

Annie sat on the edge of the bed next to Nicky. "No, do you think there are many people in the pool area now?"

"Might be a few still swimming or in the Jacuzzi. Why?"

"I want to go swimming now, Nicky. Will you go with me?"

" I will if you want. I would like to see you in your bikini."

"You'll be disappointed, Nicky. I don't have much to see."

Annie used the bathroom, changed into her bikini and put

209

her dress on over her suit. She and Nicky went downstairs to the pool area. Annie saw two guests in the Jacuzzi and two couples in the pool. She looked at Nicky and he looked at her. Annie stepped back and undid her sundress. Nick watched as Annie let it fall to the floor. Nick looked at her as she stood in front of him in just her bikini.

"Well?" she asked.

"Wow! You look fantastic, Annie."

"Oh, Nicky! You don't have to say that. I know it's not true. I have an ordinary body. I don't have big breasts like Avanna's roommates and some of your other friends."

"You are still sexy looking, Annie. Looking sexy is more than just large breasts. Come on, let's get in the pool. Maybe if I'm lucky your top will come off at just the right moment."

"I thought you didn't want to see me," she said.

Nicky smiled. "I'm only human, Annie."

Annie looked at Nicky for a moment as she thought about what he said. She looked at Nicky and they held hands as they walked over to the pool and got in. They swam for a few minutes, then Annie leaned against the side of the pool. Nick moved in front of her and put his hands on the edge on either side of Annie. Suddenly, Annie remembered the night in Peoria when she was alone in the pool with Matthew Sullivan.

"You look perfect, Annie."

"I have funny tan lines under my bikini. Do you think I should get rid of them?"

"No. I think Reid would like to see your tan lines."

"Do you want to see them?"

"I saw a little bit of them before we got in the pool. I thought it made you look even sexier. Girls who are tan all over are not as mysterious."

Annie waited to see if Nick was going to kiss her, but he didn't. They swam for another few minutes, then got out of the pool. She and Nick grabbed towels from the stack, dried off, then wrapped the towels around their waists. They sat down in a corner on a love seat facing each other. They talked for several minutes as Nicky told her stories about growing up in the city.

"Are you disappointed my top didn't come off, Nicky?"

"I would be lying if I said I wasn't a little disappointed. I did see some of your tan lines though. We should get dressed and find the other guys, Annie."

"We should go back upstairs so I can get dressed. I don't want to put my dress on over my wet bikini."

Nick followed Annie to her room. She again used the bathroom to change.

"Let's find Reid and Avanna. The night is still young and I want to have more fun. I want to dance with you again," Nicky said.

"I feel like I have more energy now than before. I guess the swim did me some good. Thanks, Nicky. Thanks for everything."

"You're welcome, Annie O'Dell. Who knows? We might have other chances in the future to use the pool." Nick smiled at Annie and she knew exactly what he meant.

Nick and Annie headed downstairs and found Reid and Avanna still watching movies with the same people as before. She saw Reid sitting in a large recliner by himself, walked up behind him and kissed the top of his head.

Reid looked over his shoulder. "Annie! You woke up. I was worried you were done for the night."

"How did you know I was sleeping?"

"Because I checked on you. I went up to the room, and you were sound asleep. I didn't want to disturb you, so I left."

"I went swimming with Nicky. I just wanted you to know," Annie said.

"Are you upset I went swimming without you?" Reid asked.

"At first I was a little disappointed, but I'm over it now. I don't care you were with the roommates."

"They don't mean anything to me, Annie," he whispered.

Annie sat on the wide recliner with Reid until the movie ended.

"Who's hungry?" Avanna asked.

"Is there any pizza left?" Drew asked.

The whole group decided to get some more food and

something to drink. They raided the kitchen and hung out in there. After finishing the last of the pizza, they headed back to the family room. Avanna turned the music up so they could dance. Avanna played a slow song and Nicky danced with Annie.

"You feel pretty good in my arms, Annie," Nick said.

"I shouldn't have had that last beer," she replied. "I went over my limit."

Annie and Nicky danced again as another slow song played.

"Nicky, I'm ready for bed," Avanna said. "Will you help me check the house?"

Most everyone had gone home. There were a few people in the pool area. Nick told them to crash wherever they wanted downstairs. Avanna and Nick met Reid and Annie in the kitchen for one last drink. Annie stood in front of Reid with her back to him. He began kissing her neck as he held her shoulders. He knew she was drunk or very close to it by now.

"Are you ready for bed, Annie?" he asked hoping she wouldn't remember to be mad at him.

"I'm ready, Reid."

"We'll see you guys in the morning," Reid told them.

"Don't do anything we wouldn't, Reid," Avanna teased.

Reid and Annie headed upstairs leaving Avanna and Nicky alone in the kitchen. Avanna's roommates along with Drew and Leslie walked into the kitchen.

"Oh, here you are," Charlene said with a smirk. "We were looking for you guys. We just saw Reid and his little friend going upstairs. He had his hands all over her. We know what they are going to be doing."

"Maybe, maybe not," Nicky said. "She is still a virgin and pretty young."

"She won't be a virgin for much longer," Kim told the others, who all laughed except for Nicky.

"We're going to bed, Avanna. You coming?" Jenny asked.

"Nicky and I will be up there in a few minutes. Did you manage to capture any guys to share your rooms?"

The three vultures shook their heads.

Charlene said, "No, we wanted Reid, but he wasn't interested. At least that's what he said. I think he just said that for his little friend's benefit."

"Maybe he will join us later. We can make it a night to remember," Charlene added.

Annie and Reid made it to their room. As they climbed the stairs, she felt his hands caressing her body. She sighed as she realized she wished it was Matt groping her instead of Reid. She used the bathroom to get ready for bed. She came out and Reid was already in bed.

"I may have drank too many beers, but I'm not smashed and I know you aren't supposed to be in my bed."

Reid sat up. "Are you really going to make me sleep on a couch?"

"Floor, couch, bathtub. Whatever. It's your choice, but we are not sharing this bed."

Reid sighed then got out of bed. "Annie, I know you aren't ready and I respect your wishes, but I hope you don't want to wait much longer."

"I know tonight would seem to be the perfect time because I'm too tired to resist, but I can't. I need to tell you something."

"What, Annie? You can tell me anything."

"I was hurt when you were with Avanna's friends. I said it didn't bother me, but it did."

"I'm sorry, Annie. I guess I wasn't thinking about your feelings. I should have stayed with you."

"Yeah, too late now." She pointed to the door. "Will you leave now, so I can go to sleep?"

"Whatever you want, Annie. I'll see you in the morning."

Annie woke up, got out of bed, took a shower and got dressed. She headed downstairs to find something for breakfast. Avanna and Nick were already up, but not dressed.

"Morning, Annie. How was your night?" Avanna asked.

"I slept fine, Avanna. Do you have anything for a pounding headache?"

"I think Avanna wants to know about something else,

213

Annie," Nicky said as he frowned at Avanna.

"I'll get you something," Avanna said.

Annie waited until Avanna left the kitchen, grinned at Nicky and whispered, "I can't tell you the details of our special night of lovemaking."

Nick looked at Annie for a time. "You didn't do it, Annie. I know better than that."

"No, I made Reid sleep downstairs. Have you seen him?"

"Not this morning," Nick answered. "I'm making coffee. Would you like some?"

"Yes, please. Is there anything to eat? I need something to settle my stomach."

Avanna returned with a bottle of medicine. "Try one of these. They work for me."

Reid walked into the kitchen, saw the medicine and held out a hand. "If that is for a hangover, I'll take one."

Avanna handed the bottle to Reid after giving one of the pills to Annie. "Someone looks like he had a rough night. Where did you sleep?"

Nick, Annie and Avanna stared at Reid waiting for his answer.

"I crashed on a couch in the media room," he said. "Do I smell coffee?"

"Yes, and I'm going to see what I can whip up for breakfast," Nicky replied.

"Thanks, Nick, I appreciate it," Reid said. He moved closer to Annie, but she backed away.

"I need you to take me home after we eat," Annie said.

"I can do that. Maybe my brain will be less fuzzy after I eat. I can't remember everything that happened last night."

Avanna frowned at Reid. "That's a good thing." She had talked to her roommates before they left, so she knew more about what happened than either Annie or Nick.

Chapter Thirty-Four

Annie and Reid stopped briefly at her house to drop off her suitcase, but no one was home. Annie figured her father would be at Grandpa's farm taking care of his father.

"Would you be able to run me out to Grandpa's, please?"

"Sure, Annie." Reid told her as he looked at the time. He seemed anxious to get back to his apartment. Twenty minutes later Reid pulled into the long gravel driveway out at the farm. He parked between the house and the barn.

"Are you going to come in with me, Reid?" Annie asked.

"I'll come in, but I can't stay very long. I have to get back to my apartment. I've got a paper to finish."

Daddy and Elisabeth were there taking care of Liam who seemed to be doing much better.

"Annie! How's my favorite granddaughter? It's so good to see you. Your father and Elisabeth have been driving me crazy. They won't let me do anything for myself." He held out his arms to hug Annie, but he frowned at Reid.

"How are you feeling, Grandpa? You haven't been overdoing it, have you? You know what the doctor told you."

"Ah! What does he know? He's still a kid."

Reid hung around for an hour but then needed to leave. Annie walked him to the front door and he kissed her goodbye on the cheek.

"I'll call you later, Annie. I had a good time at the party."

"So did I, Reid. I hope you understand why I wouldn't share a room."

"I am very patient, Annie. You know that."

Annie watched him as he turned the car around and took off. He didn't glance in her direction as he left. She turned around and saw her father waiting.

Dad put an arm around her shoulders. "So how was your weekend, Annie? Tell me about it."

"Keith, maybe Annie doesn't want to tell you about her weekend. Maybe she wants to have some secrets from you. She's not a little girl anymore."

"It's okay, Mom. Nothing happened that I can't tell Daddy," Annie said.

"So tell me!"

Annie described the weekend and even confessed about how much beer she drank. She also casually mentioned how she and Reid were supposed to share a room.

"He conveniently forgot to mention that, huh?" Dad asked.

"He told me about it after we got there. I didn't know he was staying overnight. I got kinda mad at him and told him it wasn't going to happen. When I eventually got ready for bed, he was already in it. I might have been pretty buzzed, but I wasn't too far gone to kick him out of the room. He ended up sleeping on a couch downstairs."

"I can't believe you would do that, Annie!" Dad exclaimed as he paced around the room. "What would you have done if Reid tried something?"

"That's just it, Daddy. I knew he wouldn't and I'm not totally helpless."

He stopped pacing and pointed a finger at her. "You are grounded for life! I can't believe you would even think about sharing a bed with him. You are too naïve and you were probably drunk. Are you sure he..."

"I'm sure! Don't you think I would know if we did that? I never got in bed with him."

"I don't know! Would you?"

Annie and her father argued for a few minutes until Elisabeth calmed them down.

"You're still grounded, young lady. You can't leave your room for a month."

"Daddy! I don't live at home anymore, remember? I'm going to college."

"Well then, when you come home you're grounded."

"What if I never come home?"

"I'll call North Park and tell them you're grounded," he said, let his shoulders sag and then shook his head. "What am I supposed to do, Amy Catherine?" he asked looking at the ceiling.

"Do you still love me, Daddy? I still love you," she said.

"Of course I still love you." He hugged her and they both laughed.

By now they had both cooled off and Keith realized how silly he sounded.

"You know how much I love you, Annie, and I can't help being so protective."

"I know, Daddy, and I'm sorry for what I did. I realize it was wrong."

"Promise me you will be more careful in the future."

"I will. I promise."

Dad hugged her and whispered, "You're still grounded."

The rest of the semester seemed to fly by. Reid and Annie still dated occasionally, but they hadn't taken their relationship to the next level. In fact, just the opposite. Annie didn't kiss Reid again after Avanna's last party.

One day after her afternoon classes, Annie found Reid waiting outside her dorm room. "Hi, Reid. I didn't know you were coming over."

"Hey, Annie. We need to talk. Can I come in?"

"Sure, is anything wrong?" Annie asked as she opened the door and let him inside. She knew Reid had bad news for her and she suspected what it was.

Reid walked over to her desk and leaned against it. "Annie, I don't know how to say this without hurting you so I'm just going to say it. I've met someone else."

Annie dropped her backpack on the floor and sat on her bed. She had a feeling this was going to happen after seeing Reid with another girl at the library a couple of times.

"Do I know her, Reid? Does she go to school here?"

"You probably don't know her. She's a junior from Milwaukee. Her name is Hannah Vandiver and we met in my Calculus class. We were studying and one thing led to another. I'm sorry, Annie. I never meant for this to happen."

"I know you didn't intend to hurt me, Reid. Actually, I could tell something has been wrong since Avanna's party. At least

217

we didn't have sex. That would make it more difficult," she said and then paused. "Is it because of my age or my reluctance to sleep with you?"

"I've thought about that, Annie. I really thought it didn't matter that you're so young, but in reality I guess it does. It wouldn't if we were older. In another ten years it wouldn't matter, but now it does."

"I'm glad you told me, Reid. I hope we can still think of each other as a friend."

"I'll be your friend, Annie, but we won't be close friends."

"Have you told Nicky or Avanna?"

"Yes, I talked to them last weekend on the phone. Nicky told me to tell you hi and he's sorry things didn't work out for us. He hopes you will still consider him a friend. I should go, Annie. I have to meet Hannah."

"Okay, Reid. Do you mind if I don't walk you downstairs?"

"No, I don't expect you to do that."

Reid hugged Annie briefly and rather stiffly, then left. Annie lay on her bed and waited for the tears to come, but they didn't. She looked up at the ceiling and remembered the good times she shared with Reid. *I'm so glad we didn't sleep together.* She thought about Nicky. *We had just as much fun together. I wonder if I'll ever see you or Avanna again.* She thought of Matty and Mace. She hadn't talked to Matty for a couple of weeks. She saw Mace almost every day and he would be coming over soon to study with Erin before they went to the dining hall. She waited for the knock on her door. She didn't have to wait very long. She got up to open the door and let Mace in.

"Hey, Annie! How was your day?" Mace asked as he dropped his books onto Erin's desk, picked up one of Erin's headbands and put it on. "I hope it was better than mine. My day sucked big time."

Annie stared at Mace then said, "Will you take off that headband? You look ridiculous."

He took it off. "Are you pissed about something?"

"Reid stopped by and he broke up with me," she replied.

"What!? Why? What happened, Annie? Are you okay?"

218

Annie moved close to Mace and he hugged her. Now the tears started to flow. Mace was still holding her as Erin entered the room. Mace looked at Erin and shook his head.

Erin rushed over and put her hands on Annie's shoulders. "Annie, are you all right? Is there something wrong?"

Mace answered for her. "Reid broke up with her. He stopped by after class and dumped her. If I see him around, I'm going to pound his lights out."

Annie broke off the hug and poked Mace in the chest. "No you won't, Mace Franklin. You will do no such thing."

"But Annie..."

"You will treat him civilly if you see him," Annie said as she wiped her tears away with her hands. "It's not like he broke my heart. We never had sex so I don't have anything to be all that upset about."

"Oh, Annie, I'm so sorry. Was it because you wouldn't have sex with him?" Erin asked.

Annie turned around to face Erin. "Partly, I think. He met someone else. Her name is Hannah something and she's in one of his classes. I'll get over him. He was a good guy and all, but he was never going to be the one I spent my whole life with."

"Should we go grab something to eat, Annie?"

"Mace!" Erin exclaimed. "How can you even think of food at a time like this."

"We still have to eat, Erin. Like Annie said, he didn't break her heart."

Erin rolled her eyes. "You can be such a jerk sometimes, Mace Franklin."

"It's okay, Erin. I am kinda hungry and I'm not going to pine away thinking about Reid. I sorta knew this was going to happen ever since Avanna's last party."

"Because you wouldn't have sex?" Erin asked.

Annie nodded.

Erin snapped her fingers. "I know the perfect guy for you, Annie. His name is..."

"Hold on there," Annie said. "I'm not going to start looking for another guy yet. I might just decide to become a nun."

"That'll be the day, Annie O'Dell." Mace laughed. "I know how much you like to make out and I don't think nuns are allowed to do that."

Erin smacked Mace's arm. "I don't need to be reminded that you and Annie have made out before."

Mace shrugged. "It was a spur of the moment thing, Erin. We lost our minds for a moment and it was Annie who started it. I didn't want to kiss her."

Annie tried to slug him, but he backed away just in time.

"Yeah, sure! Just make sure it doesn't happen again, Mace," Erin said and the turned to face Annie. "And you too, Annie. Don't be kissing Mace because you and Reid broke up."

"I won't. He's too much like my brother now," she said as she stuck out her tongue. "God! What will I do if Daddy marries his mother? I'll probably need therapy."

Mace crossed his arms over his chest. "If you girls are finished, can we go eat? I need to keep up my strength."

"Give us a minute," Erin said.

"Annie, are you allowed to leave the room to eat?" Mace asked.

"Yeah, why are you asking?" she asked while putting on a light jacket.

"I thought you were grounded for life. Did your dad put you on parole?"

"You are such a riot. Daddy told me to cool it with Reid and I did. I'm not a child anymore, so Daddy can't really ground me."

"We'll see," Mace teased.

Chapter Thirty-Five

"I'm going home after classes today. I need to talk to Daddy. Wanna come with me, Mace?" Annie asked as they walked out of the Jordan Dining Hall. "You got any laundry to do?"

"I do need a few clean shirts. Are you volunteering to do my laundry, Annie?"

"I'll do it, if you help me study for my Psych class," she answered.

"How? Are you going to analyze me or something?"

Annie stopped and looked up at Mace. "You can not be analyzed, Mace Franklin. There has never been anyone or anything like you before. If you carry my laundry out to the car, I'll help do it for you."

"Deal!" he said quickly before she could change her mind. "I'll meet you at Howe Hall later."

Later that afternoon Mace took Annie's laundry out to her car along with his own heavy bag of dirty clothes. Since Reid and Annie split up, Mace had been seeing more of Annie—as her friend and with Erin's full approval.

"You can come with us, Erin," Annie said.

Erin waved a hand. "Thanks, but I really have to finish this stupid paper and I can't do that if I'm with you guys."

Mace kissed Erin and then he and Annie left.

"Have you told your father about Reid yet?" Mace asked on the way to the O'Dell home.

"No, I've been putting it off. I plan to tell him today when he gets home. He really liked Reid, even though he thought he was too old for me."

Annie and Mace hauled the dirty laundry into the house and Mace dumped his out onto the floor.

Annie looked at it with disgust. "Don't you even sort it?"

"No, why? I dump it all in the washer and throw in some detergent."

Annie picked up a t-shirt and held it out to Mace. "This is the most disgusting thing I have ever seen. How can you even wear this?"

"Oh, I don't wear that one. I use it to clean the toilet."

"You are so gross!" she said as she threw it at him.

"I'm kidding, Annie. I used it for something, but it wasn't the toilet."

Annie sorted through Mace's dirty clothes and explained how he should separate different fabrics. While she was doing that, Mace was going through Annie's laundry and picking out her underwear. She finally noticed.

"What are you doing? Will you leave my underwear alone? You are so immature, Mace Franklin."

"I was just checking to see if you had any sexy underwear. You know the kind you can see through."

"If I did, you would never see it. At least not while I was wearing it."

"Whoa! Here's a pair. Does your father know you have this?" Mace held a thong high over his head.

"Let me have that!" Annie yelled.

Mace grinned. "Only if you tell me why and who you bought it for."

"None of your business, Mace Franklin," she said using a few other words for emphasis.

Annie practically tackled Mace trying to get her underwear away from him.

"I bought them to wear because they are comfortable. Not because I was going to let any guy see them," she said as she struggled to pull his arm down.

"Yeah right! Who do you expect to buy that crock of bull?"

"Are you selling crocks of bull now, Annie?"

"Daddy!" Annie turned around and froze. "I didn't know you were home." She looked at him, then back at Mace.

Mace tried to hand Annie her underwear, but her father saw it. Dad looked at it without saying a word. Mace handed it to Annie.

She immediately hid the thong behind her back. "I bought them because they are comfortable, Daddy."

"Oh, is that the crock of bull you were talking about, Mace?" Daddy teased Annie.

"Oooh! I hate all men with a passion," she swore. "Get out of here so I can start the laundry."

Later, while they were still sitting at the island after eating dinner, Daddy patted his full stomach and asked, "How is Reid? Why didn't he come with you? Not that I don't like to see you, Mace."

Mace nudged Annie with an elbow.

She frowned at Mace and then looked at her father. "I have to tell you something, Daddy."

"What is it, sweetie?"

Annie stared at the refrigerator.

"Reid dumped her," Mace spilled the beans.

Annie smacked Mace hard on his arm. "Can't you keep your big mouth shut, Mace?"

"Is it true, Annie? Did you and Reid break up?" Daddy asked as he stacked up the dirty plates.

"Yes, we did. He met an older girl in one of his classes and they started dating. He came over to my room and broke it off. He tried to be nice about it."

Mace harrumphed. "He dumped Annie because she wouldn't sleep with him."

"Mace!!!" Annie and her father yelled at him.

He shrugged and said, "Well, it's true."

"You have no tact, Mace."

"Sorry, Annie, but I'm still pissed at him."

"Daddy, I could never picture myself being with Reid for the rest of my life, so I wouldn't have sex with him. I guess he just got tired of waiting for me to grow up."

"I think you are very grown up, Annie. A less mature person would have just gone ahead and had sex."

"Hey! Why are you both looking at me like that?" Mace asked.

"If the truth hurts," Dad said.

"Or the shoe fits," Annie added.

"I have never claimed to be mature. I just like to have fun." Mace sounded hurt.

"Annie, are you okay with what happened? I know you

223

really liked Reid. He was a nice Crock-Pot."

Mace tilted his head. "What?"

"It's over your head and none of your business, Mace," Annie said.

"Whatever." Mace opened the fridge and grabbed a Coke.

"I did like him a lot and he was fun to be with, but I never told him I loved him and he never said that to me. I think we both knew from the start that it was just a temporary relationship. After all it was just a blind date."

Later, Annie and Mace studied in her room while they listened to some tunes. They were both on her bed as she read her Psych textbook. Mace was reading *Sports Today*.

"I'm going to bed, sweetheart. Thanks for dinner and cleaning up the kitchen. Are you finished with the laundry?"

"There's one more load of Mace's stuff. I wanted to save it for last because I wasn't sure if the washer could handle it. It's so gross I thought the washer might self-destruct."

"Good thinking, Annie. I always knew you were smart."

"Thanks, Daddy, and good night. We'll try to be quiet."

"Don't worry about me. Once I fall asleep tonight, I won't hear a thing. One more thing, Annie."

"What?"

"Reid made a big mistake."

"Yeah! I agree with you, Detective O'Dell. He made a huge mistake dumping Annie."

"Thanks, Daddy. I love you."

"I love you, too, sweetie." Daddy said and then watched as Annie literally jumped on Mace.

"You just have to get your two cents in, don't you?" Annie hollered as she tried to punch Mace in the belly.

Mace grabbed her hands. "Ow! Get off me. That hurts."

Daddy shook his head and walked away as Annie and Mace wrestled like they did as kids.

Two days later Annie started hinting to her father about a birthday party.

"I think I agree with you, sweetie. You should have a

birthday party since you will be thirteen and a real teenager now," he said with a grin.

"Oh, Daddy, I'm not going to be thirteen."

"You were acting like it the other day when you and Mace were wrestling on the bed."

"We were not," Annie insisted.

"I should have taken a picture. You guys were acting the way you would when you were little kids." Dad smiled as he thought about years past.

"Daddy, will you please let me have a party? I want to invite all my friends and have it at the farm. I already asked Grandpa and he said okay."

"Of course you can have a party, sweetie. I suppose turning eighteen is a big deal. Do you know how many kids you are going to invite?"

"I made a list. Wanna see it?"

"Sure."

Annie showed the list to her father. He started to count the names but gave up.

"I see why you want to have it at the farm now. It's the only place we could fit this many people. Unless we rent the stadium."

"I doubt if everyone will be able to come to the party, but I didn't want to leave anyone out. Some of them might stop by for a few minutes and not stick around."

"If you're worried about the cost of the food and beverages, don't. Grandpa and I will pay for everything."

"Thank you, Daddy. I love you."

"I love you, too," Dad said as he tried to calculate the cost to feed a hungry mob of teenagers. "I might have to take out a loan."

Chapter Thirty-Six

"Annie, isn't that Reid over there with that girl?" Elaine asked one day in the dining hall.

"Yes, we broke up and her name is Hannah something."

Victoria smirked, "I heard Reid dumped you because you wouldn't have sex with him."

Cindy slammed her hand on the table. "How can you say such a mean thing, Victoria?"

"It's true. I'm sorry if it sounds mean, but it's the truth."

"Maybe Annie isn't ready to have sex. Ever think of that, Victoria?" Cindy said as she frowned at Victoria.

"If she's not going to have sex then she shouldn't be dating a twenty-two year old guy. By the way, how was the sex with Bryce and Adrien? At least Lainey is engaged. Do you think Bryce is going to marry you, Cindy?"

Annie looked at Elaine and Cindy. "Have you guys..."

"They sure have, Annie. And Rachel and Ben, too. I guess you are the last virgin standing. Even Solomon and Ashley are doing it!" Victoria was pleased with herself for spreading gossip.

Annie stared at her friends with her mouth open for several seconds. "What about Diana Ahronson?" Annie asked.

"Oh, no one dares ask her about that. It would spoil our image of her if she wasn't saving herself for marriage," Cindy said.

Elaine put down her fork. "We didn't want to say anything, Annie. I'm sorry about Reid. He seemed like such a nice guy."

"He's still a nice guy, Lainey. I think it was the age difference more than the sex thing. The 'no sex' thing."

"Did you ever make out with him at least, Annie? You know get naked and make out," Victoria asked sarcastically.

"Victoria!" Cindy exclaimed. "Will you leave Annie alone and stop asking about her love life?"

"What love life?" Victoria asked while chewing on her burger. "She doesn't have one. She hasn't even slept with Matt Sullivan. Annie, sex is not that big a deal. Just go ahead and do it."

"I'm not like you, Victoria. I can't just grab a guy and ask him to have sex with me."

"Come on, Annie. Let's go talk somewhere without Victoria," Elaine suggested.

Elaine, Cindy and Annie walked over to the quad in the middle of campus.

"When were you going to tell me, guys? How long have you been doing it?"

"I was going to tell you, but Lainey thought it might influence you to go ahead and have sex with Reid just because we were," Cindy said.

"I didn't want our decisions to affect yours, Annie. I guess we thought you might go ahead just to be like the rest of us. I realize how silly that sounds now. You've never been one to follow blindly along with a crowd."

"That's right. I wouldn't have made my decision about sex based on what you guys were doing. Okay, now that we've got that out of the way, I want details. I want to hear everything about how it happened and where."

They spent an hour talking about sex.

Tuesday night Annie and Erin heard a knock on the door around nine o'clock as they studied at their desks.

"Are you expecting anyone, Annie?" Erin asked without looking up from her textbook.

"No, is Mace coming over after all?"

"He said he had to take care of Keyshon tonight."

There was a louder, more urgent, knock on the door.

"I'll get it, Erin."

Annie opened the door and smiled. "Matty! What are you doing here? I didn't know you were coming over."

"I'm sorry to just stop over without calling, Annie. Can we talk? Somewhere private."

"Okay."

Annie could sense Matt had something serious on his mind.

"We were ready for bed, Matty. Give me a minute to get dressed. Do you want to come in and wait?"

"I'll just wait out here, Annie. I don't want to disturb Erin if she's not dressed."

"I'm not naked, Matt. I've got my pajamas on," Erin said as she turned her desk chair around.

"Hi, Erin. I still think I'll just wait out here."

"I'll be right back, Matty. Just give me a minute."

Annie closed the door and Matt waited in the hall with his back against the wall. He rose up and down on his toes.

"Annie, what does he want? Where are you going?"

"I don't know, Erin. We haven't talked for a while. It might be about the baby."

"Are you going to put something over your pajamas?"

"Yeah, why?"

"Put on a bra at least!"

"Oh, don't be silly. Matty can't see anything through my sweatshirt. I'll have my phone with me. I'll call if I need anything."

"Dial 9-1-1 if he starts anything."

"See you later, Erin, and don't worry. I'll be fine."

Annie opened the door and Matt turned to face her.

"Are you aware I could hear you guys talking?" he asked.

"So what?"

Matt looked down at Annie's chest. She smacked his arm as they walked downstairs to the lounge.

"Don't even think about it, Matthew. There's nothing there you haven't seen before. What do you need to talk about? Is it the baby? Is there something wrong with the baby, Matty?"

They sat on a love seat in the corner of the lounge.

"It's not the baby. Joni and the baby are doing just fine. I talked to her just a couple days ago. It's about you," he said as he patted her knee. "Victoria called and told me you and Reid broke up. She seemed so pleased and made sure I knew Reid dumped you. She's so petty and vindictive. Are you all right, Annie?"

"I'm not heartbroken or anything, Matty. I kinda knew it was coming. Things were not the same after spring break. We went to Avanna's party."

"I've heard about her spring break parties. Did you...?"

"No! I didn't go skinny dipping and I didn't have sex." Annie answered.

"Did you stay overnight?" Matt asked as he watched

228

another couple enter the lounge. The couple looked around and then headed for the stairs. Matt turned back to Annie. "Did you?"

"You probably know the answer already since you're asking," Annie said. She looked at Matt, took a deep breath and then said, "I didn't share a room with Reid and nothing happened. We kissed a little, but that's all. Are you jealous?"

Matt shook his head and then used the smile Annie liked so much. "If you remember we once spent a night together, Annie."

"That was different!" Annie smiled back.

"It was special, though, even if we didn't do anything."

"I'm glad I didn't do anything with Reid now. How do you handle it when you run into girls you've slept with? Is it awkward? Do they hate you or anything?"

He sat back and thought about the questions for a moment. "First, let me get something straight."

"Okay," Annie said.

"I haven't had sex with every girl I go out with. I've had sex with some, but probably not as many as you or other people might think. There are some I made out with but didn't have sex."

"Okay, so what about my questions."

"It's different with different girls. Some of them think I took advantage of them and won't talk to me. Some of them try to get me to go out again."

She grinned. "You mean sleep with them again?"

"Yeah, I was just trying to be tactful and delicate."

"Oh, Matty, you don't have to do that for me. But it's sweet that you do. When you are with someone do you ever think of the other girls?"

"Not really, Annie. If I'm with someone I try to concentrate on the moment. I don't compare one girl to another either."

"Are you and Joni dating or anything?"

"No, if she wasn't pregnant we wouldn't even be talking. We both knew it would never work between us from the beginning. We tried because of the baby but it just didn't work. I have agreed to support the baby, but I won't try to get joint custody or anything. Joni met someone and they're together."

"What's his name? Does he go to school here?"

229

"Beverly Tramiel. Her name is Beverly and she's a senior, too," he said and then waited for Annie to react.

Annie stared at Matt for a few seconds. "Beverly?"

"She and Joni are old friends, or were old friends. I found out Joni and Beverly had been together for two years, but they had a fight. That was when I went out with her."

"You mean Joni's gay?"

"Yeah, she is. Gay or bisexual or something. I don't understand it, Annie. I think Joni just went out with me to get back at Beverly."

"That's mean. Are they going to raise the baby together?"

"That's the plan." Matt stared at the ceiling. "Maybe it was the plan all along. I think she just used me to get pregnant."

"Well, look at it this way, Matty. They can both breast feed the baby!"

"I don't think it works like that, Annie. I don't know for sure since I'm not a woman."

"You said you used protection when you were with her so maybe it was just an accident."

"Can we talk about something else?" he asked.

"How about you, Matty? Are you dating anyone now?"

"No. I haven't been on a date since the last time I was out with Joni. Before you even ask, that means I haven't had sex either."

Annie grinned as she touched his knee. "Poor baby. You must be going out of your mind."

"Very funny, Annie. You don't know what it's like," he said as he grabbed her hand.

"Not yet anyway."

They smiled at each other.

"Do you want to get something to eat?" Matt asked.

"Sure! As long as you behave."

"If I have to, I will. It might not be easy since you're in your pajamas." He pulled on the neckline of her sweatshirt and peeked underneath.

Annie let him look. "Does that excite you? Knowing all I'm wearing under my jeans and sweatshirt are my pj's."

Matt grinned. "I'll try not to get so excited that I attack you, Annie."

"Party pooper. Why do you think I came with you?"

Matt held Annie's hand as they walked outside.

"Where do you want to go, Annie? Darby's is still open or we could go over to the Lion."

"The Lion is closer. Can we go there?"

Matt took Annie over to The Hungry Lion. They grabbed a booth and ordered some potato skins and pop to drink. After talking to each other for several minutes about everything that had happened lately, they were quiet. They both realized they were very comfortable with each other even if they were not talking. Just being together was enough to make them happy.

"I should be getting back to my room, Matty," Annie said after she finished her Dr Pepper. "Erin will wonder where I am."

"I'm ready to go." Matt left enough money on the table to cover the bill and the tip. He waved to some staff as they left.

"Don't you get free food since your father owns the place?" Annie asked.

Matt shrugged. "I do, but I like to pay for my stuff if I'm not working. I always leave a tip because I know how hard they work."

He drove her back and walked her up to her room.

"Thanks for tonight, Matty," she said as she leaned against her door.

"I should be thanking you for going out. I want to kiss you, but I won't now," he said as he ran a hand through her hair. "I love how soft it feels."

Erin heard them talking and opened the door. Matt grabbed Annie's arms to keep her from losing her balance and falling into the room.

"Say good night now, Annie," Erin said as she smiled at Matt.

"Night, Matty," Annie said as Erin pulled her into the room and closed the door.

Matt chuckled as he walked away.

Chapter Thirty-Seven

"Hey, Matty. Are we gonna study at the library or are we gonna go to my house. Call me back when you can."

Annie left a message for Matt on his phone. After breaking up with Reid, Annie started dating Matt Sullivan. Annie had gone out with Matt before, starting in her sophomore year of high school.

"Hi, Annie. I just got your message. Would it be all right if we study at your house?"

"Can we take your car?"

"Yeah, I'll drive. Are you ready to leave now?"

She stuffed her books into her backpack. "I will be by the time you get over here."

"See you in a little while."

Matt arrived at Howe Hall twenty minutes later and ran up the stairs to Annie and Erin's room. Erin let him in.

"Hi, Matt. Annie's in the bathroom. She should be ready soon."

Matt stood just inside the door and glanced around the room. He smiled because he could see Annie's clothes scattered around. "How are you doing, Erin? Mace still treating you right?"

"He knows he better, or else he will be out on his butt. You can come all the way in. I won't bite you."

Matt sat on Annie's bed. She came out of the bathroom and Matt stood up and kissed her tenderly. "I missed you."

"It's only been two days since we saw each other, Matty."

"I know, but it seems longer than that."

"Will you guys knock it off! You are worse than Lainey and Adrien. I think it was better when you were fighting."

"When did we ever fight, Erin?"

"I don't remember when exactly, but you didn't use to be so sweet to each other. Are you sure you're not having sex, Annie?"

"I think I would know if we were, Erin."

Matt didn't say anything but had a grin on his face. Erin noticed Matt grinning.

"Are you coming back here tonight or not?"

"We're going to stay at the house tonight and Daddy is home FYI."

"I'll see you tomorrow night then, Annie. Take care, Matt."

"See ya, Erin. Say hi to Mace for me."

Matt carried Annie's books out to the car and even opened the door.

"Hi, Daddy! I'm home. Where are you?" Annie asked as she threw her backpack on the small table in the hallway.

"In my room, sweetie. I'll be right there." He came out of his room and saw Annie and Matt in the kitchen. "Hi, sweetheart. Hi, Matt. How are you guys doing?"

"We're doing good, Mr. O'Dell. How has work been?"

"I'm still trying to keep the city safe, Matty."

Annie gave her father a hug and a kiss on the cheek.

"We're going to spend the night here, if that's all right."

"Of course it's all right. I like to see Matthew."

"What about me?"

"Oh, you too, Annie."

Annie knew he was just teasing her.

"We have to study for a couple hours. We'll be in my room. Oh, is it all right if Matty sleeps on the air mattress?"

"It's okay as long as you leave the door open. You know my rules."

"We will. Thanks, Daddy. What do you want for dinner?"

"Would pasta be all right?" Dad asked. "I can make it while you study."

"With a salad and honey rolls," Annie said.

"I think that can be arranged. Six o'clock okay with you?"

"Sure. That will give us time to study."

Annie and Matt went to her room and studied with the door open. She sat on her bed while he used her desk.

Later, as he worked on dinner, Detective O'Dell recalled a conversation with Matt shortly after Annie and Reid broke up.

"Can I talk with you, Detective O'Dell?" Matt asked with his hands in his pockets.

"Sure, Matthew. What's on your mind?"

"It's about Annie. I know she and Reid broke up. I guess he dumped her but anyway. Would you mind if I ask Annie out on a date—a real date?"

"What about your friend Joni? Are you still seeing her?"

"I'm not seeing her except to talk about the baby. I know I've made some mistakes before, and I haven't been the best behaved guy around."

"You can say that again," Detective O'Dell said.

"I know you know Annie and I have been together before."

"I know that, Matt, and I know you didn't take advantage of her. I appreciate that."

"I really like Annie. She means more to me than all the other girls I've ever dated."

"You mean slept with."

"Yeah, I guess so. You know I've dated a lot of girls, but I haven't slept with too many of them. I know everyone thinks I have, and I haven't done anything to make them think otherwise..."

"Matt, I'm not too concerned with what you've done in the past. My concern is Annie."

"I've always been careful. I can't understand how Joni got pregnant. This is really awkward, Mr. O'Dell. I feel like such an ass. I've screwed up my life so many times and Annie has always been a friend to me no matter what I did."

"She likes you very much, Matt. She would kill me for telling you, but she finds you difficult to resist."

"I wouldn't ever take advantage of her. I swear it."

"I believe you, Matt. I know you could have, but didn't. If you promise to treat Annie with respect, I will not stop you from seeing her. If she wants to see you that is." He pointed a finger at Matt. "I will promise you this though, Matthew Sullivan, if you hurt her I will see to it you never have another chance to hurt anyone again. Do you understand me?" He pulled the trigger on his hand.

"I understand, and I promise I won't do anything to intentionally hurt Annie. What if we have an argument though?"

"That's not what I mean, Matty. If you and Annie become involved, there will be disagreements."

234

"I just wanted to be sure."

"Matty, I like you. I always have. I know Annie likes you. Go ahead and ask her out. I think I already know what her answer will be."

Detective O'Dell was putting the salad together and smiled as he thought about how happy Annie seemed to be with Matty. Matt appeared to have changed, too. He no longer tried to portray himself as the school bad boy. He knew Matt and Annie made out like normal college kids, but Matt hadn't pressured Annie into doing more than she was ready to do. She was still hurt by how Reid ended their relationship, even if she wouldn't admit it to anyone. Annie came out to the kitchen to grab a couple bottles of pop.

"How's the studying going?" Dad asked.

"Okay, but it's boring," she answered and then looked up at her father. "Daddy, do you remember my story about the Crock-Pot and the bonfire?"

He chopped the last part of the romaine lettuce and set the knife down. "I believe I do."

"Is it possible for one guy to be both a Crock-Pot and a bonfire?"

Daddy thought for a moment and then smiled at Annie. "If you ever find a guy who is both, then hold onto him, sweetie. A guy like that could be a real keeper."

Annie looked over her shoulder for a second, turned her head, smiled at her father and whispered, "Daddy, I think I might be in love."

"I think that is very possible, my sweet angel. I do indeed."

"You're not mad at me?"

"Not at all. Just be careful, Annie."

"We are going real slow, Daddy. Matty hasn't been pressuring me for anything. I'm glad you trust us enough to let him stay over."

"You have both earned that trust, Annie."

"I love you, Daddy!"

"I love you more than ever, Annie Mercer. Your mother

235

would be so proud of you," he said as he blinked his eyes rapidly.

Annie and Matt studied until dinner was ready. Dad called them out to eat when it was on the table. After finishing dinner, Annie and Matt discussed where they wanted to go. They decided on a movie.

"We're going out to a movie. Do you want to come with us, Daddy? We're going to see that cop movie with Denzel Washington you talked about."

"That's nice of you to ask, but I doubt Matt wants me along."

"It was my idea, sir. We don't mind if you are with us."

"Please come with us, Daddy. We'll buy the popcorn."

"A large Coke, too?" Dad asked.

"Sure, as long as you buy the tickets."

"Aha! That's the catch. I knew there would be one. It's a deal, anyway. Do I have to sit on the other side of the theater?"

"No, you can sit with us. I'll sit between you and Matty so you can make sure he doesn't try anything."

Matt shook his head. "You know I wasn't going to try anything, Annie."

"What time does it start? I have to be in bed before midnight."

"We'll be home before then, Daddy."

"Are you sure you want me to come with you? I could just give you the money for the tickets and concessions."

"We really want you to come with us, so stop fussing."

Dad offered to drive to the theater. Matt sat in the front and Annie was in back.

"Thanks for sitting in back, Annie. I don't like to be in the back of a squad car."

"It's an unmarked car, Matty."

"It's still a police car even if it doesn't look like one."

After a moment of silence Annie surprised her father and Matt.

"I'm the only virgin left out of all my friends. The only virgin on my floor and maybe in the whole dorm. Oh, Daddy! What if I'm the only virgin in the whole college?"

236

"I can't believe that's possible, Annie, and even if it were true would you just follow along with the crowd just to fit in?"

"No, I would never do that. I make my own decisions and try not to be influenced by everyone else."

Annie's father glanced at Matt. Matt looked over at Mr. O'Dell.

"I know what you're thinking, Matthew, and don't say a word."

"I wasn't going to say anything."

"It's not Matt's decision, Daddy. It's mine. I have to choose whether or not I want to have sex and right now I'm not ready. I'm not even on the pill."

Matt grinned as he looked back at Annie. "What about tomorrow?"

Annie smacked his shoulder.

"I was just kidding, Annie."

"You better be. When I decide to go ahead with having sex, I want it to be special. I want it to be romantic and not just something that happens in the back of a car, or in my dorm room because we get carried away."

Dad looked in the rearview mirror. "I know it's rather unrealistic in this day and age, but it would be okay with me if you wait until you're married, Annie."

"Will you still love me if I don't wait?"

"You know I will. I've told you I will always love you no matter what you do. That doesn't mean I'm giving my approval for you and Matt to go ahead."

"It might not be Matty. What if we break up and I find someone else."

"I'm right here, you know," Matt said. "Do I have any say in the matter?"

"No!" Annie's father said at the same time that Annie said, "Yes."

Annie glanced out the window for a few seconds, then said, "I think I would rather have a lover who knows what he is doing than one who doesn't."

"Wouldn't it be more important to be in love?"

237

"That goes without saying, Daddy. I wouldn't sleep with someone I didn't love."

"It's always better if that's the case. What do you think, Matt? Is sex better with a partner you're in love with, or not?"

Matt shrugged his shoulders and rubbed his arm while staring out the window.

"Well, Matty?" Annie asked.

"I'm not the right person to ask about that, sir. I don't think I've truly been in love with any of the girls I've had sex with. I might have told them I was and maybe I even thought I was at the time."

"I know you weren't in love with them, Matty. I know Victoria certainly wasn't in love. She just likes to have sex. I think I will like it, too."

"I hope you do, Annie. Your mother certainly did," Dad said and then grinned. "I shouldn't have said that out loud."

Matt was quiet for a moment as he listened to Annie and her father talk.

"Annie, how can you be so comfortable talking to your father about sex? I could never talk to my parents about that."

"I have always talked to Daddy about sex and everything else."

"I'm sorry, Annie. I didn't mean anything bad."

Dad stopped at a red light and looked over at Matt. "It wasn't always easy to talk about things while Annie was growing up. There were things I didn't know, but I learned what I could, so I could talk to her."

"Like when I started having a period. Daddy told me it would happen, so when it did I wasn't afraid."

"Jeez, Annie! Too much information."

"It's just a natural thing women go through, Matty. I feel lucky I had Daddy to talk to about puberty and what was happening to me. Some of my friends, who have mothers, weren't able to talk to their own moms. They had to learn everything from other people."

"Maybe we should change the subject, Annie," Dad said as the light changed. "We don't want to embarrass Matthew any more than we already have."

"Thanks, Mr. O'Dell. I like to have sex, but talking about it is different."

Annie laughed. "We know how much you like to have sex. You are going to be a father soon enough."

"How is everything going with the baby?" Dad asked.

"The doctor told Joni everything looked good. She showed me a sonogram of the baby and I listened to her heartbeat."

"I want to have two kids. A boy and a girl and in that order. I know I want a daughter, so if the first two were boys I would want three," Annie mentioned.

"You mean in the future right?" Dad asked.

"Yes, Daddy! After I graduate and get married."

Matt was relieved when they arrived at the theater. He got out of the car as quickly as he could.

Annie sat between Matt and her father to watch the show. Matt held hands with her and even kissed her once. Detective O'Dell was becoming more used to the fact Annie and Matt were in a relationship. Even though Matt's history would not inspire confidence in many fathers, Detective O'Dell trusted Matt with Annie. Not an easy thing to do, but Matt and Annie had earned his trust. Matt was grateful that on the way home the conversation was about the show, and not what they discussed on the way there.

"I'm going to bed, Annie. I'm tired and I have to be at the station at eight. Good night, sweetheart. Night, Matthew."

"Good night, Daddy. We'll try to be quiet so you can sleep. See you in the morning."

Detective O'Dell closed his door and was soon sound asleep.

"Are you hungry, Matty?"

"A little. What have you got to snack on?"

"Would you like some homemade chocolate chip cookies? I've got everything I need to bake some."

"Sounds good to me. Need any help?"

"Sure. If you want to eat any, I think you should help make them."

Annie kissed Matt and together they made the cookies.

"Hey, stop eating the dough, or else there won't be any left for cookies," Matt told Annie as she ate another spoonful of cookie batter.

"I've always loved eating cookie batter."

Eventually, Annie slid two sheets of cookies into the oven.

"While the cookies are in the oven, you can inflate the air mattress and I'll get the sleeping bags," Annie said.

Twelve minutes later the oven timer sounded and Annie pulled the cookies out. She set them on the island to cool.

"We have to let them cool for a few minutes. Wanna watch a movie?"

"As long as we don't disturb your father."

"Daddy wouldn't hear a bomb go off next to his ear right now."

Matt and Annie sat on the couch to watch a TV movie and eat cookies. Normally he would have taken advantage of being this close to a girl and tried to seduce her, but not with Annie. He knew she was not ready, and he was being very patient. It was the first time Matt had dated anyone and felt accepted by her parents. In this case, her father and grandfather. He realized this was worth more than adding another meaningless sexual encounter to his resume. Matt looked at Annie and smiled.

"What?" she asked.

"Nothing." He stroked her soft, curly hair and lightly ran his finger along her face.

"Watch the movie," she said.

He touched her lips and poked her nose playfully.

She pushed his hand away. "Do you another cookie?"

"No, I want to kiss you." He kissed her tenderly and felt something new stirring in his heart. He didn't say it out loud, but he realized he was falling in love for the first time in his life.

The movie ended shortly after one o'clock. The cookies were long gone and Annie felt tired. She yawned as she relaxed against Matt's shoulder. Matt placed an arm around her. He wished he could hold her close all night long.

"Are you ready for bed, Annie?"

"Yeah, I am falling asleep. How did the movie end?"

240

"The way you thought. It was the neighbor all along. You seem to be able to figure out these mysteries before I can."

"Comes from living with a detective all these years."

"As opposed to a guy with a questionable reputation," Matt said with a grin.

"Your father is not as disreputable as you think, Matthew."

Annie knew some things about Cormac Sullivan that not even Matt knew. She felt guilty about keeping this secret from Matt.

"Will you carry me to bed, please? I am too tired to walk."

"Are you too tired to put on your pajamas?"

"No, I can manage that by myself."

Matt stood up and lifted Annie into his arms. She put her arms around his neck as he carried her into her bedroom. He plopped her down on the bed and bent over to kiss her. She kissed him back and tried to pull him onto the bed.

"Stop it, Annie! You need to get ready for bed," he whispered quietly afraid to wake her father.

"Fine then. I'll be in the bathroom getting ready. It won't take me long, then you can use it. If we are ever living together, married or whatever, I want a place with two bathrooms."

"I'll see what I can do."

"Thank you, Matty. You're so sweet to me."

Annie got ready for bed, then Matt used the bathroom. Annie was wearing real pajamas instead of her normal gym shorts and a t-shirt. Matt slept in boxers and a t-shirt. Annie was already in bed when Matt entered the room. Matt kissed Annie good night and thought about how good it would be to be able to get in bed with her.

Annie knew what he was thinking and smiled. "Maybe someday, Matty."

"I can wait, Annie. For you I can wait. Night, baby."

Chapter Thirty-Eight

"Are these seats taken?"

"I'm sorry. We're saving these seats," Elaine answered.

Elaine, Cindy, Rachel and even Diana Ahronson were sitting in the dining hall waiting for the Roosevelt High grads.

"Mace, we're over here," Cindy shouted and waved.

Mace and Erin saw Cindy and sat down. Solomon and Ashley ate quickly so they could head to the computer lab. Adrien and Bryce joined Elaine and Cindy. Elaine and Cindy looked around trying to spot a couple of missing people.

"Have you seen or talked to Matt and Annie today?" Cindy asked.

"I called her and left a message earlier, but I haven't heard back from her," Elaine answered then ate another bite of salad.

"You don't think they're avoiding us do you, Lainey?"

"I hope not, Cindy, but you did upset her when you called Matt an irresponsible womanizer the other day."

"Well, it's true and sooner or later he is going to take advantage of her. I just know it!"

Christopher and Randy Braun showed up with Victoria Madison and Leila Fanaka and stuck around for a few minutes before leaving. Trish Eiffert and Tyree Boyce stopped to say hi—a very rare occurrence.

Mace came to Matt and Annie's defense. "When did anyone take advantage of Annie O'Dell? Do you really believe she is so naïve that she doesn't know what she's doing?"

"She thinks she's in love with Matthew, so she isn't thinking clearly," Cindy said.

Mace waved a finger at Cindy. "I think you're just jealous because Annie has not slept with Matt the way you let Bryce sleep with you."

"Come on, you guys!" Elaine stood up. "Let's not argue. This is our last dinner together. Let's just try to get along."

Cindy frowned at Mace.

"Yeah, I'm sorry, Cindy. I shouldn't have said what I did," Mace apologized.

Cindy sighed and said, "It's okay, Mace. You might be partly right."

"That almost sounded like an apology," Bryce said.

Cindy turned and frowned at Bryce.

"There they are over there by the vending machines," Erin said as she pointed.

Mace stood up and whistled loudly. Annie heard him and turned around. She waved at Mace. She took Matt's hand and they joined their friends.

"Where you been, girl?" Mace asked.

"Sorry we're late, but Matty had a late final. He just finished a few minutes ago. How is everyone doing? Is anyone totally finished with finals?"

No one answered Annie's question for a moment.

"Ashley and I are finished," Solomon said. "We're taking summer classes and we've found an apartment."

"Where?"

"It's actually in the same building where Reid and Ron live, Annie. I hope you will come and visit us anyway. I know you won't want to see Reid, but we want to see you and Matt."

"We will come for a visit after next week."

"What do you think about the changes in the residence halls? I think it's a good idea myself," Elaine asked.

The college made a few changes and Howe Hall would no longer be strictly for freshman girls. Annie and Erin would be sharing a room again next year. They didn't know which one yet, but it would probably not be the same one. Elaine decided not to transfer, much to the chagrin of Adrien Coyle, who would be in Kansas City next year. She and Cindy would be roommates again. Mace decided to stay in the dorms because his scholarship covered room and board. He would have a new roommate though. Matt Sullivan would commute from home to save money.

Mace finished eating, stood up and pointed to the other side of the dining hall. "Erin, I need to go say goodbye to Kevin and Scott. I probably won't have a chance to see them again before they leave."

"Say goodbye for me, too."

"Can I go with you, Mace?"

"Sure, Annie. Kevin always asks about you whenever I see him."

Mace and Annie walked over to where Kevin Murphy, Scott Cavanaugh and their girlfriends Holly Cavanaugh and Lisa Kamen sat. They hugged each other hugs and said goodbye. Kevin and Holly would be teaching in South Boston. Kevin would also be coaching basketball. Scott and Lisa were moving to North Trenton where they would have teaching positions at Wesclin County High School. Kevin and Holly were getting married on July 18 in South Boston. Scott and Lisa were getting married in St. Louis two weeks later.

Mace and Annie returned to their friends.

"That might be us in three more years, Mace," Annie said.

"I hope you don't mean we will be getting married to each other," Mace teased.

"No, doofus! I can't marry my stepbrother," she said as she playfully poked him in the side.

"So you think we will be brother and sister by then, huh?"

"It could happen. I meant that we will be engaged and graduating... you know what I mean." Annie bumped his hip with hers. "Stop teasing me."

By Friday afternoon everyone was finished with finals. For the SoHam kids it was easy to move out of the dorms and back home. Erin Bezick would take a train back to Nebraska. Before that happened though, Erin would stay with Annie for another week. She was able to store her things at the O'Dell home. Erin was sticking around because Annie's eighteenth birthday was on May 29 and Annie was having a big party at Grandpa Liam's farm.

Matthew Sullivan became a father on Monday, May 25. Beverly was with Joni in the delivery room. Joni's timing was perfect as she and Beverly had just graduated a few days earlier. Beverly called Matt with the news.

"Thanks for calling, Beverly. Are Joni and the baby all right?" Matt asked.

"They are doing fine. We are naming her Jennifer Lynn,"

244

Beverly said, then added other details.

"Would it be too weird if Annie and I came to St. Bart's to see the baby?"

Beverly hesitated a moment, then said, "You are the father, so I suppose you have some rights."

Matt was filled with pride, but also some sadness because he knew he would not be a part of his daughter Jennifer's daily life. Joni and Beverly combined their last names with a hyphen for their daughter's name.

"Do you feel as weird as I do, Annie?" Matt asked in the elevator.

She shrugged. "I try not to think about you being the father."

They found the right room and Joni let them both hold baby Jennifer.

"You won't break her," Annie told Matt.

"She's so tiny." Matt handed Jennifer to Annie after a couple minutes.

Annie knew just how to hold Jennifer. Matt looked at Annie as she held his daughter. Annie smiled at Matty and he kissed his daughter, then Annie. Matt and Joni had reached an agreement as to his involvement with the baby. He would be allowed limited visits but only with Joni present. He would be helping financially as much as he could and was determined to earn enough money to support Jennifer and even put her through college. Joni and Beverly did not need his financial support, but he insisted on helping.

Chapter Thirty-Nine

May 29 took forever to arrive, at least to Annie. Matt came over early in the morning before Annie was awake. He made breakfast for her and took it to her room. Erin was semi-awake and saw Matt come in the room. She slipped out of bed to let Matt move close to Annie. He kissed her cheek and whispered softly, "It's time to wake up, sleepyhead."

Annie opened one eye and looked at Matt. She smiled and stretched her arms above her head. "What time is it?"

"It's eight o'clock. Happy birthday, Annie. I made some breakfast for you."

"It smells good. Did you really make it by yourself?"

"Your father helped a little, but I did most of it myself."

Annie sat up in bed, and Matt kissed her again. He placed the tray on her lap and sat on the bed next to her. Erin went into the bathroom to take a shower and get ready—also to give Annie and Matt some privacy. A few minutes later there was a knock on her open door.

"You can come in, Daddy."

Her father sat on the edge of her bed to talk to her.

"Happy birthday, sweetheart. I can't believe my little girl is eighteen now."

"Oh, Daddy! I'm still your little girl."

"I know. You'll always be my little girl no matter how grown up you are. I'll let you and Matty have your breakfast."

"We need to be at Grandpa's by noon. We have to get everything ready. I told everyone to come at three. Not everyone will get there that early, but some of them will."

Annie finished her breakfast and got ready.

"Annie, you need to come into the living room," Dad said.

Annie walked out of her room. "Why?"

"You need to open your presents," Matt said.

She ran into the living room and sat on the couch between her father and Matt, giggled and said, "You didn't need to buy me anything."

"Yeah, right," Dad said as he shook his head. Matt and Erin

looked at each other and laughed.

"She's such a child," Erin said as she settled into the recliner.

"Open this one first," Dad said.

Annie ripped open the package. "Is this a new cell phone?"

Dad nodded. "Matt said you needed an upgrade. He helped pick it out.

"Thank you so much." She kissed them both on the cheek.

"What's in this one?"

"You need to be careful," Matt said.

Annie took her time with the wrapping paper. She opened the feathery light box and said, "It's empty. There's nothing in here."

"Look closer," Dad said.

Annie removed the paper. "It's a gift card."

"I thought that might be better. You can pick out your own clothes."

"Thank you, Daddy. You have done all right in the past, but you still shop in the kids' section."

Matt handed her the last gift. "You really need to be careful with this one."

She was even more deliberate with the paper. She opened the box and put a hand to her mouth. "Matty, it's beautiful."

Matt took the necklace out of the box and helped Annie put it on. "I want to take you to Ciao Bella soon."

"I'll let you," she said. She got up and ran to the bathroom to look in the mirror. "I love it," she hollered. She came back to the living room and stood in front of Erin.

"Let me see it, Annie."

"Did you pick this out?" Annie asked.

"We went shopping together. Matt saw this gold chain and loved the heart on it. You need to be careful with it. It's rather fragile."

"I won't wear it if I play basketball," Annie said.

Matt grabbed her around the waist and pulled her onto his lap. "You better not."

Annie, Erin and Matt arrived at Grandpa Liam's farm shortly after noon. Annie and Erin wore jeans and a t-shirts, but brought dresses to wear later. Matt wore black jeans and a light blue dress shirt just for Annie. Dad arrived with Elisabeth, Mace and Keyshon a half hour later. Keyshon was starting to accept Matt as Annie's boyfriend. He always hoped Annie would marry Mace and live with him so they could play together. Keyshon liked Erin more now that he was familiar with her.

"Hi, little buddy! How are you today?" Annie asked.

"I'm fine, Annie. How are you and Matthew Sullivan doing? Did you get married yet?"

"Not yet, Keyshon. I'm too young to get married."

"I'll marry you!" he exclaimed. "I don't care how old you are."

Matt pretended to be upset. "Are you trying to steal my girl, Keyshon?"

"I'm just teasing, Matthew Sullivan. I know Annie wants to marry you."

Keyshon always called Matt by his full name for some reason.

"Me and Grandpa are going fishing later. Do you want to join us, Matthew Sullivan?" Keyshon asked. "Sometimes me and Annie go swimming in the lake in our underwear, but Grandpa said we can't today."

Matt glanced at Annie and shook his head.

"Keyshon, that's supposed to be our secret," Annie said as she put a finger to her mouth.

Guests began to arrive shortly after three o'clock. Annie was running around the house to get away from Mace and Keyshon when she saw Elaine, Cindy, Adrien and Bryce get out of the car. She waved and ran over. "Hi, guys."

"Are we the first ones here?" Elaine asked.

"Yes, but it's all right."

"Why are you out of breath?" Cindy asked.

Annie shrugged. "Those guys were chasing me."

Adrien looked at Bryce and asked, "Is she really eighteen?"

"Only in physical age," Bryce answered.

By four all of Annie's close friends had arrived at the farm. Annie mingled and talked to everyone. She saw Diana with Damon Barclay. In a few days they would be in Europe with their families. Victoria Madison and Christopher Braun walked around holding hands. Randy Braun made an quick appearance, but then left for Milwaukee to see Leila Fanaka. Dad and Grandpa used two grills to provide food for everyone. Matt helped them and kept busy running food to the tables set up in the backyard. There were tubs filled with ice and beverages. Some of Annie's friends brought food and presents even though she told them not to. Annie saw Derrick and Kristen Keasling talking to Tony Bertucci and Emmy Colasanti, who had been dating since Kristen Keasling introduced them at the beginning of the school year. Annie giggled as she looked at Emmy and Tony together.

Annie pointed. "Matty, look at Emmy and Tony. He is so big and she's even smaller than me."

"It does seem a bit humorous to see them together."

After everyone stuffed themselves with food and drinks, Annie opened her presents. Erin kept track of who gave her the gifts so she could send thank you cards. The DJ arrived at six and the music began shortly after that. Annie danced with Matty, then dragged her father out for a dance. Matt didn't dance very much, so Annie was free to dance with other guys. She even danced with all her girlfriends as the DJ played a song just for the ladies. The guys watched all the girls dancing. Annie danced with Mace a few times and even danced with Keyshon, who held her close. Keyshon had grown several inches over the last year and was now as tall as Annie. Annie saw Emmy and Tony dancing. Later, she asked for a chance to dance with him.

"Where did you learn to dance so well, Tony?" Annie asked.

"Mama made me take lessons. It actually helped with my football. It improved my balance and flexibility."

"I watched you dancing with Emmy. You look good as a couple even if she is so tiny."

"Thanks, Annie."

Tony had always been shy around girls and today proved

249

that to still be the case. Annie saw Emmy sitting by herself and walked over to talk to her. Emmy smiled at Annie and waved.

"Hi, Emmy. Thanks for coming. I wasn't sure you would."

"Thanks for inviting us. We're having fun."

"I heard you graduated early and started working full-time."

"Yes, I did. I need to earn some money for college and to pay for my apartment."

"Are you living on your own?" Annie asked.

"Yes, I found a furnished apartment close to work."

Annie didn't say anything for a moment. "Are you considering North Park?"

Emmy looked embarrassed as she answered. "I really can't afford North Park. I'm going to Paul Frank Junior College now. After I finish there, I will take classes at North Park, but only when I can afford it. Kristen is going to North Park. I will come over to see her when I can."

"Kristen and I will be in the same dorm," Annie said as she saw Mace dancing with three of her girlfriends. "I hope we can see each other whenever you stop over."

"That would be nice, Annie."

Tony came over to dance with Emmy again.

"I'll talk to you later, Emmy," Annie said as she watched them walk away. She giggled as she thought of Emmy and Tony in bed. *He would squash you.*

Annie danced with Matty a few more times, then she dragged Grandpa Liam onto the grass for a dance. She saw Derrick Keasling and he asked for a dance.

"Do you remember when we were in junior high and I kissed you?" Derrick asked.

"I seem to remember it was a dare, or a bet or something, and you lost."

"My friends thought I lost, but I looked at it as winning the bet," he said with a smile.

"That's very sweet of you, Derrick. How is Arizona?"

"I really like it. I like the school and even the hot weather. Do you know Kristen will be going to North Park?"

"Yes, we will be in the same dorm. I'm really glad I decided to live on campus."

"Do you mind if I ask you a personal question, Annie?"

"I suppose it depends. What did you want to ask?"

"Are you and Matt as happy as you seem?"

"I think we are very happy to be together. You probably know his reputation, but he has been so sweet to me. He's not really like everyone thinks. He did have a baby with a girl from school though."

"I heard about that. How do you feel about it?"

"I saw the baby in the hospital with Matty. Since it happened before we were together, I accept it and don't hold it against him."

"I wish you guys all the happiness in the world."

"Thank you, Derrick." Annie smiled at him and surprised him with a quick kiss.

"Did I win another bet, Annie?" he asked while grinning.

"Maybe this time I won the bet," she said. *You look like that movie star I saw a couple weeks ago. I bet you have your choice of girls down in Arizona.*

Some of her friends stuck around to help clean up the place. Eventually, all the party guests left. Mace took Erin back to his house. Keith O'Dell and Elisabeth Franklin were staying at the farm with Keyshon who was already asleep upstairs.

Annie found her father on the living room couch and walked up to him. "Daddy, Matt and I are going home now. I want to thank you and Grandpa for the best party ever. I love you both so much."

Dad stood up and hugged her. "You're welcome, sweetie. Grandpa went to bed already. I'll tell him what you said in the morning."

"Good night, Mr. O'Dell. Thanks for everything," Matt said and then he whispered to Annie's father so she couldn't hear. "We will follow the rules tonight. I wish I didn't have to, but I will."

"Thanks, Matt. I appreciate it. I know it's not easy to wait."

"Not really, sir. I think I've become more mature and I can wait for Annie."

251

Matt took Annie back to her house. They were alone at last.

"Did you have a good time, Annie?"

"It was the best party I've ever had, Matty. Thank you for everything. I really love the necklace. It must have cost you a lot of money."

"Not really, I stole it."

Annie gave him a dirty look but then smiled. "I know you're kidding."

They got ready for bed. Matt stood in the space between her bed and his sleeping bag and the air mattress. Annie was on her knees at the edge of her bed.

"Do you want a good night kiss, Annie?" he teased.

"Maybe just one quick little kiss."

They shared one last kiss, then Matt held Annie close. He didn't want to let go, but he did. Annie looked at him and smiled. Matt smiled back at her. He took a step back, lost his balance, fell onto his butt on the sleeping bag.

"Are you all right?" Annie asked while trying not to laugh.

He bounced back up. "I'm fine. I meant to do that."

He almost kissed her again, but didn't. Instead he put a hand on her cheek.

"Annie."

"Yes, Matty. What is it?"

"I just need to tell you something. I've never told anyone this before and meant it."

"And what might that be?" Annie asked. Her heart fluttered hoping she knew what he would say.

Matt hesitated long enough to take a deep breath and then said, "I love you, Annie Mercer O'Dell. I really love you."

She launched off of the bed and tackled Matt to the floor. "I love you, too, Matty Sullivan. I love you so much."

Check out these other titles by the author

The Emmy's Story Series

1. We We're 'posed to Get Married
2. One Of The Guys
3. A New Friend
4. Did You Like the Ravioli Tonight?
5. Completely and Forever: A Wedding
6. It's Time To Go!
7. How Difficult Can It Be?
8. Forever... Isabella... Forever
9. The Forgettable Year
10. Turning Thirty

The Annie Mercer O'Dell Series

1. Roosevelt High

Stand Alone Books

1. Growing Up In Kinmundy Junction
2. Grandpa, Lions and Kitty Cats: A Collection Of Short Stories For Children Of All Ages